Biker's Surrogate

BWWM Dark Motorcycle Club Romance

Rebel Barbarians Motorcycle Club

Book One

Jamila Jasper

WWW.JAMILAJASPERROMANCE.COM

ISBN: 979-8-3302-2951-2

Thank you to my Patreon subscribers for your support with this book.

❀ Created with Vellum

Rebel Barbarians Motorcycle Club

Description

A gorgeous black woman with a beautiful head of natural hair struts into the gas station and catches the bigoted biker's eye...
Southpaw throws a punch and draws blood to snatch innocent Anna away from everything she knows while saving her life from a gas station creep.

He needs her womb... <u>urgently.</u>

After losing his future first-born in a series of lost pool games, Southpaw needs a surrogate that will deeply offend the rival he owes a baby.

Anna is perfect. Soft. Easy on the eyes. Even easier to knock up.

There's only one problem with Southpaw's plan to pay off his debts and quit his addiction to playing fast and loose with his bloodline.

Anna's different from other women. She's not a part of the biker lifestyle.

His reluctant prisoner is smart as a whip with a butt that stops traffic.

And one night between her legs is enough to make a man fall in love...

This is a dark interracial romance story with potentially triggering content. Enjoy this motorcycle club/biker gang romance, the first book in The Rebel Barbarians MC Series.

Thank you for being a part of my journey and for bleeding into what I write. I needed your help for Anna & Wyatt to ride off into the sunset together.

The female lead in this book is named after my lovely patron, Anna. Click here to subscribe: www.patreon.com/jamilajasper

Played out by the band
Love is a losing hand
More than I could stand
Love is a losing hand
Self-professed, profound
'Til the chips were down
Know you're a gambling man
Love is a losing hand

Though I battle blind
Love is a fate resigned
Memories mar my mind
Love is a fate resigned
Over futile odds

And laughed at by the gods
And now, the final frame
Love is a losing game

– Amy Winehouse, Love Is A Losing Game

Shaw.

Wyatt "Southpaw" Shaw

Rank: Junior Officer
Son of the Rebel Barbarians President, Harlan "Harley" Shaw
Patched In: June 2016

THE REBEL BARBARIANS MOTORCYCLE CLUB ALPHA CHAPTER CHARTER

The democratic organization of the Rebel Barbarians Motorcycle Club permits club operations within 100 miles as the crow flies from the old Route 66 highway on the traditional Rebel Barbarians bike route.

Club headquarters decided by committee are located in the basement of Hollingsworth's Chicken Basket, run by Deb Hollingsworth-Shaw.

Section I Purpose

Our club monitors and protects the safety and purity of families and associates of the Rebel Barbarians. Members share a passion for patriotism, respect for authority, a desire to protect tradition, and maintain the sanctity of the American race across the Midwest.

Section II Membership

Eligibility: *Eligible members must be over 18 years old, white American males, & receive three references from active members. No* *women. No homosexuals. No niggers. No spics. No immigrants. Once recruited into the Rebel Barbarian's organization, initiates receive their first brand or tattoo prior to a year long initiation.*

After the year-long initiation, recruits may become permanent active members, requiring them to pay 15% of their legitimate earnings to the club and 30% of illegitimate earnings. New recruits participate in an 18 month initiation ritual into the organization and during that time, they must follow a strict code of conduct, show respect towards the organization, and demonstrate loyalty to the motorcycle club.

Club members must have several years of riding experience assessed by the club officers and their membership must have the support of active due-paying members. Junior club members have 5-10 years of membership, senior members have 10+ years of membership.

Recruitment: *Recruitment period begins every year in Pontiac, IL club headquarters with the annual July 4th summer barbecue followed by the charity ride for veterans with leukemia and local food banks. The recruitment period ends on Labor Day when all potential recruits must put in an official bid with the club officers.*

Potential recruits must meet the requirements for eligibility and dress in club colors during the recruitment period to signal loyalty to the organization. Once becoming a "recruit", said recruits must spend 18 months in service of the club before becoming full members.

Code of Conduct: *If you're gonna start a fight, make sure you finish it. Never let another man speak ill of your club or brothers. Never touch another rider's old lady. Never cheat a club member. Never touch another man's bike. Never sit on another man's bike.Get drunk. Fuck. Fix bikes. Have fun.*

Section III Club Structure

Officers: *The current officers of the Rebel Barbarians are as follows. President - Harley , Vice President - Randy, Enforcer - Doc , Treasurer - Cash*

Meetings: *Quarterly meetings are held at club headquarters in Amarillo, Texas and they are presided over by the club president. Attendance is mandatory unless you are serving a prison sentence, the military, or an equivalent commitment.*

Rank:

Recruits - Fresh recruits are the newest members of the club. Barring special circumstances, recruitment lasts 18 months before graduation to "newbies"

Newbies - Recruits who survive their 18 month trial period with the club participate in the initiation ritual to become newbies. The newbie period lasts five years.

Juniors - 5-10 years of club membership.

Senior members - 10+ years of club membership

Officers - Elected club officers hold the club leadership positions

Junior Officer - Officers appoint one family member to apprentice under them for their position in the club however, the final decision on officers relies on a club election.

⅔ quorum must be reached for all club elections pertaining to membership & officers.

Section IV Rules & Regulations

Riding Rules: Fuck pigs. Stay armed. Shoot if you must. Never ride alone. Never ride without club colors.

Club Colors: All riders must wear a Rebel Barbarian's MC patch dependent on their rank and position within the organization. All club tattoos must be prominently and proudly displayed.

Club Dues: All active members pay club dues of $250/month to maintain club membership. If dues are unpaid for over 90 days, they fall into collections.

Section V Amendments

All amendments must be decided by a 75% member vote and there must be a quorum - over ⅔ of all membership present for any voting to take place about matters pertaining to the club.

Section VI Dissolution

In the event of the tragic end to the Rebel Barbarians, all club assets should be liquidated and proceeds split up amongst the four founding families. S. S. H. B.

Underneath the position on the wall where the 18 x 24 poster of the club rules hangs, four bullet holes pierce the wall from a fight that happened some time ago between two bikers over an old lady. It's hot as ever in Amarillo, Texas and this joint houses the natural predator of an ice cold beer. The thick smell of marijuana smoke, cigars and chain-smoked cigarettes hangs in the air even after the building stays empty for months.

The smell of chicken grease from the restaurant overhead has always permeated the clubhouse, firing up the appetite for fucking and fighting amongst the bikers.

...

This is how their story begins.

CHAPTER ONE
SOUTHPAW

Addict? I'm not a damn addict. I don't care what Hawk thinks. Just because I pushed myself a little bit and got us into this fucked up situation doesn't make me a junkie. Green dice roll over the tops of my fingers on my left hand as I straddle my bike and watch the Jew's door. Junkies suck dick for a hit of a drug but all I've ever done is believe in myself. Maybe a little too hard.

A bunch of criminal redneck bikers stealing a half million dollars of pills off a Jew is just as much of a gamble as anything else. What's the difference between this and what I did? The whole country is a shake of the goddamn dice. I just have the balls to take my chances at winning big. Except this time, I lost. And the time before, which is why I went double or nothing.

I just got a little too drunk. Or Reaper got a lot better at pool since I last played him. That must've been two years ago at the annual tournament in Amarillo. Goddamn, he was lanky back then.

My back tenses. I hate jobs like this. A stick up is easy. You find the motherfucker behind a gas station, talk like you're in an action movie and ride away while the bastard figures out what to do with soiled trousers and no cellphone.

I shouldn't be here. I promised myself a couple years back that I wouldn't end up in another situation like this one. I wouldn't call myself an addict, but I definitely have a problem. Never saw a game I didn't want to win. Dice. Roulette. Poker. Pool.

Problems start when you stop winning, when the debts pile up, and when you need to bet everything but the shirt off your fucking back to get the same high. Gamblers know winning feels just as good as losing. I can't explain my desire to self-immolate but my older brother Ethan doesn't think I hate myself at all.

"You're a goddamn selfish bastard, Wyatt. You don't know how to love anyone but yourself."

Strong words from the older brother who put his first dog down himself.

PEDESTRIANS WALK past the black door we're watching, but we're invisible to them, even if I feel like a fucking germ in this city with every goddamn antibody potentially becoming aware of my presence. The constant sound of sirens from every direction keeps me on edge and the sound of motorcycles reminds me if any of our enemies hears the Barbarians strayed so far from our territory, there could be consequences.

The last thing we want is a bunch of Blacks and Hispanics going all gangster on our asses. *Could this motherfucker hurry up?* After a family of five walks past me and definitely notices that I am way out of place in this nice ass neighborhood, I get paranoid. Hawk made me promise to stay away from liquor or pills to make this trip, but I can't help but feel like I need something.

My gun burns the skin on my back from the unrelenting heat. Could we have had bad intel? Dad claims to have a connection with some double-crossing police informant named something-Biederman who gave him this information, and I'm not in much of a position to question him since I gambled half a million dollars that I don't have.

It's either this, dad sells the family home to help me out, or asks Uncle Mikey or the Sinclair family for help. Not gonna fucking happen on my watch.

My back is against the fucking wall, although I question my dad's sanity associating with a damn Jew.

"I question your sanity gambling away half a million fucking dollars your broke ass doesn't have," he'd raged at me. Our fight that night was one of our worst, and we've had some bad ones over the years.

I don't fuck with a Biederman or any "-man" for that matter but right now my job ain't questioning him. I have a time limit before the Blackwoods take offense. The last thing you want is to cause an outlaw biker any offense.

Where the hell is this goddamn Jew?

My phone buzzes and I check nervously, even if I don't want to take my eyes off the door. I asked dad to let me do this alone, but to avoid another blowout argument, I agreed to my babysitters. He sent me with a couple Sinclairs... Hawk and his cousins Ghost and Condom Sinclair join me and my brothers, Ethan and Owen to complete this errand.

(For club business, I call Ethan, Bear, and Owen, Scrap.)

Once we have the money, I'll have some peace of mind.

BUT I WON'T BE free. Just free *for now.*

IF ONLY IT was just money I'd lost. Once we're done here, I'll have that part sorted out... but the Blackwoods want more than that. The smug look on Doc's face when Reaper won told us everything we needed to know about their intentions. *Utter humiliation.* Dad thinks Doc wants his son wearing the President's patch.

I say let him have it if he wants. Only a fool would want to lead this band of outlaw hooligans who only care about drugs, liquor, fucking and our goddamn bikes.

Bear: Both in position. Give the word.

Southpaw: No movement.

I DON'T DESERVE their help. The sun beats down on the back of my neck so hard I must be red already. The die rolls back over my fingers. There's too much traffic here. It's too hot. Chicago is too noisy and it's not the familiar roar of a bike between my legs.

The city is unsteady. Unpredictable. Loud in all the wrong ways and filled with too many people. Black people. Mexicans. Puerto Ricans. Jews. Cities packed with leeches that suck every last dollar out of our country and fill these filthy fucking cities with more crime than the cops know what to do with. The cops aren't any better than the scum they preside over. Just having bikes and wearing a cut out here attracts instant attention from pigs.

Once they see my patches and my tattoos, I'm guaranteed a night in jail on some trumped up charge. A fly lands on the back of my neck. I swat it away as a strong craving for beer sets in. How late is it? I wish I could have a drink. God, I miss drinking. The last time I got properly drunk was the Rebel Barbarians Motorcycle Club quarterly meeting out at the clubhouse in Amarillo a couple weeks ago. I could use some Hollingsworth bourbon. But dad's right that I need to keep a clear head.

Dad's right about a lot. This should be simple. Once I have the money, I can worry about the bigger problem, so I just gotta get through this simple job – getting four duffel bags of shrink-wrapped pills from downtown Chicago all the way back out to Pontiac, the head of the old Route 66 highway that crosses the Southwestern

United States. With the recent bike tune-up, we can move this shit quickly – as long as we get the duffels out of the Jew's apartment without incident.

FINALLY. Movement from the Jew. The black door opens and a short, balding man with tortoiseshell glasses and a long black trench coat exits. He doesn't look like a big time drug dealer. I guess the M.D. types in this line of work like to look the part. Their clientele ain't like ours. They're junkies with Porsches and second houses.

I REACH for my phone and shoot off a text to the group as I watch him walk up the street, oblivious to my position. He doesn't know he's being hunted – which is good. At least we aren't riding into a trap. I wonder what baldie did to piss off Biederman and make him betray one of his own...

> Southpaw: Jew on the move.

Hawk: 5 minutes, then enter. Condom.
Ghost. Move to look out points.

Bear: Coast clear. Coming with Scrap in 5 minutes.

HE DOESN'T LOOK like the type of guy to get involved in our dirty business. I watch the Jew as he stops at a crosswalk. His clothes are clean, expensive, and he's clean-cut and clean-shaven. I guess you never know what people get up to just by looking at them. You definitely wouldn't peg him for a drug dealer. I guess it's just like dad says. *Jews are sneaky.*

I wait for the Jew to cross the street before I move, confident I can get everything done in my allotted five minutes. I straddle my bike where I have it parked illegally behind a Dodge Caravan, watching the oblivious man until he disappears around the block.

Once he's out of sight, I hop off the bike and hurry across the street to the apartment as fast as I can go without running and drawing too much attention to myself. His wife and kids are inside – along with four duffel bags of shrink-wrapped 20 mg fentanyl pills worth about $500,000. We're gonna have to do something pretty fucked up, but unlike the Jew, the wife isn't likely to be carrying a piece on her. According to our source – if you believe him.

The door to their pre-war brownstone is old enough that I don't need to engage in high tech locksmithing to break the lock open. I've been doing this shit since I was a kid anyway, robbing kids' houses and flipping their shit back to them in high school. Messed up, but I made a lot of money back then.

I open the glossy front door easily and the house smells like pancakes and bacon, like they live in a freaking movie set apart from the rest of Chicago, which distinctly smells like hot dogs and piss. When I enter the narrow, constricted hallway, I hear a woman's voice calling from upstairs.

"Barry? Barry is that you?"

I stick the green die in my pocket where it rattles around with the matching one to the pair of dice. *Good luck. I could use some good luck right now.*

My phone buzzes in my pocket again. High heels click across hardwood nervously. The bitch knows I'm not Barry. I wish I could say I was nervous in situations like this, but the truth is, I'm calm as fuck. I put a bullet in the chamber and raise the pistol to the top of the stairs, accurately predicting to the second when Mrs. Goldstein will emerge.

She screams as loudly as her lungs will allow once she sees me and the last gasp of oxygen almost squeaks out of her as her knees knock together and she faints. Her kids come running and although they scream their little heads off, I gotta give the little brats credit for holding it together a lot better than their mom.

"SHUT THE FUCK UP!" I yell at the little Goldstein kids. Poor motherfuckers. They scream and the older one covers her brother's eyes. She's a pretty little girl with curly brown hair in a tangled mess and wide gray eyes round with fear.

"Don't shoot us!" she says. "Well, if you have to shoot us, shoot me and let Oliver go."

Oliver starts bawling his fucking head off, which kinda pisses me off since I have no intention of killing the kids. I expected them to be a little more obedient. Or younger. This isn't what dad promised. I shut off the part of my brain that gets fucking livid at my father for his inhuman tendencies and focus on my job. I'm here for pills – not to be the good guy.

Fuck, I've never been the good guy and if there was even a shred of hope for me, I wouldn't be in this situation in the first fucking place. *I bet everything. I bet everything I had and lost like a fucking idiot and the worst part is, I'd do it again.*

"Stop crying and shut the fuck up," I repeat. "I'm not gonna kill you unless you keep crying like a couple of babies."

She tightens her grasp over her brother's eyes. The protective, selfless action tugs at my heartstrings just for a second before I harden myself to the possibility that I might have to get rid of those children. Not kill them but make them... disappear.

"I'm ten," the girl says sassily. "I'm not a baby."

The more I talk to her, the higher the chances of my guilt kicking in.

"Where's the bathroom?" I respond brusquely. *If I show any weakness, the rest of the Barbarians will know and I'll never hear the end of it from dad.*

The little girl gestures to the bathroom with her chin. I just need them out of the way.

· · ·

I SHOVE the kids in the bathroom and prop a chair up against the door so they don't try anything and get shot in the process. They're quietly sobbing by the time I lock them up, but at least they're safe. What the hell is taking Hawk and my brothers so long?

Loud footsteps downstairs interrupt my train of thought followed by an even louder Oklahoma accent. It's a funny accent that mixes Midwestern and Southern sounds in a way that shouldn't be possible, but it tells me that my accomplices have finally arrived.

"I'm upstairs!" I call down to them.

Ethan is the loud walker, so I hear his stupid ass crashing up the stairs first. He hasn't kept his disapproval about this entire situation to himself. If dad didn't order my older brother to join me, he might have sold me out to Reaper by now. He's that pissed off. Luckily, I still have Owen on my side. He yelps loudly and then swears to himself in a much more masculine sounding voice.

"Don't tell me he killed the Jew bitch," my younger brother says loudly enough for the kids to hear. Great. I close the distance between us and try to speak with a lower tone of voice.

"She's not dead," I growl from the hallway. "Just passed out."

We come face to face in the hallway. Hawk and Ethan look worse off from the heat than I am.

"Should we do something with her?" Ethan asks. "Looks painful."

He shoots me a glare like I was supposed to do something with the woman when she passed out in front of me. I ignore him. I've done my fair share of shit for the club and for my older brother, despite his selective memory.

Hawk and Ethan pick which sides of the Jew's wife to grab her from and they grunt as they lift her together, careful not to smash her head against those perfectly decorated walls.

Hawk carries her to the master bedroom, which suits me just fine since this is where the duffel bags are. I begin the search immediately while they situate her on the bed.

"Where are the kids?" Ethan asks. Owen doesn't seem to give a fuck. While my older brother Ethan paces angrily, Owen stays focused on the search for the pills. As the youngest, Owen always feels like he has something to prove and he's right.

Ethan on the other hand, is a constant hard ass about everyone else and ignorant about his own flaws. I glare at Ethan. Does it look like we have time to discuss this shit? He doesn't see any fucking kids. Why does he care?

Owen picks up two watches from the dresser and shoves them both into his pocket. Rolexes? Pateks? I'll ask later. I don't bother hassling him for his kleptomania, and I still have Ethan glaring at me for answers I don't have the goddamn time to give him.

"Locked up," I grunt impatiently. "They're out of trouble."

Hawk searches just as fervently as Owen, throwing open dresser drawers and tossing panties, thongs, sex toys, and more boring pairs of underwear onto the bed. I can't remember the last time a duffel bag fit in a dresser, but I assume he's looking for any loot that could make this errand worth his time.

Ethan seems hell bent on finding a mistake I've made. Finding out the kids are safe doesn't stop him from fault finding. He's like a goddamn woman. Ethan flings open a closet door and throws coats, dresses and wool sweaters on the ground as he searches for the duffels.

"Did they see you?" he asks.

The question pisses me off.

"Of course they saw me. What are they gonna do about it? Nothing."

OWEN TAKES a couple thongs out of the lady's underwear drawer and shoves them in his pocket.

"Can you do something useful you fucking pervert?" I snap at Owen to stop myself from saying something worse to Ethan as I cross the bedroom to search for the duffel bags in the master bedroom's *third* closet. How many closets do two people need? Hawk gets on his knees to look under the bed.

"Nothing here," Hawk calls out with a grunt. "Just a gun locker…"

Owen ignores my chastisement as Hawk drags out the gun locker.

"Fingerprinted," Hawk says. *Great.* Hawk presses his fingerprint to the keypad – stupidly. My heart does an excited little flip when I open the closet door. They're right out in the open. Four duffels, just like dad's Jew informant suggested. The weight on my chest shifts just slightly.

"I found the shit."

Owen and Hawk lose interest in the gun locker. We have less than fifteen minutes to get the fuck out of here.

"Holy shit. Are the pills in there?" Owen asks. *Where else could they be?* Still, it doesn't hurt to double check. Scrap's idiotic comments have saved our asses multiple times in the past. Bear and I haul the duffel bags onto the bed.

We check for the pills, peeling open the zippers and shedding enough of the bubble wrap to make out the sandwiched pill casings. I stand back and watch Bear and Scrap double check each pack, my fingers reaching into my pocket just beyond my awareness for the pair of dice that I flip between each finger over and over, using the ritual to calm my mind from the sheer euphoria brought on by this motherlode of drugs.

"This shit is gonna move fast," Hawk says. "Let's get the fuck out of here."

We each grab one bag. I leave the kids barricaded in the bathroom as we walk past with the loot. Ethan glances over his shoulder at me one last time.

"Are you sure we shouldn't shoot the bitch?"

"No point," I tell him. "Let's get the fuck out of here."

We're not in any mood to argue. The last members of our crew, the lookouts, give us the go ahead once they see us leaving the house.

Now... *we run.* I quickly fix the duffel to the back of my bike. I don't worry about my brothers. We've done shit like this dozens of times. We grew up in the life, desperately wanting to be like our fathers who seemed so fucking free compared to other dads.

Our fathers lived for freedom. The open road. The original American dream of conquering the wild west, obeying nobody's rules, and living without the laws of a king. Other dads seemed boring. Bankers. Doctors. Teachers. None of them were bikers. None of them wore cuts. Or patches. Had tattoos. Our dads were cool and when we grew up, we planned to be just like them...

My bike roars to life, becoming one with my body as I zip off into traffic, weaving around cars and trucks with confidence that anyone else might think borders on stupidity. I won't know if my brothers made it out of the city okay until I get to Pontiac, but that's just fine with me. I leave Chicago from the West before looping around and finding the Old Route 66 highway that connects the Rebel Barbarians chapters across the Midwestern and Southwestern United States.

DAD HAS BEEN SO FUCKING DISAPPOINTED in me lately. This will help take his mind off things. I guess I shouldn't blame him. The old man is getting old. Doesn't help that Hollingsworth and Blackwood both have grandkids.

HE WANTS AN HEIR...

BUT HOW THE hell can I give him an heir when I gambled my unborn first-born child... *and lost?*

CHAPTER TWO
ANNA

He won't stop following me. I thought I was lying to myself enough to actually believe it. Women love doing shit like that, don't we? Ignoring our instincts for the sake of making other folks happy. I'm not a weak woman by any means, don't get me wrong. I can take a punch and I can throw one too. But I'd rather not throw a punch if I don't have to, and I don't know if throwing a punch would get Gary off my back or make the entire situation blow up in my face.

It's been four weeks since I turned down his awkward advance towards me in the gym parking lot. What rational woman goes on a hike with a complete stranger several miles from our town, I might add, to some place with ponds and bogs and all manner of locations where a man could dispose of a woman.

Turning Gary down for the hike only seemed to have activated his curiosity with me. At first, I understood where he was coming from. Rejection hurts, I get it. My sympathy for his annoying ass quickly vanished when he started popping up at my regular spots. I let the first three times slide. Then that pair of glassy blue eyes kept popping up at my favorite gas station, Aldi, Walmart, the park closest to my house, and then twice, I saw this man outside of my job.

I thought that crossed the line but again, I had no proof. But here it is. This man must have got in his car and followed me as I headed north back towards Chicago from a mutual friend's party. What the hell does he think he's gonna get out of following me?

I already blocked his ass on Instagram and I tried to take a detour to get him off my tail but there's nothing out here, so maybe this was a bad move. Keeping track of traffic and getting this weirdo off my tail gets me thrown off. I know I'm going the right way, but I don't normally take random weird highways when there are faster ways to get back to my part of Chicago.

Where the hell am I? I hope I can find somewhere to stop and maybe hide in a bathroom until this weirdo gets bored and drives off. I don't want him following me home. Living alone makes me crazy paranoid about creepy dudes knowing where I live.

Turning into the next gas station I see, I glance at the signs and see I'm somewhere along the old Route 66 highway, but I can't tell what town I'm in, or if there are enough people this far from the city to constitute an entire town.

All I can see from this gas station is a chicken place with hella motorcycles parked out front. The chicken smells good, but judging by the bikes parked outside, I don't want anything to do with that spot.

I avoid bikers for obvious, smart reasons. There's a reason half the towns this far west are considered "sundown towns" and fat ass white guys on motorcycles with shriveled dicks and a point to prove are most of it.

Gary doesn't notice me hiding behind the salty snack aisle at the gas station. Bastard. I knew he was following me, but now that I have confirmation, my plan to confront him seems crazy. The man might be excessively thin and creepy looking – like a walking grim reaper – but that doesn't mean he can't threaten me. Or shoot me. This is Illinois after all. Anyone in this place could have a pistol.

He straightens his back, scanning the aisles. Shameless as fuck! I'm so damn focused on Gary that I don't notice anyone else in the gas station. Completely oblivious, I stumble backward and land against the broad chest of a grown ass man. I yelp, not just betraying my position, but sounding like a scared child as I quickly turn around to apologize to the person my clumsy ass just walked into.

But when I look at the man, no words come out. I've never seen someone so simultaneously terrifying and handsome in my entire life. It feels wrong. He's easily six-four, with thick, short black hair. The scar on his face draws my attention to his thick, full lips that look recently bruised and cut up, like he just got in a fight. A pair of green dice roll between the fingers of his left hand unconsciously, and he scowls when he notices me with immediate disapproval and frustration.

"I...I..."

Words just won't come out. Tall, terrifying... and built as fuck. This man either lifts weights or he spent his formative years in prison. Either way, the results speak for themselves. His exposed biceps are larger than my thighs and covered in tattoos.

"Yes?" he responds, gazing down at me with imperious bemusement. It's just enough time for Gary to spring into action and (in his own mind) save the day.

"Anna!" Gary calls my name. I ignore him, my eyes locked with the green-eyed muscular giant standing in front of me. He smells like a car engine, the highway, dirt, and money balled up in your pocket for too long. Plus sweat. It's still early spring, but with all the layers of leather and the boots, the smell of pungent masculine sweat is strong off him.

I don't bother looking at Gary, but I can see him in my peripheral vision approaching me and calling my name again. His arm snakes over my shoulder, making my skin crawl as his fingers cup my shoulder. The strange man's scowl deepens.

"Is this guy bothering you?" Gary asks, his fingers curling possessively into my shoulder and twisting my stomach into an uncomfortable knot. The craziest thing about the worst case scenarios you come up with in your head is that in real life, the embarrassing situations are normally way worse. Life is funny that way (and by funny, I mean fucked up because come on now...)

The strange man smirks a little and then his lip quickly stiffens.

"Is that your boyfriend?" he asks me calmly, his gaze never once leaving mine, like Gary's presence is both annoying and irrelevant. His eyes are only made more beautiful by the way they draw attention to his sharp, aquiline nose that defines his rigidly masculine face with a statuesque quality. I have to crane my neck back just to see those eyes...

"No," I breathe out, although the word is so gently expressed that it's almost a whimper instead of an actual word. Gary's fingers tighten on my shoulder, deepening my nausea at his closeness and my desire to escape. Gary always smells like garlic. It's the first thing I noticed about him when he approached me in the parking lot but now that his arm is over my shoulder, the garlic smell seems to be mixed with onions and the terrible mixture of body odor you get when you mix vegan males and natural deodorant. I gag a little bit.

"Okay," the strange man says. "I need you to get the fuck away from her. Right now."

I glance over at Gary, finally breaking eye contact with the stranger but only for the sheer pleasure of seeing how the hell he reacts. His arm falls away from me quickly and he looks indignant. And red. I take a step to the right just in case it gets ugly.

"Excuse me?" Gary says. "I'm a friend of hers, buddy, so just watch it."

My instincts tell me this is the wrong move. Panic surges through me as Gary talks to this giant like he's a middle schooler and not towering over both of us with biceps the size of a gigantic ham. The man's gaze flickers with barely suppressed outrage. He shifts a little closer to Gary, allowing me to really look at the tattoos he has tracing up his arms..

I move closer to the stranger, even if he's clearly dangerous. Far more dangerous than Gary. I can tell from the mean look on his face. The scars on his pale skin. He looks way too muscular, dirty and mean to be anything other than an outlaw. I don't know much about outlaw bikers, but how much do I need to know? It's the same with all criminal elements. I treat them in the hospital and ignore them in the streets.

I don't like the way he looks at Gary. His eyes are cold and empty, so dark in the evening light that they're almost black. I can see him considering something cruel with emotionless purpose. He could rip Gary's head off just for inconveniencing him. I can sense it. Why can't Gary?

My palms sweat and my tongue grows heavy in my mouth. The man tried to protect me, so maybe I can intervene before this spirals out of control. The man's gaze darkens. It's too quiet in this place. I convince myself to calm down by telling myself once I thank the stranger for scaring Gary away, he'll head right out on his business.

This doesn't have to explode into violence.

"I'm not your buddy," the man says. "Now do what I say and step away from the lady."

That barely suppressed rage no longer appears to be suppressed. The man's cheeks darken visibly. I can't make myself look away from him. Maybe I should be looking at Gary or for a method of escape, but the strange man's face captivates me instantly. *Why is he standing up for me like this when he doesn't even know me?*

Gary gives me a desperate look. "Anna?" he says. "Come on. Let's get out of here."

Let's? Has this man lost his cracker jack mind? We are not together. His weird ass followed me out here and now he's talking about let's? I'm not taking my chances with Gary or the biker.

I'm taking my chances with the gas station CCTV. I fold my arms, pop my hip and kiss my teeth so long and loud that my Antiguan grandmother would have given me a trophy if she could have. But I'm not stupid. I keep my body positioned just behind the strange man in case I need to make a hasty getaway.

The strange man sticks his hand in his pocket and when he removes it, the green dice are gone, and I notice the large rings on his hand. Thick, silver rings twisted around large masculine fingers. His hand looks like a bear paw and he looks more dangerous than ever before with tattooed knuckles and cuts all up and down his arms like he's been in plenty of fights. And he enjoys them.

"She doesn't want to leave with you, buddy," the man says. "Don't make me ask you twice to get going."

The cashier at the front of the gas station doesn't seem to care. But then again, she's a short, pale woman covered in tattoos which may very well prove her allegiance to the tall man standing in front of me.

"You're not the boss of me," Gary says weakly. "This is a free country whether you backwards, ignorant, *racist* rednecks want it to be something different."

I don't anticipate the biker's next move because really, Gary's remark was a rather benign diss that was more weak than offensive. But the stranger moves without a second of hesitation the minute Gary defies him, grabbing him by the shirt and balling up the fabric in his fists, nearly knocking Gary off his unstable footing with his violent grasp.

Gary's mouth moves like an awkward, suffocating fish. I take a step to the side and let the big guy do his thing. Blood rushes past my ears as the situation escalates out of control immediately.

"Hey!" I call out half-heartedly, fighting the contradictory feelings rushing through me. I want Gary to learn his lesson but I have no idea what this unpredictable stranger is capable of. He could really hurt him. The stranger ignores my call and the woman working the front of the gas station convenience store apparently doesn't give a shit.

Holding Gary by his shirt, the biker quickly thrusts his head forward and headbutts Gary. It happens so fast that I hardly want to believe that's what happened, but Gary immediately loses consciousness and falls into the salty snacks, sending a downpour of Doritos and Cheez-Its onto his head as he slumps over. The woman at the cash register begins filing her nails. Now I'm scared.

You don't have to be an expert in behavioral science to sense a fucked up situation. My throat tightens. Calling out to her will be useless, but someone has to do something.

The man grunts and turns his attention towards me. This time, I'm not so amused. Gary groans on the floor and tries to collect himself but it's clear that he's finished.

"Southpaw," the man says. *He's introducing himself.* I make nervous eye contact with him but as soon as our eyes meet, those nerves disappear, replaced by an instant calm that spreads through me and fills me with an irrational trust in a man who has just proven himself to be unstable.

"The name is Southpaw," he repeats in a surprisingly gentle country accent. With Gary, he didn't sound that gentle. But Southpaw? What the hell is he talking about?

That can't be a name.

"Excuse me? First name?" I stammer out foolishly, trying to make sense of everything and glancing over at Gary's semi-conscious body on the ground. Gary's lashes flutter open and he groans. *Southpaw* ignores him.

"Southpaw," he repeats, sticking out his meaty tattooed hand. The hand he sticks out to shake is clean, but his left hand is covered in blood. Okay. Southpaw. It's a nickname. My heart still pounds. Pissing this man off further isn't a good idea.

"Anna," I answer, sticking out my hand reluctantly to find out that I'm trembling with terror that this man notices, his face wrinkling with disgust like my reaction isn't normal. He grabs my hand and a strange energy passes between us. I want to ignore it, but when you feel that energetic exchange, it's impossible to ignore. The connection begins with eye contact, but that first touch always does it. Our souls have a way of knowing who our lives will get all tangled up with.

We might not have conscious awareness of God's plan for us but somewhere deep down inside us, something does.

I pull my hand away from his quickly, the sickly feeling in my stomach intensifying as Southpaw's gaze leaves mine, but only to travel slowly down to my cleavage, where he lingers purposefully. He runs his tongue over pink lips that look baby soft in stark contrast to how harsh and rugged the rest of him looks.

"You're coming with me," he says with a grin as he runs his fingers through a trimmed dark beard. "Now."

His commanding tone scares the crap out of me, but he doesn't stand a chance of me listening to him. I'm not going anywhere with this man. If I had to guess, a man like that wants to take me back to some redneck dive bar and revel in his conquest for ninety seconds before dropping me off at a truck stop somewhere. No fucking thank you.

"What? No. No, I'm not. I have a shift in two hours back in Chicago," I respond firmly, but kindly. "I'm not going anywhere."

He screws his face up, gives me another once-over and guesses my job on the spot. I don't even know how he does it, since I'm not in my scrubs, so I could be anything from a homeless person to a massage therapist.

"Nurse?" Southpaw grunts. My face gives it all away and I can tell because of how he smirks. *Damn it.*

I just told a crazy man where I work. Am I mentally ill? Despite my instant regret at revealing too much information, I can't exactly back out of this conversation now. He takes his left fist and examines the blood dripping all over him before wiping the blood off on his jeans where I suddenly notice several more suspicious brown stains that are more likely to be blood than dirt now that I'm paying attention.

I nod slowly.

"Good," he says. "I need a nurse. Come."

"No," I say firmly. "I'm sorry but if you need a nurse, you're going to have to go to the hospital."

He raises his eyebrows and smirks like a man who has never heard the word "no" before.

"That's funny," he says.

"I don't see what's funny about it," I respond, glancing at the woman at the cash register, who will surely help out another woman in need if necessary.

Both entrances to the gas station open and three more bikers enter the place. *Fuck.* I go into panic mode. I just watched this man knock another man out over nothing and now I'm surrounded by them.

"You want me to kill that guy?" Southpaw asks me, pointing casually at Gary.

I shake my head.

"No."

"Too bad," he says, reaching behind his back for a pistol. My stomach churns. I think I scream. I cover my ears. But it doesn't matter. He shoots him right in front of me. Three bullets in rapid succession. The girl at the cash register doesn't even flinch. She just calmly turns around and takes four peppermint Zyns off the rack behind her, sliding them under the glass.

WHAT THE FUCK. What the fuck. What the fuck.

MY HANDS ARE SHAKING, but I'm not crazy. This is a crime. I reach into my pocket for my cell phone because if this guy plans on killing me, nothing I do is gonna stop him. Apparently that bitch at the front doesn't give a shit either. The second my phone emerges from my pocket, Southpaw snatches it from me.

"Unlock this and call your boss, cupcake. You're quitting your job."

CHAPTER THREE
SOUTHPAW

We stop at a Flying J after another ninety minutes driving southwest on the highway because if I don't stop, this crazy bitch is gonna kill me. I stop the bike and then have to pry her fingernails out of my body before climbing off the bike and flinging her over my shoulder. Thankfully she isn't wearing anything with a lot of fabric that could get caught up in the bike – just tight ass leggings and one of those tops that exposes her entire stomach. As long as I keep the bike upright, we'll both be fine. Clearly, she doesn't feel that way judging by the way she's looking at me once we stop riding. I got her there safely, so I don't see what the big deal is.

Once I have her off the bike, throws one hell of a punch at my face that I duck to block. I grab her around the waist, but that doesn't stop her from throwing another punch at me back like she wants to send her fists straight through my heart.

"Settle the fuck down!" I scream at her.

That only makes her fight harder. She screams her ass off while I yell at her and figure I better let her down so I can calm her because she won't stop fighting, no matter how tightly I hold her around the waist. *Christ.*

I set her down, watching her throw her helmet off before she attempts punching me until she can't scream anymore and she just looks like a crazy ass black lady punching the fuck out of a big white boy in a parking lot. It takes her a while to notice how the entire situation must be coming across. Her screams slowly fade out and then she sniffles, wipes her eyes and glances all around her at the mostly empty parking lot.

Bear and Scrap go ahead with all four duffel bags. Truthfully, none of us can afford to stop but considering my situation, they'll understand if I'm a bit behind. Everything is fucking catching up to me. My older sister took me aside last year and warned me it might end up like this.

You'll run out of that gambler's luck and then what? The club is important... You can't lose the club.

Maybe my luck will run out. But not today. Not as soon as my sister Tylee thought. Because fuck... stumbling upon this creature was beyond lucky.

"Where am I?" she says through sobs, trying to sound strong despite the fact that I clearly scared the fuck out of her. She told me she had never been on a motorcycle before, but I didn't expect her to scream her fucking head off the whole way or hold onto me so tightly that she drew blood.

"It doesn't matter."

"This is a crime," she says. "The police will report me missing and they'll track my phone and then you and your band of human traffickers will be sent to prison."

It would sound believable if you didn't know anything about US law enforcement. We're already over the Cook County, Illinois boundary, which is already enough to slow down Midwestern law enforcement. Add to that Anna fits a demographic of women whose disappearance rarely rattles anybody.

If she didn't have anyone else to put that sorry motherfucker out of his misery for her, she doesn't have anyone to save her ass from me. She glances behind her like she's looking for an opportunity to run or more landmarks to ground herself. Either way, she shouldn't bother.

There is no fucking way I'm letting Anna out of my sight for the rest of her life – at least not until she's done what I want.

"That's not gonna happen, cupcake."

She glares at me when I call her that. Her dark brown skin doesn't have a single line on it. I can tell from how she carries herself that she's around my age, maybe a couple years older, but if I had to just look at her smooth walnut skin, she doesn't look a day over nineteen. She has a great body too.

Black women don't make good wives on account of running their mouths way too much, but she'll do just fine for paying off my debts.

I can feel my tongue jutting out of my mouth unconsciously, running over my lips as my darkest thoughts enter my head. *Why wait?* Another part of me rises to the occasion, instantaneously aroused by the thought of what I need from her. Why I brought her out here. The darkest part of me takes over.

"WHY ARE YOU DOING THIS?" she says. "I appreciate you saving my life but you've done enough. Please... Just let me go back to my job. I have an apartment. I have a life."

She sounds desperate. So fucking desperate. Unfortunately for Anna, the desperation in her voice only arouses me more.

"I can't do that, cupcake."

"Why not?"

"Because I need you."

THE VISIBLE TERROR on her face intensifies. There's no way for me to get through this situation without scaring the crap out of her.

"Listen. I can tell you're some sort of crazy biker with some gang affiliations, but I am not about that life. I'm a nurse. If you have someone that needs patching up, I can point you in the right–

"Quiet."

She looks at me like I have three heads.

"Excuse me?" she says with a lotta fucking attitude.

See what I mean? Black women are always talking back at you. I don't need to have any experiences to know that they're a problem but Anna is just proving me right.

"I don't need anyone patched up. I need *you*. And we're gonna go into that gas station bathroom and you know... I'll do what I need to do."

Her eyebrows raise about an inch and her mouth drops open.

"Oh hell fucking no," she says. "You do not mean that."

Great. At least I don't have to worry about the kid being stupid. Not like it matters, since I'll be giving it to Reaper when we're done with the entire process.

"I need a baby."

"What?" she says. "Are you on PCP? Methamphetamines? Something stronger? I'm not having a baby with you. Please... whatever the hell is wrong with you, I'll help you."

She takes a suspicious step back. I don't want her natural African American athleticism to kick in just when my alcohol withdrawal is at its strongest. My hand clamps around her wrist and she yelps in pain as I close around her tightly. The yelp only serves to stiffen my cock more.

"LET GO OF ME! SOUTHPAW!"

I drag her body against mine. She shoves her hands against my chest in a last-ditch effort to fight me off. I've never been nervous before kissing a woman. I guess it's just that her lips look so different up close. And she smells different from any other woman I've been with. Her skin is different.

"LET GO!" she shrieks in a husky, sexy voice.

I don't let her go, but I do respond. Holding onto her more tightly, I silence Anna's screams with a kiss. At first she emits a muffled scream and then a noise halfway between a scream and a yelp. I don't stop. Those lips are mine. They became mine the second I killed her previous suitor and took Anna for myself.

She stops screaming and after a few seconds of fiercely kissing her lips... she moans. I can tell the sound embarrasses her because she follows it up with a sharp inhalation and then subdued silence. I pull away from her and run my thumb over her wet lips. They're so... full. They feel like they're going to burst with fullness. I lean forward and bite on her lower lip until she screams and slaps my cheek.

I pull away with a grin, maintaining a tight hold on her forearm.

"Come," I murmur, relaxing a little to give her an opportunity to choose me.

Anna's pretty face twists in disgust. It's almost enough to make me cum in my pants. I don't know why I'm fucked up like this. I just am.

"No. I'm not letting you knock me up in a gas station bathroom when I don't even know your real name," she protests. Again, she makes an effort to yank her arm away from me, but it doesn't work. I pull her tighter against my chest so I can smell her better.

So she can smell me.

"How would my real name help the situation? It's a Flying J. The bathrooms are clean," I tell her. "I need you now."

Truth be told, it will be a lot easier to justify her presence to the rest of the club if she already has my cum inside her. Anna still doesn't understand what the hell she just stumbled into and I find her confusion and desperation for escape amusing. It's been a long time since I've been close to someone who didn't have a place in our world. Who didn't want my place in our world...

Anna looks at me like I'm repulsive and not the son of someone important and powerful.

"I am a nurse, not some back alley hooker," she protests without breaking eye contact for a second. "I'm not letting a guy who smells like a sweaty ballsack fuck me in the bathroom. Period."

"Fine," I growl, reaching for my belt with my free hand. "We can do it out here."

"Are you crazy?!"

"No," I growl, but I don't feel well. My head hurts. I need beer and my dick is now so goddamn hard that I can't think. I don't know how this happened to me. I just kissed her. It was just one kiss to shut her up and now... *I really do need her.*

"You're going to walk in there with me and you won't make a fuss. When I'm done with you... I'll protect you. I promise. Because where we're going, you're going to need my protection."

"Or I could call the police and get their protection."

"You think the pigs in bumfuck Illinois give a shit about some black chick's problems? They don't. I have your phone and everything that connects you to the outside world." I can tell from the look on her face that she wants to kill me, but the outrage only gives me an opportunity to look at her differently as her lips, nose and lines in her face all draw out exactly how she feels about me.

Disgust. Not a single whiff of attraction. She doesn't know who I am and something tells me if she really did know who I was underneath the cut, all the way down to my roots and core, down to the pure blood driving through my veins, she wouldn't give a fuck. I shouldn't drag her into my underworld. The disgust she feels now is nothing compared to what she'll witness if I abandon her here.

I have a debt to pay.

AND IF I don't pay it with her, I'll have to take one of the girls always hanging around the club and one of those girls won't do something like that for nothing. This woman doesn't give a fuck about club politics. Her skin color makes the situation an added 'fuck you' to Lyle Blackwood.

He doesn't want a mixed race bastard child. He wants to take something to punish me. Teach me a lesson for what I did to his daughter. But I never promised her anything. It's not my fault the

Blackwoods thought they had an easy way into the club leadership. Not like any of that matters right now. I placed the bets and I got too drunk to play the way I normally do, losing more money than I had access to.

I'm lucky dad didn't kill me. He's killed for less.

CHAPTER FOUR
ANNA

Southpaw stares at me with an intense and animalistic fixation keeping me positioned firmly against his chest. I wish I was wearing something more than a crop top and leggings. I feel dangerously exposed, especially pressed up against this stranger.

I couldn't move if I wanted to. But I don't know what I want right now. Escape? Where the hell would I go? *This man killed someone and I witnessed it. I'm lucky that I'm not dead yet.*

But I'm not having his baby. He's a stranger. A murderer. And worse, his murky green eyes terrify me. He won't let me go. I can feel it. His heart races as he holds me against him and the scent of his sweat finally overpowers the smell of engine grease all over him.

"Will you do what I say or will you make trouble?"

I give him the fiercest, most hateful look I can muster up, but my survival instincts are even stronger than my loathing this time.

"I'll go with you," I answer, my voice completely strained as I agree to sign my life away to this maniac. "But you have to promise not to kill me and... when you have your baby, you let me go."

"Deal," he says. "I want nothing to do with you personally. You're just a convenient woman with enough tits and ass to make me cum fast."

His face hardens as he says this, like he's being intentionally cruel to push me away. I swallow slowly, fighting the urge to knee him in the balls. He's easily six-four and I watched him blow a man's brains out, something I wish I could forget. Southpaw runs his tongue over his lips again. There's no reason for any person to be this big.

He turns me around and pushes me towards the gas station entrance. I glance up at the CCTV when we enter, but I suspect this man knows what he's doing, just like he did at the first gas station where we met each other. *It's some type of hillbilly mafia out here.*

My stomach drops when we enter the Flying J together. The guys working at the front counter obviously know Southpaw. They address him by his name and give him some sort of strange salute. They don't have leather jackets but they have tattoos and they all look like they were raised on a combination of methamphetamines and Mountain Dew.

I feel like a hooker. Heat starts behind my ears and spreads over my neck. By the time Southpaw drags me into the cramped but strangely clean bathroom, the walls seem like they're moving in closer. And closer. My breathing grows shallow and he lets go of my arm, which should make me feel better, but it doesn't. After shutting and locking the bathroom door, he just watches me, odd satisfaction spreading across his face as panic heightens within me. Blood rushes past my ears and I'm panting like a goddamn dog.

This isn't right. I'm not this person.

"You don't have to do this," I plead with him weakly, even if he obviously doesn't give a single fuck. "I don't want to have your baby and... you don't want me to have your baby. For all you know, I could be crazy. I could give the baby my mental illness."

The words spill out of me senselessly. This man isn't listening to me. He's only listening to the bulge in his crotch and the demented instincts flooding his criminal mind. I thought he was helping me with the Gary situation but clearly... *I was wrong.* It feels like my heart is beating against each of my ribs and the pain is sharp. Logically, I know it's just a panic attack, but that doesn't stop it from happening.

I suck in air sharply and almost lose control of myself. He closes the distance between us again and cups my cheeks.

"Breathe," he says slowly and for a split second, I forget that he's the monster who shot a man in front of me and then dragged me into a gas station bathroom to knock me up. My response to him isn't logical. He presses his forehead to mine and just as easily as he induces a panic attack, he takes it away. I breathe in slowly and then he kisses me. My lips part to kiss him back. I feel a burst of energy from his lips. They're so warm.

I gasp for air.

"Good," he mutters as he drags his lips down to my neck. The stubble on his beard tickles my neck. I cry out with an involuntary moan. What is this man doing to me? Why am I moaning? My heart races and panic tightens my chest again. Without me saying anything, he wraps one of his gigantic bear arms around my waist. I should feel more threatened, especially because this draws our bodies against each other and forces my nipples against his firm chest through my clothes.

His lips move over my neck again and then his tongue juts out as he sucks on my flesh, forcing another moan out of me. I try to stifle it by pressing my face into his shoulder, but I just end up forcing myself to inhale every scent mixed into his t-shirt and leather cut. It's overwhelmingly masculine. The engine grease. His sweat. Something stronger than that and a little sweeter seeps through. I hold him back as he pulls me closer and kisses my neck.

"I won't hurt you," he murmurs in my ear, his voice getting lower and huskier, sending a gush between my legs. I suppress my awareness of the disturbing response to this kidnapper and murderer kissing my neck in a gas station bathroom. His voice just sounds... *hot.* And it's been a while. The thing with being selective about the guys that you date is that sometimes your dry spells last a long time.

But this isn't what I wanted to break my dry spell. I promised myself I would never let another guy get intimate with me who I wasn't head over heels in love with – who didn't love me. There's no love in this situation, just a killer's animal lust.

"I killed for you," he continues. "I promise you sweet Anna, I won't hurt you. I just need somewhere warm and wet to cum..."

He sucks hard on my neck until I moan loudly and then, as if he's trying to punish me for enjoying his kisses too much, he pulls away and commands me sharply, "Take your pants off and bend over the sink."

The sink faces a small bathroom mirror and the entire space is a cramped family-style public restroom with a baby-changing table behind us and plain brown tiles all over the floor and ceiling. *At least it's clean.* When I don't turn around immediately, Southpaw flips me around. Our eyes meet in the mirror.

He towers behind me, his gigantic body making me feel like I'm truly small and powerless for the first time in my life. My breath catches as I brace myself against the ceramic sink. My fingers grip the sides of the sink as Southpaw begins executing his commands.

"Please..." I whimper. I sound like I'm begging him to continue instead of begging him to stop. He aggressively yanks down my leggings and underwear away in one swift motion and the yelp I make sounds like a yelp of pleasure as everything slides to the ground. I want to say "no". I definitely mean for the words to come out of my mouth. But Southpaw's menacing figure is suddenly behind and underneath me as he drops to his knees.

I shudder as his body's closeness spreads warmth all over my thighs. Adrenaline rushes through me as I get past my surprise and realize what he's about to do. *No.* I have never been able to get a boyfriend to do this so a stranger getting on his knees terrifies and confuses me.

"You smell good," he grunts and my stomach knots. Southpaw

pushes his head forward, kissing my thighs slowly at first and scraping his beard along my soft flesh before he slides his tongue between my lower lips.

He has to notice how wet I am...

Hot shame courses through me as he makes a low grunt of pleasure in the back of his throat and continues sliding his tongue between my legs. I moan again because this man barely knows a damn thing about me but he comfortably licks every inch of me from my clit all the way to my asshole.

The yelp I make when his tongue gets to my back door only encourages him and a large amount of spit slides out of his mouth and lubes up every inch of me from my asshole to my lower lips. When he gets me completely soaked, he sucks on each of my lower lips. I cry out loudly as he takes the left one into his mouth, teasing it with his tongue and then sucking hard until my moans become shrill and even more untamed.

Southpaw pauses the torturous teasing of my outer lips by running his tongue over my clit in slow, smooth circles that cause a tightening sensation between my thighs and makes it extremely difficult to breathe. He grips my thighs and spreads my legs apart, completely taking control of me like I belong to him. His tongue moves to my asshole again, just when I thought I would cum from him teasing my clit.

This isn't what he said would happen here. Quick sex. He needs a baby. Why the hell is he eating my pussy?

Southpaw pulls his tongue away from my asshole and in a deep, husky and completely serious voice, he says, "I've never seen one so dark before. I like your pussy, woman."

Before I can tell him that I've never heard anything so crude and inappropriate before, he adds a finger. His roaming finger slides deep inside me with an immediate and cruel stroke. The noise I make is ungodly. Juices gush from my tightness all around his thick, meaty finger. His tongue returns to my clit and my response is beyond my control.

I cum hard. The pleasure in my core feels just as uncontrollable as my panic. I can't release my death grip on the sink as Southpaw smacks my ass and keeps running his tongue in slow circles along my clit as I climax. The waves crash into me ceaselessly for several minutes. He doesn't stop licking me and sucking me. My thighs are soaking wet.

I block out every thought in my head because if I have to think critically, I'm going to freak the fuck out about how I just got the best head of my entire life from a psychopathic biker who kidnapped me and hauled my ass off to a Flying J bathroom to make a baby with me. He keeps kissing my thighs until I moan again. His tongue feels good but his thick beard tickling the back of my thighs feels even better.

There's something that drives me fucking wild about having a gigantic man like that on his knees behind me licking every inch of me like a dinner plate he wants to wipe clean with his tongue. He doesn't hold back. That tongue goes wherever he wants. Including my ass, which he still licks with slow, tentative licks like he's trying to tease me or torture me in an entirely new way.

I shudder as I feel strange new pressure building in my core from the way Southpaw licks my ass. A tongue in my ass has never been on the menu before, so this gritty biker treating my butthole like a five-star appetizer sends a forbidden thrill straight through me. He wraps one of those large hairy biceps around my legs as he props me up a little to get better access to my ass and lower lips.

I cry out even louder than before as his tongue slides from my ass back to my pussy. I bite down on my lower lip to stop myself from moaning, but it doesn't work. I can't escape how fucking good he feels and my common sense has completely evaporated. This hot, tense, terrifying moment between us feels like the most important thing in the world. I just need the release. More release. I just want to cum again so fucking badly. It's like he awakened some hibernating sexual creature with a voracious appetite for the most messed up orgasmic pleasure imaginable.

I just can't think about the fact that he's a monster or that he shot someone in front of me. I'm a nurse. I see trauma every day... I can just block it out. I grip the sink tighter as Southpaw's tongue returns eagerly to my clit. His index finger pushes against my entrance again and I greedily push my hips back against him, yielding to him intentionally for the first time since he pressed his tongue between my legs. The guilty knot in my stomach tightens but I try not to care. I can't let myself care.

One orgasm doesn't feel like enough to process the fucked up shit that happened before Southpaw locked my ass in this bathroom. My cries grow louder as he sucks on my pussy lips more sensuously, drawing each one into his mouth and making out with my pussy until the juices dribble down his chin and I explode with another powerful orgasm. He withdraws his fingers from my pussy.

I hear him shoving his finger into his mouth and sucking my juices off of it with a loud smack when he withdraws it from his lips.

"Mmm," he growls. "You taste fucking good."

More of my juices squirt out of my pussy and drip down the backs of my thighs. His tongue scrapes across the back of my thighs, allowing every inch of me to feel not just his soft, warm tongue but the prickling from his beard.

"You have the sweetest pussy I've ever tasted," he murmurs. "So fucking sweet and tight."

I whimper as he puts his finger against my entrance again. I thought he was done, but apparently I'm wrong. The thick, fat finger stretches my entrance again. I lean forward as another involuntary moan escapes my lips.

"You sound hot when you moan," he says. "If this is how you sound with my finger, you're gonna love my big white dick."

His what?

My body tenses at his uncomfortable mention of our race. I obviously thought about it. I know where the fuck I am and I know enough about biker culture to know that most of these motherfucker are country ass racists and proud of it. This man projects powerful racist vibes. He runs his tongue over the back of my thigh again and chuckles.

"That make you uncomfortable, cupcake?" he murmur. "Talking about putting my big white dick in your pussy? Because it gets me hard thinking about knocking you up..."

He releases my thighs and rises to his feet. A pang of panic surges through my chest. Having his tongue between my legs allowed me to detach from the situation and throw myself into the pleasure I feel. Having his dick between my legs represents something more permanent.

I can feel his giant body moving behind mine. Edging closer. There's no room in this bathroom for me to escape from him even if I wanted to. The man is a pillar of chiseled muscle and physically larger than me just because of his height. I know how easy it is for him to overpower me too.

He touches my ass as he moves in closer behind me. My thighs shudder. I look into the mirror again, making the mistake of glimpsing the man's face. Southpaw can't be his real name. Our eyes meet and he quickly looks away from me, his strong brow pinching over his straight, aquiline nose. He has a *very* handsome face beneath the beard, the tattoos and the bruises from whatever physical fights he must have been in lately.

"You have a great ass," he grunts, as if he feels like he has to say something. It doesn't matter what he says. Nothing will change the truth of this situation.

I'M HIS PRISONER – a woman he kidnapped and brought to a truck stop bathroom to use as his personal surrogate. There's nothing romantic or normal about this moment between us.

CHAPTER FIVE
SOUTHPAW

I can smell her pussy lips on my mustache. I am drunk off Anna's scent, which fills every inch of this room. This woman is incredible. I don't know what the fuck I've been doing the past decade or so, but I should have tasted some black pussy years ago if this is what I was missing. Her body is different from other girls I've been with.

She's small, which I have always liked. There is something very sexy about a woman much smaller than me who I can easily throw around. Anna has curves, though. Nice tits. A firm, full ass with plump cheeks like two pillows that I desperately want to jiggle around my dick. Her sweet ass makes me desperate to slide my tongue back against her asshole and taste it again.

She has the sweetest, full lower lips that make me want to plunge my cock deep inside her tightness. I can't waste time sliding another finger between those lips. I need to cum. *I need that baby.*

"I'm not gonna be romantic, cupcake. This is breeding, plain and simple."

I don't need her getting confused or getting any strange notions about our arrangement here. She's just a convenient pussy for me to cum in. Luckily for me, she's a very sexy convenience. I touch her lower lips, letting my cock stiffen as I feel how sticky and wet her entrance is.

She grips the side of the sink and makes eye contact with me in the mirror again. Under other circumstances, I would feel guilty. Unfortunately, I'm too goddamn hard to give a fuck about guilt. I want Anna's pussy right now. My cock has total control over me and my desires twist up in a way that I don't even fucking understand.

I want to knock her up. I want to feel her pussy wrapped tight around my dick. I want to cum inside her. I want to feel her soft ass thighs. I can't wait to feel Anna's tight ass pussy wrapped around my dick. Her soft butt cheeks jiggle as she adjusts herself slightly. Anna's juices dribble down her thighs and I don't think I've ever been this hard in my life.

Undoing my belt and sliding my black jeans and underwear over my ass, my dick springs forward on its own. There are no thoughts in my mind at all. There's nothing in the room but our heavy breathing, Anna's scent, and pure lust coursing through my veins. She smells so fucking good. Lining up my hips behind hers, I grab her hips forcefully.

She emits an uncomfortable moan in protest, but she doesn't dare defy me now. Her body is so fucking tiny compared to mine that I don't have to worry about Anna escaping my clutches. Placing one hand on her lower back, I press the head of my cock against her slick entrance. Heat from her dusky entrance envelops my cock instantly and I have to fight the urge to slide into her with one swift stroke.

Once she feels my dick edging threateningly close to her tightness, Anna unconsciously eases forward, pulling her hips forward so I can't get to her. My fingers sink more tightly into her hips.

"Don't move."

I push the head of my cock forward slightly. *Holy fuck.* She is so fucking tight. It's like having a hand wrapped tightly around my dick. Even tighter than that. Thrusting a little deeper provokes a full-throated moan from Anna, although I barely have two inches of dick inside her.

"Damn, you are so fucking tight, woman."

"It hurts," she gasps. "It hurts... I can't..."

SHE CAN'T? I have way more dick to go and every intention of getting every last inch of myself inside her. I lean forward a little more, ignoring her protests and getting another inch inside Anna's pussy. She cries out louder. More of her juices coat my cock but it doesn't matter how wet she gets, nothing can change how tight she feels.

"What's wrong?" I growl. "Never had a real dick inside that pussy before?"

"I'm not talking to you," she gasps, glaring at me via harsh eye contact in the bathroom mirror. This woman fucking hates me and something about having her bent over the sink with nothing but pure hatred written all over her face gets me so hard. She squirms uncomfortably as she can feel my cock stiffening inside her and the veins bulging out of the underside as blood rushes to the head from Anna's tight pussy wrapped around me.

My threatening look in the mirror does nothing to quell her defiance. The woman is a goddamn witch and she just keeps glaring at me, daring me to say another word when she specifically told me not to. I lean forward until I reach for a handful of her hair and wrap it around my hands before slowly craning Anna's neck back as I rise to my full height and take complete control of her.

Her body tightens as she realizes now that I could just slam every inch of my dick into her in an instant – and without warning.

"Look at yourself, woman," I growl, tilting her head to force her to make eye contact with me in the mirror again. "You look so fucking hot taking my dick. Is this the first time you've bent over for a white boy?"

Her nostrils flare with blatant fury. I drive another inch of my cock inside her, forcing her to moan as I assert my dominance over her dripping hole.

"Answer the damn question."

"Or what?" she growls. "You already have your dick inside me."

"You have another hole," I remind her.

"Yes," she gasps. "Yes, you're the first white boy."

I DON'T KNOW why I thought I would be able to hold back after that. I shove the rest of my cock inside her. I must have hurt her from the ear-splitting cry that emerges from Anna's mouth. I can't control myself. I thrust into her ardently, taking her from behind with possessive urgency.

The sound of our hips smacking together and Anna's heavy breathing as she makes desperate efforts to stifle her moans drives me wild. I can't say I ever fucked a woman so hard in my life. I smack her ass a couple times as I enter her dripping pussy and watching those soft cheeks jiggle around my dick tightens my balls against my body.

I'm gonna cum.

My climax tightens in my balls but I stay on the edge without cumming as I reach between Anna's lower lips and easily find her clit between soft, smooth lips that are completely wet and sticky with juices from our fucking. Once my hands reach for her clit and I rub her pussy in slow, smooth circles, Anna explodes.

It feels so fucking good to make her lose control like this. Her pussy tightens around my dick as she cums. The sexy ass moans escaping those full lips and the way her pussy grips the fuck out of my cock makes it impossible for me to hold back a second longer. I push all the way inside her sweet black pussy and empty every drop of my cum inside her.

How fucking long has it been? The last time I had sex, I must have been drunk as fuck because it didn't feel anything like this. Her soft, wet pussy easily accepts my load and as more ropes of cum erupt from my dick, I can feel my seed soaking into her walls as they grip my dick and milk me for more cum.

This is fucking heaven. Her pussy is pure relief. Euphoria. I groan and push forward even deeper, following my body's instincts to give every drop of my cum to the woman positioned in front of me. Her legs spread submissively as she gasps for breath bent over the sink, careful to avoid eye contact with me in the mirror.

I pull out of her and immediately push two fingers into her, causing Anna to yelp in surprise.

"I need you pregnant."

I offer no other explanation and she doesn't ask. I rub her inner walls slowly, pushing my seed into them and feeling my cock already sprouting another semi. If I didn't have shit to do, I would definitely fuck her again. When I remove my fingers, she remains bent over and I watch some of my cum drip out of her pussy. My cock gets fully hard again, but I try to distract myself with the fucked up ride ahead of us and how I'll have my hands full keeping this mouthy piece of ass out of trouble.

"Get your clothes on."

No kissing. No cuddling. I don't want this woman getting the wrong idea about what we're doing here. She doesn't look to me for any affection. If anything, fucking her only makes her hate me more. Sounds about right for me and women. I get dressed and smack her ass once I'm done and she's sliding into her leggings. She says nothing.

"Hey," I growl at her before we leave the bathroom. Why the fuck hasn't she looked at me? She came at the very least, that should have fixed thirty-percent of her attitude. Anna finally looks at me with nothing but loathing – again.

"Yes?"

"That was some good pussy."

"YOU CAN STILL LET ME GO," she says hesitantly. "If it was so good."

"Nice try, woman, but... I need you."

I pat her belly and she swats my hand away, unconcerned with the potential consequences of hitting me. I let her get away with it, this time, but the next time I want to touch any part of her, I'll expect compliance.

"I strongly doubt a tall muscular white man can't find someone better to have sex with," she mutters to herself. But she clearly doesn't want to engage with me judging by the way she stares at the door. I open it and Anna rushes past me, her shoulders sinking with relief once she's away from me. It's better if she hates me anyway. There's no room in my life for a woman to like me.

Won't stop me from fucking her, won't stop her from staying. Fact is, I've got debts to pay and Miss Anna's gonna help me pay them.

CHAPTER SIX
ANNA

My legs shake and shudder the entire ride to the honky tonk. It's painfully cruel that Southpaw leaves me so damn sensitive that I cum during the ride to the bar. Thankfully, I don't think he notices since the only outward signs I give him are sinking my fingers deeper into his sinewy side muscles when the waves of orgasm become too intense to handle.

I hate everything about riding. My legs are completely stiff for how long we've been on the road. It should be illegal to not be sitting in comfortable and *heated* leather seats for that much time. Southpaw's speed down the highway doesn't make the landscape any less flat and boring, even if he scares the crap out of me. I don't get the motorcycle thing.

I can't imagine why anyone would voluntarily do something so goddamn dangerous with their free time. When Southpaw parks the bike, I leap off of it, quickly unbuckling my helmet before dropping it to the ground. The only reason I don't run away from him completely is because he throws me a sharp look and then whistles at me harshly, like I'm some type of farm dog. I glare at him but stop dead in my tracks, still quaking with the adrenaline coursing through me.

He takes his helmet off, letting his thick black hair fall out of it in messy waves down to his shoulders. If he weren't a sociopathic murderer, maybe there would be something handsome about his sharp jawline or his dark raspberry colored lips. He reaches into his back pocket for those disgusting Zyn things and then gives me an annoyed look.

"You should stick close to me. Shit gets pretty rowdy in there."

"Where exactly are we?"

"Doesn't matter," he says. "This is all our territory but you stumbled into the middle of a civil war and I don't have time to explain everything to you."

"You had plenty of time to fuck me in a rest stop bathroom," I snap at him.

His face clouds with anger but he can't possibly hate me more than I hate him. This man shot someone in front of me, kidnapped me and now I'm hours away from home without my phone, wallet, keys or a goddamn clue where I am.

"That was for both of our safety, woman. This place doesn't allow blacks."

He spits the word like it's a slur and I find myself oddly grateful that he didn't use a harsher word. The man gives off a vibe like it's on the tip of his tongue.

"I don't have to go anywhere that doesn't allow me," I respond.

He smirks. "You're coming with me because you have what I need to hold up my end of a deal. That load I put in your belly will be the only thing keeping you safe. My family will protect you."

I hate the way he looks at me. It's worse than a dog eyeing a piece of steak. There's something dark and twisted wrapped up in Southpaw's desire for me. *He was so rough after he ate me out – like he hated me for the fact that he wanted me.*

When I don't budge, he commands me firmly. "Come."

I move towards him, expecting him to give me another stern warning or otherwise threaten me. But he just leans in and kisses me again. I hate kissing him. He's tall, firm everywhere, I can smell his sweat on his clothes and of course, the intense scent of leather. I forget that I watched him blow a man's brains out over a minor slight.

I forget that he "fucked a baby in me" as he put it several times very crudely when he didn't even tell me his real name.

His intense olive eyes gaze deeply into mine once he pulls away from the kiss.

"You're a nurse," he says, running his thumb over my lips. "Means you're smart. Means you're useful. Your color doesn't matter for what I need."

He crudely pats my pussy from the front through my pants. I lurch away from him in disgust and hit his forearm again but that only makes him laugh. He puts his arm around me possessively. I don't feel an ounce of affection from him, just control. He drags my body against his, once again reminding me of his sheer physical strength. I couldn't escape him if I tried. I lean into him.

"Don't get the wrong idea," he says. "This doesn't mean you're my old lady or anything."

"Your what? I'm not anybody's old anything," I snap at him. He laughs again even if I definitely didn't say anything funny.

His demeanor stiffens as we approach the door and if anything can make that hunk of muscle uncomfortable, I am definitely concerned. The bar is just off the old Route 66 highway, I can tell that much as we get closer from all the tacky ass signs outside announcing the honky tonk bar like it's Las Vegas and not just a dive off the side of the highway.

We must be in Missouri. Only other Midwesterners will understand, but different states have a different smell and feel to them. This place smells like Missouri and judging by how long we were on the road, and a faded out road sign I attempted to read while Southpaw swerved like a maniac, I suspect that's where we are.

Missouri is a big state, so I can't exactly narrow that down but... It's my best guess.

I quickly scan the parking lot and lose count of the bikes parked out front. The lengthening days mean that the parking lot is covered in a dusky gray and orange sunset light that would be pretty if we weren't in flat ass Missouri.

"Are we in Missouri?"

"Don't say a fucking word when we get in there," Southpaw responds. I guess we're done fucking laughing with each other, huh? His fingers curl around my biceps as he pulls my body against his. He kisses my cheek firmly and a confusing shiver goes straight through me. This man is not right in the head. Once I hold on to that truth, I will – eventually – find some way to escape him.

Southpaw shoves the doors to the bar open and that shit is straight up like a saloon from an old school western movie. The thick smell of tobacco, vape juice, marijuana, beer, urine and hard liquor of every flavor hits me like a bus with no brakes. I don't recognize the music. It's some honky tonk shit, that's about all I know. When I enter the room, everybody stops talking. Like... everybody.

He wasn't exaggerating when he told me to stay close. It's clear that nobody in this damn room expects this man to walk in here with a black woman. They're gawking. One man in the back of the room coughs loudly and I pray silently to myself that it cuts the tension, but it doesn't. The hacking cough settles back into silence and it's just us against the room full of bikers with some damn country song on the radio.

The beast who's kidnapped me here finally opens his fucking mouth after silence that feels like it lasts forever.

"I'm here. I have the money and the first born child I promised... right inside this pussy right here."

He pats the front of my crotch again and sharp humiliation courses through me. This time, I sense better than to smack him. His crude action sends a murmur rippling through the room full of

ANNA

bikers which feels more claustrophobic than before. Tobacco smoke drifts towards me and chokes my lungs.

A man steps out from the crowd with a clearly antagonistic expression towards Southpaw. The energy in the air is thick and adrenaline surges through me. Shit is about to go down. They gaze at each other like they're out for blood. Considering I'm about to witness another fucking crime, maybe it's a good thing I don't know the guy's real name.

"What the fuck is your problem? Is this a joke?"

The man who spoke parts the crowd and as he gets closer, I notice he towers over Southpaw, which is truly a genetic achievement since the crude beast standing next to me was previously one of the largest men I had ever seen. He's significantly older than Southpaw, which is just about the only thing giving me any comfort in the situation. Bullets don't care how old you are, so I just have to hope these assholes prefer settling things with their fists.

My body tightens and I try to look disinterested and most importantly, I try not to look at anyone in particular.

"It's not a joke, Doc. I came inside her. I'm gonna knock her up and in about 39 weeks, you'll have your first born."

"She's a goddamn nigger, Southpaw."

I've never heard anyone just drop the word like that. I know it seems unlikely to certain folks or a certain generation, but it's just never happened to me. Maybe I'm privileged or just blessed. I'll take that. But to hear someone just drop the n-word like that... My ears ring and the pain is physical. I start to say something, but Southpaw gives me the meanest look I've ever seen and he speaks instead.

"I know."

That's it? I freeze, completely paralyzed. This isn't who I am. *It's the trauma, girl. You're a nurse. You know that.*

It doesn't matter what I know logically. Too much has happened for me to diagnose myself, far less treat myself. Right now, I'm just surviving.

The man he called Doc runs his fingers through long, gray hair and even if he's trying to hide his feelings from Southpaw, he makes no bones about hiding his utter disgust with me.

"You're a fucking cheat," Doc says.

Southpaw glances around at everyone in the room. They're all captivated by the conversation and when I get a hold of myself, I realize that this could go way worse than I thought. Half the men in this room are armed. Most are drunk. In the very back of the room, there are white lines cut on the bar counter.

"Not a cheat, Doc. You never specified the kid had to be white."

Doc spits on the ground and then he seems to feel quite comfortable turning his ire on Southpaw. All the men in the room glance anxiously at each other's hands. One move for your weapon and you're fucked. It's gang shit. Doesn't matter if it's the Italian mob, the crips or this hillbilly mafia. You get a bunch of testosterone filled fuck-ups in a room together with liquor and guns, some shit is bound to pop off.

At least we're close to the entrance. Not like it matters, since I have yet to meet a motherfucker who can outrun a bullet. I don't like how this could escalate or that the only person in this room I can cling to for protection is Southpaw, the man promising my "unborn child" to a bunch of racist bikers who don't seem happy about it.

"You got a problem, Doc?" Southpaw asks with a shit-eating grin on his face. Can this man not read the room? The man he's calling Doc cracks his knuckles, drawing my attention to the rings on his fingers, even more tattoos than Southpaw and healed scars that suggest he's been in ten times as many fights.

But he's not alone. Two more men appear behind him and they look like they could be his sons or at least his blood relatives. But Southpaw doesn't have any backup and now shit is getting real enough that his eyes are glued on Doc's and he isn't even looking at me. The country music croons throughout the room, but there's nothing honky tonk about the energy between the men facing off.

A few men peel away from the crowd and stand behind Southpaw. Okay. He's not alone. I think I recognize a couple of the men

47

from the ride over, but a lot of these white guys look alike to me. They're all tall, smelly, hairy, muscular, wear leather and sunglasses, have tattoos up and down every bare inch of their skin and they're white.

I'm not bothered by that. But I can tell it's going to be a problem for me.

The man standing to Southpaw's left puts his hand on his shoulder. He has a couple inches on Southpaw and the patch on the back of his leather cut says "Junior Officer". They look like they're roughly the same age. Maybe the taller guy is a little older. He has grey eyes that are almost clear, messy hair pulled back in a half-assed ponytail and his eyes are bloodshot from liquor or some other drug.

He has his nickname patched onto his jacket — Hawk. He has a commanding presence that captures the attention of everyone else in the room. Him moving over to Southpaw's side clearly means something. I just don't know what or how bad this is gonna get. The tobacco smoke gets thicker.

Southpaw's patch also says "Junior Officer", so judging by my powers of deduction, they have a similar rank, which doesn't help me figure out how the hell this is gonna go down since I don't know how the lines are drawn here or what could happen next. I don't want to die here and if I thought I was in danger around Gary, I'm in way worse danger now.

"This doesn't have to turn sour," the man standing to Southpaw's left says. "He's paying his debts. We gotta end this shit, Doc. Our families have too much history for us to let this tear the club apart."

"The Blackwoods aren't the ones tearing the family apart. He's got a problem. A huge fucking problem."

Doc gestures with his chin towards Southpaw and takes a long drag from his cigarette.

"We all have fucking problems," Hawk says. "Are we really gonna let money fuck with our family? It's not worth it, Doc."

"Easy for you to say when some piece of shit redneck ain't cheating you out of $500,000."

I'm guessing Southpaw is the piece of shit redneck. He smirks, like he doesn't even seem mad about it. This man is crazy. I knew that when he shot a stranger for no damn reason, but watching him stare down a pack of men ready to beat his ass and smirking as they call him a piece of shit has to take the cake.

"I won't apologize for having balls of steel, Doc. No risk, no reward."

That response turns Doc's face bright red. He clears his throat, moving mucus around slowly and disapprovingly before taking a long drag from his cigarette and spitting on the floor in front of Southpaw again. And then it's quiet again. Doc grunts.

"You're not the only one with balls of steel, boy. And I don't take kindly to your disrespect. I'll give you a chance to win your bitch back."

A man even taller than Southpaw steps a little more into the light and immediately, I can tell he's Doc's son. They look alike with the same slim nose, mean sorrel colored eyes with hooded lids and thick brows. Both men look country as fuck, but the young guy who steps in front of Doc could possibly take Southpaw, the asshole I'm currently relying on for defense.

The new contender has a patch on his jacket with his nickname – *REAPER*. He's another Junior Officer. I don't like how he looks. If he "won me" in whatever sick bet these men are making with my life, I have no doubt he would do the most twisted things to me.

He looks me up and down slowly and I can feel his eyes lingering on my boobs. I want to sink into the ground, but I end up edging closer to Southpaw, smelling the gentle peppermint on his breath. *Goddamn it, why do I feel safer close to him? It's totally fucked up.*

This might be the night I die. And I'll never find out how *Empire* ends. Life is so goddamn cruel.

"I'll play you for her," Reaper says. "Hot piece of ass like that... Shit, we all look the same color with the lights off."

The off-color comment earns a laugh from his audience. Fear surges through me again. I have no escape. Southpaw puts his arm

49

around my shoulder. It's the first real gesture of affection he's shown me since we walked in here. Not like I really want his *affection* as much as I want him to get me the hell out of here.

"Maybe you shouldn't do that," Southpaw's friend advises him. But I can tell from the look in that man's eyes that he's going to do it. With his free hand, he rolls the green dice between his fingers and I can see all over his face that he's hooked on the challenge. The thrill.

"Do *not* gamble me, Southpaw," I hiss. "Your ass has done enough."

No point holding back my mouth if I'm going to die regardless of what I do or say. But he doesn't even acknowledge me. His eyes lock onto Reaper's and I can tell that he is going to do it.

"You think I give a fuck about her?" he says. "I'll play you for her, another 25 grand, and that solid gold Harley Davidson ring on your index finger."

Doc shifts uncomfortably and glares at his son, but this conflict has become personal between Southpaw and Reaper. Nobody else in the room exists and they're like two male lions on the savannah fighting for territory.

"Got it. I'll be sure to make your bitch scream when I fuck her on the pool table after I win her."

"Deal. Easiest deal I've ever fucking made, because there's no way in hell you're winning this."

Before I can react, they shake on it. *Holy fuck. Holy fuck.* I still have Southpaw's cum in my pussy and he's already gambling me away.

CHAPTER SEVEN
SOUTHPAW

I can tell she's pissed, but I can't look at her right now. I have to get my head in the game so I can beat Gideon Blackwood, also known as 'Reaper' at a game he's consistently kicked my ass at for the past two years. Tonight is different. This fresh pussy standing next to me will bring the winner out of me because I have every intention of hitting that sweet ass pussy again and filling her up with another load of my cum.

There was something special about the way she moaned and if we can stop in one of the motels for the night, I would love to do a hundred different things to Anna in a king-sized bed. First thing I gotta do is win her ass in a bet, make an extra $25 grand off Gideon for humiliating my ass in front of her and top it off with some added humiliation of the Blackwood family by winning the heirloom ring Lyle 'Doc' Blackwood gave to his eldest son for his twenty-first birthday.

I can feel my best friend's angry gaze on the back of my neck. Every time I raise the stakes, each time I get to this point, I promise him that I'll never go back on my word.

I keep promising that I'm done gambling. That I'm done risking everything just to chase a high I haven't felt since my very first win – my bike. I still have the lucky dice from that game and even if I haven't had much luck at pool since then... I didn't have Anna.

Tanner Hollingsworth, AKA 'Ghost', steps forward to act as mediator. He's been the official referee of these pool games since the start. Except, there wasn't supposed to be another pool game between me and Reaper. I promised dad and I went through hell to fix shit... so why the hell am I rising to another challenge.

Ghost's expression seems to be asking me if I really want to do this, but I don't want to keep my eyes off Reaper for too long. This will only escalate into a civil war if these motherfuckers keep challenging our authority. That's what got us here in the first place. The club has always had a structure where you earn your position. Leadership ain't patriarchal and it has nothing to do with money.

The Blackwoods think if they marry into enough Hollingsworth money they can buy more power in the club than they rightly deserve. Our club used to be about brotherhood, not winning at the expense of lifelong friendships that stretch back generations amongst our families. Dad would say I'm just as much to blame as they are because I can't ever back down.

But why should I? The Shaws and the Sinclairs have taken just as much heat for this club as anyone else. We might be shitty with money, gambling bastards, alcoholics and a couple of us might even be deadbeat dads. But we put our brothers first. *Always.* Money isn't more important than family. Period.

"Y'all know the rules," Ghost says. His unkempt, curly black hair smells like pungent marijuana smoke. "Ten minutes to get ready. I'll check the balls and your pool sticks with the help of one member representative from each family. But I swear to fucking God... I've had it up to here with the two of you."

I'm not the only problem. Gideon wouldn't keep testing me and my authority if it weren't for his father. Doc has aged into a bitter man who wanted more for his sons than marrying into

Hollingsworth wealth. He wants some sense that his legacy will be strong but the strongest of his brood is Gideon.

Everybody knows Gideon has one screw loose. He kills for fun. Most of us fight and most of us have killed but none of us take pleasure in it. The man has a special kind of darkness that makes his sorrel eyes look black like a demon's. We could never let that type of man take control of the club. We would devolve into even more bitterness and fighting than we're going through right now.

Hunter 'Hawk' Sinclair thumps me hard on the back.

"In the fucking bathroom."

"The bitch stays with me," Ghost says firmly before Hawk can get her in the bathroom with me. Better that she doesn't see the lucky potion Hawk gives me before every pool game. He drags me off to the restroom at the back of the bar which smells like piss. They need to get Ruth back here to clean this shit up.

Hawk reaches into his pocket for some pure white. I can feel the burn in my nostrils just from looking at the powder in the clear white baggie. Before I can snatch the bag of coke out of his hand, he holds it away from me.

"Not so fast, you fucking idiot. What the hell were you thinking? We should be moving out of here in case the Jew mobilizes people to come after us. You promised your dad you were done gambling."

"I was. But the Blackwoods need to learn their place."

"You are such an egotistical fuck. You settled the debt. You could have just let it go. The way I see it, you found the perfect solution. Gideon wouldn't let his dad touch his pet. There would be so much infighting that they wouldn't have time to fuck with the club."

Hawk sounds more like the President's son than I do sometimes. I have no attachment to leading the club and I wonder if he'll eventually take the spot dad thinks I deserve. Hawk doesn't have a gambling problem. He doesn't have an ego problem. He thinks things through... He's smarter than I'll ever be.

"Doesn't matter. I already shook on it. I have to play."

Hawk gives me a disappointed look but then my best friend gives in – like he always does.

"Fine. I'll cut us a couple lines. Have some liquor to loosen your joints up and remember, you're a fucking lefty. That should be a goddamn advantage."

"I've just been off my game lately."

"Hopefully some fresh pussy will improve your game," Hawk says. "I don't know why you had to go and bother with a chick like her."

"What does that mean?" I grunt.

He works on cutting the lines without looking at me. I reach for the flask he left on the bathroom counter and finish off the rest of the liquor in there. The moonshine tastes pretty damn good. It's made out of peaches and sugar, fermented on the back of Hawk's bike with a few pieces of cinnamon bark in it for spice. Disgusting, but it gets the job done faster than Everclear.

"She's darker than burnt charcoal," he says with a flat, Oklahoma accent. "I didn't know you were into that type of thing when we have perfectly good women crawling over every bar on Route 66 begging for a ride on your cock."

He sniffs up a line of coke and I want to get my fill before I deal with Hawk's prying questions. Why the fuck is everyone up my ass about who I fuck to pay my gambling debts? It's not like I'm making her my old lady or keeping the damn kid. She's just a warm, wet hole to put my cum in.

It's not my fault she had a tight ass pussy and soft brown ass cheeks that jiggled so perfectly around my dick that I feel fucking addicted from just one hit. *I need more.*

"Is there one piece of pussy across this highway that hasn't had six or seven bikers in her quest to become an old lady? Maybe I don't want biker skanks involved in my personal business."

Hawk laughs and delivers a hearty, 'oh fuck' as he does another line before moving out of the way and presenting me with two freshly cut lines. They're both going to hurt like hell. It's been a couple weeks since I last did any coke. I had to stay clean to plan the pill heist, but now that I have to play another game of pool, I definitely need something strong in my system.

I snort one line and then Hawk hits me on the back.

"You can trust people in our circle. They know what's good for them. You can't trust that woman because she's not one of us. You let your ego get ahead of you back at that gas station with the creep."

"It wasn't my ego. That guy had a bad look in his eye."

"You sound like Gideon when you talk like that. Schizo ass Gideon."

I don't need a Sinclair giving me a lecture about what's crazy and what isn't. The Shaws have their problems and the Sinclairs have theirs. The second line of coke burns its way to the back of my throat and the rush of energy eliminates the entire impact of alcohol. I raise my head and Hawk hands me his flask.

"More moonshine. Play to your strengths. Gideon is sensitive and paranoid."

"Hm."

I grab the flask and tip it down my throat.

"Don't get attached to that woman," he says. "You can't keep her. Your dad will never let that shit slide."

"I'm a grown ass man."

"He's the president of our club, Southpaw. And we took vows."

WHEN WE GO BACK OUT THERE, the bikers in the room have rearranged themselves around the table. I'm sure the bets have already been placed on which of us will win. I'm the dark horse here. Gideon doesn't look at me when I enter the room. He looks stiff and sober but that doesn't mean anything. Gideon is never completely sober – hasn't been since he was thirteen years old.

He's been hearing voices since he was a kid too. I can only hope to hell some of those voices start acting up today. *I don't know what I'll do if I lose, but when you gamble you don't plan on losing.*

I break and get three solids in before missing the hole. *Damn it.*

THE ROOM IS quiet except for the country music on the radio. I should be 100% focused on the table, but I can't help taking the occasional glance at the woman I'm gambling, seated safely next to Tanner Hollingsworth so this simple game doesn't escalate into a gunfight over a woman.

I WISH I could tell you what happened next.

Chapter Eight
Anna

I can't believe this is happening. It's bad enough *one* biker kidnaps me, now he gambles me to another one. *A scarier one.* I can't keep track of the highway signs anymore. My only thoughts are survival, although I doubt I'll make it through the night. Doesn't matter how scared out of my pants I am... *I'll do whatever it takes to stay alive.*

I shake uncontrollably as I cling to Reaper's body and pray quietly that he's dumber than Southpaw and gives me an opportunity to escape. How the hell could anyone be dumber than the asshole who just lost me in a game of pool? My stomach sinks. I don't even know if the man who bent me over a bathroom sink earlier today survived the bar fight.

Idiot. Reaper put his arm around me and the man saw shades of rage that I've never seen him express before. He turned into an animal and the beast lunged foolishly into a fistfight he didn't stand a chance of winning as drunk as he was. A pair of tall, blond-haired twins who must have been Reaper's cousins or brothers took care of Southpaw.

I screamed my head off as they hauled me off and fought as much as I could to see what happened to him, but that didn't help.

Reaper swerves his bike to the right so hard that I nearly throw up. My fingers sink into his jacket. It's older than Southpaw's and smells different – like very alcoholic cologne and Irish Spring soap. If I didn't know better, I would say he was sober – and not just because of how easily he won me in that game of pool. He just has a cool, quietly terrifying demeanor. Like he could snap at any moment.

After two more of those sickening right turns, he guides the bike onto a barely paved road that passes through rows and rows of infinite corn. The potent smell of swampy animal manure hangs heavily in the air as bugs smack against my helmet. When he finally stops the bike, I stop clinging to him and jump off, removing my helmet and tossing it to the side.

We're in a nearly empty motel parking lot in the middle of nowhere. *Oh God.* I don't have time to process my surroundings before motion sickness smacks into me like a bus.

"Hey!" he yells at me. But I don't care. We make brief eye contact before I bend over and empty the contents of my stomach. I cry out expecting a slap when I feel a hand on my back.

"Get it all out," Reaper says with an oddly soothing voice. I obey his command. When I'm done, I wipe my mouth and meet his gaze. We're at a motel. Instant panic sets in at what this man's intentions with me might be. *Sex. He's just like the other one. He wants sex.*

My fear must be obvious because it makes him laugh like a jackal.

"Don't look at me like that," he says. "I'm not gonna fuck you with Shaw's seed still inside you. He wasn't lying, was he?"

I wait a beat too long. His expression steels. The shift is slight, but enough to send a slow chill down the length of my spine. He touches my cheek gently, but curls his fingers just enough that I know he wants me to perceive his potential for violence. His hands, after all, are terribly close to my neck.

"Answer the question," Reaper asks, reaching into his pocket and withdrawing a vape pen. Seriously? The vape pen explains why he doesn't smell like cigarettes. He takes a deep inhalation and I answer him.

"Yes. He did it."

"Are you ovulating?"

I glare at him and he glares right back.

"Answer the question," Reaper says again.

"Possibly."

"Good," he says. "What's your name, pretty lady?"

"Anna."

"Anna," he says. "Simple name. Are you a simple lady?"

What the fuck kind of question is that? His eyes travel over my facial features, avoiding direct eye contact as he focuses on my lips and then his gaze moves down, stopping at my boobs before he takes another hit from his vape pen.

"I don't know if I understand the question."

"I consider myself a simple man," he says, like he didn't really care about me answering the question or not. "I like football. Bikes. Getting drunk. Shooting dice. And a good woman."

My chest tightens. He does that jackal laugh again.

"Don't worry," Reaper says. "You ain't a good woman. Look at your skin. It's dirty. Just like you."

Fighting him would only lead to him killing me. He can't stop me from glaring daggers at him or wishing I could put a knife in his chest and show him just how goddamn dirty I can get. I bite my tongue. Survival first.

"That pissed you right off," he says, continuing to talk to himself. "Listen, if you were the last pussy on Earth, I might test it out. But I haven't got any interest in your cunt unless it would hurt that impulsive motherfucker."

Southpaw.

My momentary relief at his disinterest must have been too much for him to handle because he closes the little distance between us and kisses me. There's nothing romantic about the kiss. It's a forceful and possessive threat – to let me know that he could take me if he wanted. He squeezes my cheeks together painfully, thrusts his tongue between my teeth and then when he removes himself, he licks my mouth like a dog and bites my lower lip until I cry out from the pain.

"You disobey me even once, I'll shove my pistol up your cunt and fuck you with it," he says. "I'm not a Shaw boy, Anna. Remember that."

REAPER BARRICADES us in Room 106 after a brief interaction with a small red-headed girl working the front desk. Reaper calls her June. She asks him how Jairus is and he glares at her, telling her to shut her whore mouth and give us the room key. *Harsh.* The woman quietly obeys his command and hands him the key.

The tattoo on her wrist stops me dead. *PROPERTY OF BISHOP.* I only stop panicking and make an effort to absorb some of the details around me when I see the tattoo. I try to make pleading eye contact with the woman, but she doesn't look at me. She clearly has an affiliation with the motorcycle club but I hope that I can make the silent, deep-eye-contact women make to signal trouble.

She just won't make eye contact. I have no choice but to give up and focus on the man standing next to me. And what he wants. My stomach churns as dark thoughts about what a biker might want with me in a motel room. Southpaw didn't take long before ripping my clothes off.

This man only took me to humiliate Southpaw, so I can only imagine what's in store for me.

He unlocks the motel room door and ushers me inside. Blood rushes past my ears as we move from the humid Missouri outdoors to the confined, musty motel room. I have no ideas for escape and no clue what type of person I'm dealing with.

Reaper looks happy. He grins from ear to ear like we just landed at the Four Seasons.

"Long time since I slept in a bed," he says, glancing around before walking over to the motel room mini-fridge and pulling out a can of Old Milwaukee. Whoever runs this place knew he was coming. For all I know, maybe he runs the place. I don't take my eyes off Reaper and he doesn't take his eyes off me.

He cracks open the beer can as he sits on the edge of the motel's king-sized bed with his legs spread. I stand awkwardly near the window – he obviously wants me nowhere near the door.

After pouring nearly half the beer down his throat, he adjusts his balls in his jeans crudely, throws off his leather jacket to expose a black t-shirt fitted around unreasonably large arms, and then he acknowledges my presence again.

"June is a bitch that knows her place," he says. "That's what I mean when I say a good woman. Good white pussy."

I assume he's talking about the woman at the front desk – and trying to offend me. I don't change my facial expression.

I don't know what he expects me to say. He finishes the rest of the beer in one more tip of the can down his throat. When he crushes the can, my stomach leaps into my throat. The metal succumbs effortlessly to the slightest pressure from Reaper's meaty fingers and I can't help but imagine those hands around my throat.

"Get in the bed," he says. "You're gonna be here until I see a positive pregnancy test."

"Where are you going to be?"

HE GIVES ME AN EERIE SMILE.
"Handling business."

CHAPTER NINE
SOUTHPAW

I pretend I can't hear my brothers whispering around me or dad's footsteps plodding impatiently in front of the couch. I thought I had enough Hollingsworth whiskey in me to knock me into next week, but instead, I'm here. On the couch of our family home. Where I've been for the past few weeks, trying to figure out how the fuck to get her back.

"He can't quit gambling," dad says. "He'll never quit. That stupid motherfucker gambled his own kid. His own fucking kid. I should put a bullet in his head."

Owen pipes up quickly, "You can't kill him, dad. He just got his ass in a little more trouble. That's all."

"He's always in trouble," Ethan adds bitterly. I can always count on Ethan to take dad's side. Not like it does him any good. He did three years for taking Xanax across state lines to keep dad's ass out of trouble but he still doesn't have the higher-level club patch he wants so damn badly.

"Can you all shut up?" I groan, groping around madly for the bottle of Jim Beam. I don't have a gambling problem. I have a family problem. On top of that, I have a new problem – Anna.

"We know where Gideon has her," Ethan says. "We should storm the stupid motel and take the bitch back. The Hollingsworths don't want problems anymore than we do. But the old man had a bunch of daughters who saw fit to tie themselves to Blackwood degenerates."

"Watch your mouth," dad says. "Doesn't matter what problems we've got. Those are your brothers."

I sit up because I don't think there's any other way I'll get them to shut the fuck up. My father and brothers stare at me. I must be a mess, but it can't be worse than how anyone looks their first day out of county jail.

"If we aren't going to get her, I don't want to listen to this."

Dad grunts. He can barely muster up a complete sentence to me that isn't laden with cuss words and more disapproval than he's thrown my way in ages. If he weren't my old man, this would have come to blows ages ago. We all share dad's height. He played college football before grandma got cancer, forcing him to drop out and fill his life with rage and cuss words. I wasn't supposed to be his biggest disappointment. My life ended up spiraling out of control. I don't know when my bad habit turned into a compulsion. I've never met an addiction I couldn't quit.

I don't want to look at him, but I can't avoid my father's piercing gaze forever. He stands stiff and straight when I look at him. The anguish on his face pierces me fresh.

"What the fuck happened to you? What the hell did I do that could make you throw everything you've worked for away like this?"

The Jim Beam churns in my stomach. Owen defends me.

"Gideon Blackwood struts around like he fucking owns the place. Doc has those motherfuckers so far up their own ass, they forget that none of this shit would be held together if it weren't for the Shaws and the Sinclairs."

"None of that should matter," dad says. "We're all family."

His words have a slightly hollow edge to them. Dad and I have a close enough relationship that I can tell when he's covering something up. Burying some emotion he feels guilty for having because he's the one in charge of keeping us all together and stopping shit like this from happening. He's always been a good leader...

"Right," I respond, staring at him, hoping to draw more out of him.

"But old wounds have a way of cropping up, especially as us old boys approach our retirement. All of us are preoccupied with our legacy."

When an opportunity to take a jab at me presents itself, Ethan takes it.

"Your legacy is currently in some black chick's pussy in the middle of nowhere Missouri because our brother is a goddamn idiot. He lost the bet. Best thing to do is move on and let the bitch go."

"She's not a bitch," I snarl at Ethan. I swear, I want to strangle the life out of my brother. Technically my *half*-brother but you can't use words like half-brother in front of dad. *Family is family. Blood is blood.*

"Might not be a bitch, but she ain't an old lady either," he says. "Let her go."

"You don't understand."

I'm drunk as fuck and truthfully, I don't get it either. There was just something about that woman. Her soft ass flesh. How her body felt smacking against mine as I took her from behind. I can still hear the sound of her moans no matter how much whiskey I drink to drown out the phantom sounds.

One moment with Anna was... addictive. I need more of her. I didn't think it would be like that. I thought it would be a quick and easy release that I could easily put behind me to pay off the debts, kill the feud between me and Gideon, and get through this shit.

But now I'm in deeper than ever. I want Anna back.

"Maybe I should play for her again," I suggest. "Go back with fifty grand and sort my shit out."

"You fucking suck at pool," Ethan spits at me. "Gideon Blackwood is a goddamn moron."

"Your brother might be right," dad says, tossing Ethan the bone he worked so fucking hard for. "No more pool. I don't know if I can even trust you around dice."

"I could play for her," Owen says. "Convince Gideon I'm doing it to spite him."

Dad perks up at that suggestion, but he doesn't immediately agree with Owen. *He's thinking of something different.* I watch my father's face as he churns through all his emotions and all the possible solutions. One day, Harlan Shaw wants me to take his role but quite frankly... I don't know if I have it in me to think things through the way he does. My best friend does a far better job at that than I do. Hawk has more patience from all his time kneeling in church with his mama. I don't like to think things through. I don't pray.

I just don't have the patience for any parts of the job.

I LIKE life to be just how it feels on the back of my bike. Impossibly fucking fast.

"What about Hawk?" dad asks. "I know he doesn't gamble but... if he can win the girl back, we can find a way to turn this all around and bring the club together."

"He wouldn't do it. He's too responsible."

My best friend isn't a fuck up like I am. I won't say that he doesn't have a dark side, but he's far more responsible. It must be the religion.

"His father will convince him."

"You sound pretty sure of that."

"Randy Sinclair and I agree on the future of the club. We want it to have a future. Not just shares in a whiskey empire but a real brotherhood... Your mother is a Hollingsworth but she sees the flaws in that side of the family. Money can't rule our lives."

"Tell that to a fucking gambler," Ethan says. To my private delight, dad doesn't respond. Dad has two daughters from his first marriage, and Ethan is his eldest. He still hasn't forgiven me for coming along two years later and taking the spotlight from him.

"Don't be a dick, Ethan," Owen says calmly, giving me a sympathetic look. I've broken my younger brother's heart so many times that I don't even know how he still believes in me. I want to be the older brother he thinks I am.

"I'm not being a dick. Who gives a fuck if Gideon Lockwood puffs out his chest? Those unstable bastards would lead us all into trouble and the club would never vote Gideon in as a leader if and when dad steps down."

"Let's not get ahead of ourselves. I'm not going anywhere. Right now, we need everyone on good terms so we can get the club down to Amarillo and attend to our real business."

"I'll talk to Hawk," I groan. "Please... just get me more liquor."

"No," dad says. "No more liquor. Sober your ass up and tell me what the fuck you plan to do with that woman once you win her back. Because you can't make her your old lady. I won't let that shit happen."

"She's just a hot piece of ass I'm trying out, dad," I groan. "I want her because I'm a man. I don't like the idea of another man touching pussy that belongs to me."

He shakes his head.

"You really knock her up?"

"Yes."

I fucking hope so. I don't even know why because a baby would only make this shit even more unbearable. If our time together worked... she might be pregnant right now.

"Why would you do something like that?" dad asks me with a scowl on his face. But I can tell he's not as angry as the front he's putting up.

"I saw her. Shot her suitor in front of Tylee and... I don't know what came over me. I just had to have her."

"Crazy sonofabitch."

"I know. I know," I respond. Just thinking about the moment I met Anna sends blood straight to my dick. The second I saw her, I wanted her. Who the fuck can you blame for two magnets coming together? It wasn't her fault, but it wasn't mine either. Pussy has never had me acting this reckless before. There's something different about her.

Ethan, naturally, shows no understanding for my predicament. Still desperate for dad's attention, Ethan says, "The smart thing to do would be dropping the bitch off in a cornfield and let nature run its course. She seems to have a talent for spreading her legs."

"Don't talk about her like that," I snarl at Ethan.

"You met the cunt and knocked her up all in one day. A slut is a slut."

"I'm gonna fucking shoot you."

"Quiet," dad snaps. "What were you thinking?"

"I wasn't thinking. I should have never done what I did. I shouldn't have bet her."

Dad glares at me. "You have fucking problems. But this time, I'll let it slide. Get the pussy back and when we get to Amarillo, you sit with her until she pops the bastard out. I'll send the kid to Mexico, send her to Jamaica, and we'll wipe this stain off the family and move on. We have club matters to attend to. I can't let your dick screw us out of our family's future."

"Any child I have will be family."

"Our family is white," dad says.

There's no discussion there. His word is final.

HAWK MEETS me at the cemetery. I recognize his black metallic Indian Scout in the parking lot. Randy Sinclair passed that bike down to his son a few years ago and whenever I'm not getting his ass into trouble, Hawk works on it, keeping one of the last original Indian Scouts in near mint condition.

That's his baby.

When we need to meet about personal, best friend shit on the road, we've always met here. Every Sinclair and Shaw we know was buried here. We used to get drunk and smoke weed out here when we were kids, talk about girls, our dads and getting the fuck out of our small town outside of Springfield, Missouri for good. Boys from Ozark ready to take on the world.

Shit didn't work out quite the way we planned but at least we've seen parts of this big, beautiful country that most redneck assholes like us could only dream about.

That's all thanks to the club. Hawk leans against his uncle's gravestone smoking an American Spirit. He's kept the same brand since he stole his first one from the same uncle we're standing on right now. Hawk already put a few fresh cigarettes on the headstone by the time I get there.

"Took you long enough," he says. "Trouble with the old man?"

"Trouble with myself."

"Want one?"

What the hell. Considering what I'm about to ask him, I might as well accept. Hawk laughs once I accept the cigarette.

"Oh brother. Must be big if I'm getting you to smoke."

"It's big."

"You want the girl back?"

Am I that goddamn transparent? There's no winning when you show people what you care about in our line of work. Caring is a goddamn cancer. I answer him by taking a long drag of the cigarette, andHawk nods his understanding.

"What the hell is wrong with you?" he asks, tilting his head and looking at me very seriously from behind his pale blue eyes. All the Sinclairs are white as winter with black hair and eyes either blue, violet or gray. They call him Hawk because his eyes feel like they're preying on you and right now, his penetrating gaze heats my neck.

"Nothing."

"It's a woman, Shaw. A goddamn woman. You want to challenge Doc, put the whole club at risk just for her? You lost. It's over. I doubt she's worth it."

"What if she's carrying my child?"

He gives me a steeled, angry look rather than softening with sympathy the way I expect.

"You came inside her, you fucking idiot. If she's carrying your child, take her to a goddamn clinic and end it."

"Isn't that against *your* religion?"

"God don't approve of a lot of shit I've done," he responds, taking a few stressed-out puffs from his cigarette. He keeps watching me for more of an explanation.

"I need her back. Reaper won't play me again but... dad thinks you can convince them to settle this on my behalf. Treat me like the royal fuck up and once you win, I leave Doc and the rest of the Blackwoods alone."

Hawk scoffs. "Are you capable of doing that? You haven't been the same since..."

He trails off because of the pact we made the last time we stood here. There ain't much we can't talk about directly, but the incident that caused the rift between me and Reaper has to stay quiet.

"I promised to let that go."

"But you can't," he says. "I can see the way it eats you up inside, man. You have to let it go."

Our club rules every square mile of the highway. Every part of the road that was once part of the old Route 66 has become slowly dominated by barbarians. The Hollingsworths made the first initial investments in whiskey production and farms stretching from Chicago to St. Louis.

Blackwoods control land, property and a chain of motels from St. Louis to Oklahoma City. But the Blackwoods and Hollingsworths are so intermarried, it's hard to know one family from another without having a pretty good handle on club history.

Power in the club wasn't always about who had the most money. Randy and Harley started the club out west in Amarillo, where dad is from. Randy Sinclair comes from Albuquerque and he's rumored to have a little bit of Indian in him, though I don't know how much of that holds true. When the club started, we shared power and used that power to build a strong network of families who looked after each other.

We all seem to have become a little too prosperous. With weak rival gangs and an impotent police force so obsessed with blacks and Mexicans they leave our asses alone, our bloodlust seems to have turned on each other.

I smoke a little more, considering his advice. Doesn't matter what dad wants, I still think Hawk would be a better leader than I ever could be.

"Are you going to play for her?"

"Not for free," he says, tossing his cigarette butt next to the grave and stomping on it. "Not even for you, Southpaw."

"What do you want?" I ask him, my body tensing as I search Hawk's face for signs of what he might take from me in exchange for saving Anna's life.

Money? My bike? A new pair of boots? He could ask me for anything and I know I would give it to him. I just don't know what to expect from him. Hawk might be my best friend, but we're guys. I don't know what he wants outside of an ice cold beer, the Cowboys to win the superbowl, and time alone to work on his bike with George Strait playing on the shop speakers.

"I want a favor," he says. "Not now but... I'll need one and when I need it, I'll ask you to do something and you won't be able to say no."

"That's it?"

I make nervous eye contact with him to see if this is the Texas boy's idea of a joke. But he ain't smiling. I fidget with the dice in my pocket, but messing around with the dice doesn't give me the answers I hope it will.

"Yes," he says. "But don't think you're getting off easy."

"I wouldn't expect that from you. Yes. I agree."

Hawk shakes his head, getting his black hair well out of his eyes before he looks at me again as if he has to get a good ass look at my crazy.

"Your dad won't let you keep her."

"I'm a grown ass man. If I want to keep her, I will."

He laughs. "I've seen her. She won't want to be your 'old lady'. She's a city slicker. A Chicago girl. Look at us, Shaw. Smoking American Spirits in a cemetery. That woman doesn't want our life. She wants cocktails and rooftop bars..."

He stops talking and reaches for his flask. His last girl left him for a job out in Palo Alto, so I try not to take his cynicism personally.

"I never said she was gonna be my old lady. But right now, she's mine and who knows how many times Reaper stuck his dick in her by now."

"Don't worry about that," he says. "You worry about laying low. Tell your daddy I'll do your dirty work for you."

"Thanks."

"Don't thank me," he says quickly. "Thank me when I get your girl back and let's hope it ain't a suicide mission or you'll owe Randy something for getting his son killed over a nigger."

Chapter Ten
Anna

After three painful weeks of sitting in the motel room with only the TV to keep me company the majority of the time, Reaper makes me pee on a stick and keeps the results to himself for another week before he tells me what I already know. *I'm pregnant.* Reaper hasn't touched me, so the baby is definitely Southpaw's, but that doesn't make me feel better. Nightmares whirl in my head every night. Those dreams were my first sign that I was pregnant. It's an old Caribbean folktale. You get *weird* dreams when you bring new life into the world.

It just amazes me how early the little clump of cells growing inside me *feels* like new life before I officially know the results. Maybe I would have figured out the truth without the results. Reaper would have no reason to keep me alive if I weren't pregnant.

I have a routine in my motel prison cell, even if I don't feel 'adjusted' to imprisonment, I count the days and keep myself grounded. Reaper arrives at 11 a.m. every day with "breakfast", coffee and fresh clothes 'from his ma'. There must be a McDonalds nearby because that is all he brings for breakfast. I know everything on the breakfast menu now and have a trauma bond with the nasty, watery coffee. Who knew I would miss the Nespresso machine at the hospital nurse's station so damn much.

Reaper barely talks to me and sits on his phone as he half watches me eat. Occasionally, he'll ask me how I feel but he does it explicitly in a way that suggests he doesn't care about me, he just wants to make sure I don't die. If I complain, he stares at me with blank, empty eyes. He only responds when I talk about bikes, Jesus or the food at McDonalds.

It's not like I want to be the motherfucker's friend, but I have nobody to talk to. The motel phone doesn't work, there isn't any internet here and the television here seems to be connected to the worst form of cable I have ever experienced. Where is the Netflix? The Disney Plus? The Hulu? Complaining about my entertainment only earns more blank stares from Reaper.

He stays in the room with me until 5 or 6 p.m. when he drives out to get me dinner from some shitty Mexican drive-thru, drops it off and then leaves again, locking the door and barricading me in with something on the other side that makes it impossible for me to escape.

I've tried everything possible to escape. Once he leaves, I eat, take a shower, and dress in the fresh clothes. I'm happy to have clean clothes but Reaper's mom and I have a very different idea of style. I don't know if I'll ever adjust to wearing stretchy capris and oversized floral tops from Walmart every day.

I don't know where Reaper goes all night but he always comes back in the morning having had a shower, smelling like cologne, and with a fresh vape cartridge that cycles through two or three different flavors. It's amazing how much I notice about him without anything else to entertain me.

My excessive attention to Reaper-related details comes in handy when he shows up with purple bruises all over his pale cheek. His lower lip is fat and he scowls before slamming my breakfast down on the table.

"Who pissed in your cornflakes?" I ask him, snatching the coffee and pouring as much of it as possible down my throat. Even if he gets me the biggest size, I miss having fresh piping hot coffee to sip on all day. I seriously hope this man doesn't plan on keeping me here throughout my entire pregnancy.

"Nobody," he says. "Keep your ass quiet and eat."

I don't want him to take the food away like he has threatened before, so I eat everything as fast as I can and then watch Reaper patiently make his way through his second double bacon cheeseburger, punctuating every couple bites with french fries and loud sips from his McFlurry.

I can't wait for him to finish before pestering him.

"Reaper?"

He glares in anticipation with glassy, empty eyes. I think he's trying to be scarier than he is. If he wanted to hurt me, he would have done it by now, not just threatened me.

"What do you want? I'm in no mood to listen to women and their goddamn whining today."

I bite my tongue to stop myself from providing Reaper with a measured and educated response. That's just not something his wild ass could ever relate to. I just have to answer his question.

"I'm a nurse and I can tell someone hit you."

"Congratulations. Must be pretty smart to notice a bruise on translucent skin."

I bite my tongue. He's not Southpaw. I don't know how far I can push him before he snaps. The details I've noticed about this man haven't only been physical. There were obviously signs that he wasn't right in the head from the bar but those signs only become more pronounced the more time I observe him up close. He hears voices occasionally, has paranoid tendencies and his antisocial behavior disturbs me.

Maybe it's trauma. Maybe he's a sociopath. The diagnosis doesn't matter and I'm not completely qualified to make one. The best I can say about the man is that he just isn't right in the goddamn head. He has pockets of sanity and he isn't downright cruel to me. That's just because it suits him, I bet.

I just need to keep the beast calm until I have a chance at escape or a chance to get back to Southpaw.

"What happened?" I press him, using the voice I save for my most stubborn patients. .

"Doesn't matter. I wanted to finish my breakfast before mentioning it but since your ass won't stop pestering me... Hawk wants you."

"Who?"

I don't remember all the biker nicknames. I would need a chart and a crash course to keep track of all the ones I overheard. I know Reaper, Southpaw and Reaper's father is Doc. That's about all I can keep track of.

"Doesn't matter who. He fancies playing me for you in secret. Just you. Guess he heard good things about your pretty pussy."

He chuckles and dips a french fry into his milkshake before eating it slowly and making disturbingly long eye contact with me. I drop my eyes quickly before Reaper gets any ideas. He laughs at my discomfort. Unstable motherfucker.

"Okay."

"It means you're seeing daylight, Anna. Best hope my daddy doesn't find out what I'm up to... so don't try running off."

"I wouldn't dream of it."

I'm trying to stay calm but really, I'm so excited that my heart wants to burst out of my chest. I haven't left this goddamn box in weeks. When I feel the sunlight on my face, I might just cry. Showing that kind of weakness in front of Reaper is obviously out of the question, but my emotions remain the same.

Reaper makes me take a shower as he waits outside the door. I can hear him whistling to himself and occasionally talking to himself as I get ready. When I'm done and finally open the door, he acts like he wasn't doing anything weird and maybe to him, he wasn't.

"You look like... my ma."

"Thanks," I mutter.

"Well," he says. "Can't say who you would be better off with. I won't fuck you but I can't make any promises about Hawk."

"Can you at least tell me who he is? Please? Don't you feel even the slightest bit sorry for me after weeks of spending all day with me?"

"No," Reaper says without a moment of hesitation. "If you were smart, you would have stolen Southpaw's pistol and fucked his ass up in that gas station bathroom. You're green, Anna. I don't have time for the innocent."

"Great," I respond, my voice tightening as I try to contain my anger. How dare this asshole judge me for my predicament? It's easy for a man twice the size of a normal human to imagine overpowering Southpaw but for me, that was entirely out of the question. He doesn't even seem to notice that he annoyed the fuck out of me. As we walk outside into the blinding sun, I push my luck just a bit more.

"Just explain who he is."

"He's the man who ought to lead our club, not the idiot who knocked you up."

I roll my eyes. "Seriously? All of this is about who gets to lead your stupid club?"

"It's not stupid and if you don't watch your mouth, I have no problem smacking a woman around."

"Do you think that's something to brag about?"

His nostrils flare and I question my sanity for testing him. Reaper isn't right in the head. He shoves his tongue into his cheek and I watch his face go through several shades of red before it settles back to its natural, sunburnt pink. I might have gotten away with sassing him this time.

"This club is about family and money. Ain't you in a gang?"

"Why are you asking me that question?"

"Nevermind," he says. "Point is, Southpaw is a gambling addict

76

too full of himself to lead us anywhere but straight off a goddamn cliff. Look at what he did to you. He would gamble away his own flesh and blood for the rush. He's more dangerous than I will ever be."

It's almost a bonding moment between us. But Reaper spits on the ground in the most disgusting manner and I turn away from him so I don't dry heave. The sun feels better than I thought, but I'm not used to it, so my eyes hurt before I put the helmet on.

My body still shakes uncontrollably with fear from riding on the back of those things. I don't like the idea of clinging to Reaper again either, but considering he gave me a heads up about this Hawk character, I suppose I owe it to him to behave myself for the time being. I climb on the back of the bike and nestle close to him.

Southpaw. I suppose there's no chance of me running into him again. Not like I want to run into that crazy motherfucker again except maybe to slap him up a bit. Still, I wonder if there's a chance. Doesn't matter if I hate the bastard because apparently, he's still gonna be the father of my child.

WE HEAD BACK to the Old Route 66 highway – East. Reaper doesn't tell me where we're going, but I observe everything in case I get even the slightest chance at an escape. We take a barely marked exit off the highway and I shiver as I notice the sign littered with bullet holes. I think the bikers use the highway signs as target practice, but I've never witnessed it myself. Just something Reaper mentioned off-hand one day and then quickly backtracked when I questioned him.

Based on the signs with bullet holes in them, we aren't exactly in Beverly Hills. The air thickens with typical Missouri humidity and black flies slam into my helmet visor at an alarming rate as we approach what looks like a creepy ass abandoned bowling alley. Most of the letters on the tacky neon *Route 66 Bowling* sign are dim. Only "66 Bowl" lights up the parking lot red and orange.

Flies and various insects nearly black out the light from the single lamp in the middle of the cracked parking lot by the time we get there after a couple hours of riding. My ass hurts from Reaper's uncomfortable bike seat and every part of my body screams out for relief. He doesn't seem to mind. Reaper stops his bike and rolls out his shoulders nervously, but the length of the bike ride hardly seems to affect him.

That's not good. The man is 6'7" tall. If anything can make him nervous, I don't want to find out what it is. He swings his body to get off the bike, so I follow his lead. Once he's on his feet, Reaper's hand rushes to his pistol immediately.

"I don't like this," he says, although his body language pretty much told me that. He takes his helmet off. I follow his lead. It's so goddamn hot out considering how late it is. The sun is staying up longer, which means it's not pitch black yet, but it soon will be. The dark corners around the parking lot seem to be closing in around us as the sun descends.

"Stick close to me," he says. Where else would I go? The abandoned bowling alley doesn't look appealing. I hear a drawn out raspy hiss and my head snaps around nervously to one of those dark corners of the parking lot. It's only a vulture picking at a possum carcass. Nasty, but not exactly dangerous.

Reaper has his pistol out, but his finger isn't on the trigger. I sidle up next to the giant, who barely seems to notice I'm still standing next to him. Something has him all wound up and I don't like it.

"What's wrong? This doesn't look like a pool hall," I say, hoping to break the ice. Maybe he's having one of those little "visions" or hearing voices. But Reaper's movements are smooth and controlled, not jerky at all. I have a brief thought that maybe it's Southpaw staging some insane rescue attempt. The thought disappears pretty quickly when Reaper starts talking.

"It ain't a pool hall. But this parking lot ought to be filled with Indian Scouts. Sinclair family's bike of choice. Nobody's here."

"Just us…"

Reaper reaches into his pocket for his phone. I hear a high-pitched whistle, a gunshot, and then the lamp in the parking lot explodes. Reaper yells out a series of cuss words and then, "Get down!"

I didn't need him to tell me. The second I heard the gunshot, my body responded instinctively from years growing up in Chicago and working in the emergency room. Reaper yells something else and then fires two shots from his pistol. Covering my ears hardly works to absorb the sound.

My heart beats so fast and air can barely get into my lungs. As I gasp for breath, I can taste metal on the back of my throat. The shooting stops. I can see Reaper's feet from my position on the ground but I don't dare look up or raise my head. A faint roar in the distance draws closer. Bikers.

More than three.

BRIGHT LIGHTS FILL the freshly darkened parking lot. The bikes are here and there are more boots on the ground than I expected. Reaper drops his gun and puts his hands up. I don't know what exactly is happening, but I know it isn't good.

CHAPTER ELEVEN
SOUTHPAW

The second Reaper calls Hawk with the news, I get accused of blowing our cover with Reaper. No more pool match. No more betting for Anna's life because... Anna's gone. He won't say anything over the phone, according to Hawk. He's just cussing a lot and demanding we come out there.

I suggest to Hawk it might be a trap, even if that kind of behavior would go against our way of doing things. It's something dad would call yellow-bellied. Cowardly. We don't have to go through anything underhanded to get our point across.

"Trap or not... those motherfuckers took your girl."

Reaper doesn't tell him *who* took Anna which makes me think he doesn't know. Considering our issues are with each other, I can't easily conjure up any other suspects. No choice but to ride out there. Dad won't like the change of plans but I don't have time to ask his permission or leave this up to a club vote.

I text him that we're headed out to Route 66 Bowling and that somebody jumped Reaper. No point getting into the details until we know more. I also text my brothers an SOS and the coordinates. If we believe Reaper and a rival group of one-percenters wearing masks and riding Kawasaki bikes stole Anna, we'll need backup. If he's lying and this is some bullshit Blackwood plot... we'll definitely need backup.

Not knowing kills me. I wanted to have Anna back by tonight. Instead, the ride to Route 66 Bowling heightens my awareness of the shifting sands beneath us. When did we all grow up? I remember playing with Reaper during the summers. He was a skinny little kid with asthma, too close to his mother, and we only saw him when the Rebel Barbarian chapters met up once a year in California for the annual drag race. Settling shit back then was so much easier than it is now.

It helped that back then we didn't have any women to fight over. It was just BB guns and makeshift toys we made out of shit we stole from our dads. We all wanted to grow up to be just like them. We got what we wanted but there has been one hell of a cost to this lifestyle.

Hawk leads the pack, consisting of both of my brothers as well as both of his, to Route 66 Bowling and we luck out by avoiding any state troopers on the highway. The parking lot is completely dark, but as we draw near, Gideon Blackwood's unmistakable figure draws into view. He leans against his bike, puffing on those pussy ass vapes he thinks are gonna save his life.

"Took you assholes long enough," Reaper says calmly once we stop the bikes. He doesn't sound angry.

"We got here as fast as we could," I answer as I get off my bike. "What happened? Where did the motherfuckers get to?"

"The twins are coming down," Reaper says, referring to his twin brothers Jairus and Jotham. "We shouldn't leave without them. No clue who the bikers were or where they went."

"This isn't the location I sent you," Hawk says. "How the fuck would I get a pool table to Route 66 Bowling?"

Hawk heavily implies the 'you goddamn idiot' at the end of that sentence. Gideon scowls at him as the last headlights from the bikes dim.

"Who the fuck sent me this, then?"

He hands his phone to Hawk who squints and then answers. "Not my number."

"What?"

"The numbers are switched. But it's a damn good spoof."

"What the fuck is going on..." Reaper says before letting out a loud groan and doubling over in pain.

"Hey," Hawk calls out to him, putting his hand on his back. "You okay, man? What the fuck..."

"I'm fine," Reaper groans. I take my tactical flashlight out of my cut and cast the beam over Reaper. That motherfucker isn't fine at all.

"Look at his shoulder," I say to Hawk, pointing out the blood seeping through the idiot's clothes.

"It's just a graze," Reaper says before letting out another anguished groan that doesn't make his injury sound like a graze.

"Keep the light on him," Hawk says. My brothers crowd around, along with Ghost and Condom. I keep the light on Reaper's injury as my younger brother helps Hawk lift Reaper's shirt to get a closer look at the wound. My brother retches when he sees the ripped flesh.

"Graze, my ass," Hawk grunts. "Someone nearly blew your fucking arm off."

"I said, I'm fine. We need to find that woman," Reaper says with urgency that immediately unsettles me. They spent weeks together. *Weeks.* And I don't know where this bastard kept the prize he won from me, but if she wasn't locked away in isolation, he had plenty of time to get to know her.

Reckless rage churns inside me, even if it's a bad time. I'll worry about what Reaper did to Anna later. We need to get her now. Working on Reaper's wound would be easier if we had a nurse. Jairus Blackwood learned some medic training from his dad, so we have to wait for him before we make any progress.

"I can shoot with either hand," Reaper says. "Just give me some goddamn whiskey, wrap me up and let's get the fuck out of here."

Hawk hands him some whiskey while we wait for Jairus to show up.The rest of us search the parking lot and all over Route 66 Bowling for clues about who could have come here and why exactly they wanted Anna.

I SCOUR my quadrant of the parking lot with a tactical flashlight alone. Cicadas scream not far off from where we search and the mosquitoes out here are the biggest I've seen yet in Missouri. A shiny glint reflects from the asphalt compelling me to crouch down for a closer look. Winchester 9mm bullets. Cop bullets.

Not all cops. But I've been in enough shootouts with Missouri cops to recognize the bullets. I pick up six from the ground. One of those could have grazed Reaper's shoulder, but that doesn't explain the other six. Just before I yell out to the club about the bullets, Owen yells that he found something on his end of the parking lot.

I put the bullets in my empty pocket and my left hand in the pocket with my dice so I can turn them around with the possibilities of what might have happened here.

"One of them must have dropped this getting out of here," Owen says as we draw closer to him and get a closer look at what exactly he found. It's a wallet.

"How much of a stupid sonofabitch do you have to be to forget your wallet," Reaper says, grunting through the last couple words.

"Could say the same about you getting shot," Hawk says. Reaper smiles. For the first time since the pool game that got this shit started, we're almost getting along. I don't say a word poking fun at Reaper since I'm the most likely person to mess this shit up.

I bring up the bullets while Owen opens the wallet. "I found six bullets. They look like cop bullets."

"I'll be damned," Owen says, pulling out some form of police identification from the wallet. "Some motherfucker named Mike MacEachern."

"Or it's a plant," Hawk responds thoughtfully.

"Cop bullets. Cop name," I say with a shrug. "Could cops have done this?"

"I know we hate pigs," Reaper says, "But does it really make sense to y'all that a pack of them would come here on motorcycles to fuck with our club? Why?"

You can trust a member of the Blackwood family to consider the hidden political motive in just about everything.

"They're cops," Owen says. "They do shit because they can."

"Why the hell would they come out to the middle of nowhere to kidnap some nigger when you can grab any that you'd like off the streets of Chicago?" Reaper says, giving me a sympathetic look before adding, "No offense."

"I don't know," Hawk says calmly. "You tell us. Did you take a crack at her all the time you had her?"

Has Hawk lost his mind? If I find out Reaper laid one fucking finger on Anna, I'll rip his arm off myself. We can't discuss this now... But Reaper shakes his head.

"No. I didn't. I swear on my daddy's life."

"Great, I don't have to kill you. Doesn't explain why pigs would get involved in a kidnapping though."

Reaper narrows his gaze towards me.

"I don't know. I'm wondering how you came up with $500,000 on such short notice."

I don't appreciate Reaper's tone. Does it matter how we came up with the money? It's no secret that each family has several business interests on either side of the law. You need legitimate books to run criminal enterprises. Running a body shop can be a good cover for trafficking unmarked semi-automatic weapons across state lines – that sort of thing. I don't want him suspicious of how we actually got the money.

"You got your money and we didn't fuck with any cops to get it, if that's what you mean."

Hawk throws me a dirty look because the last thing he wants is for this to turn into another foolish fist fight. Personally, I don't mind

84

throwing a punch at Reaper. He might reign at the pool table but I could definitely kick the lean blond bastard's ass in a fight.

"I never said you got it from the cops. But y'all have a habit of operating on impulse," Reaper says. "It's a family trait."

Hawk throws me another sympathetic look because Reaper means the Shaws, not the Sinclairs. They have their vices. We have ours. I suppose there's no point denying it, but I'm not in the mood for criticism. Hawk knows where we got the damn money.

"The money ain't connected to the cops. We're an outlaw biker club. It's safe to say all of us have made our fair share of enemies over the years. We'll get more answers if we track them down."

"Let's split up then," I suggest. "Cop motorcycle clubs have their watering holes and hunting grounds. Shouldn't be too hard for us to find."

"You don't want to stumble on a nest of cops alone," Hawk says, giving me a sharp glare as if he senses me on the verge of an impulsive suicide mission to save Anna. An impulsive suicide mission isn't my preference, but I can't think of a single thing I wouldn't do to get her back.

I don't like the thought of another man getting his hands on my property. It's bad enough when it's a man in your own club, but the thought of a dirty pig putting his hands on Anna pisses me the fuck off.

"We need the club," Reaper says. "I'll go to Harley myself and announce our truce. If you agree to it, that is."

I get to keep Anna and the baby as long as we help him out. The situation could have played out much differently. *I can't say no to this deal.*

"Of course I agree," I grumble. "What other way do we have of getting Anna back?"

"Shake on it," Hawk says. "Now. I'll call your dad, tell him to call a club meeting."

CHAPTER TWELVE
ANNA

Cold wind wakes me up from my light sleep. Last night, the bikers who kidnapped me lowered me into a deep hole with a sleeping bag and covered it with a large wooden board that has some holes in it. I think they killed Reaper. The noise he made after I heard the volley of gunshots could have woken the dead. I've never heard a grown man emit such an anguished scream.

The drive to the middle of nowhere lasted a few hours. Maybe three. I still hate motorcycles but that particular drive was so brutal I almost threw up and pissed myself. They rode over 90 mph the entire time and I didn't have a helmet, just a black ski mask. The man I had to hold onto was a fat, short guy who reeked of sweat and shiitake mushrooms.

The bikers rode in a convoy with me in the middle of it. It was an intentional attack and I don't think the folks who snatched me away from Reaper have anything to do with Southpaw. There would have been no need to grab me the way they did and anyway... I have a feeling Southpaw would have come for me himself.

It's not a sentimental feeling but a gut instinct. If there's one thing I know about the man it's that he's dangerously and impulsively possessive. It still hasn't hit me emotionally that I'm really carrying the biker's baby... I wonder what will happen now that Reaper isn't alive to claim his prize.

Running away has never been a greater priority, but the dark early morning hours don't give me enough light to properly assess my situation. The hole is deep enough that I can't climb out of it. I think it might be an old well, but I'm only guessing based off of movies, not any real knowledge of wells. It's not wet, just humid, so maybe it's just a hole. I'm too scared to call out and attract attention, so I spend the next hour making efforts to climb out of the hole before the ground vibrates and I hear the loud engine roar of an approaching motorcycle.

The bike stops and the ground continues to shake. I hear coughing and then someone hacks something out of their throat. Gross. The giant plank of wood covering the hole shifts to the side and tears well in my eyes as too much sunlight slams into me at once.

"Shit, good morning. Here's some breakfast. And a bucket to piss in."

He tosses down a paper bag and an empty five gallon bucket. My stomach churns. This cannot be real...

"What do you want with me?" I yell up to the man as my vision slowly returns. I think he's the same one I rode with last night because he has a similar height and build. With sunlight still burning my eyes and with my desperation for breakfast propelling me forward, I can barely think about keeping my head on straight.

My thoughts are foggier and more irrational than normal. Hunger from my time in the hole messes with my head. I have been down here for over 24 hours. Maybe two days. I am way too hungry to keep track. I wish this wasn't happening. I'm pregnant for a criminal biker and this is the second time I've been kidnapped in such a short span of time that I'm beginning to feel hopeless about my chances of getting out. I haven't *seen* a chance to get out. But then, just when I'm giving up and asking my desperate question... I get something in return.

"This ain't about you. It's about the men you associate yourself with."

"Me? I'm not associated with them! I'm not... Please, you have to believe me. If you can get me back to Chicago, I will give you as much money as you want. I have nothing to do with any bikers or motorcycle clubs. I don't even have tattoos!"

I know I sound desperate, but this man doesn't look particularly threatening. If I could get myself out of this damn hole, I'm sure I could do enough damage to get a chance to run away. Outrunning an obese biker like that would be a piece of damn cake, honestly.

"Listen, ma'am. It doesn't matter. You'll be next in the next 36 hoursYou'll be next in the next 36 hours. Your motorcycle club stole $500,000 worth of goods from one of ours... That has a price."

"That has nothing to do with me," I plead desperately. "Please. You have to let me go."

"You got half a million dollars?" he asks unsympathetically.

"No, but I didn't steal a half million dollars either. I'm not a damn biker!"

Screaming at him doesn't make the situation better. The man grunts impatiently and kicks the sheet of wood over the hole a little. My screaming intensifies. I don't want to be left alone in the dark again.

"WAIT!" I yell at him. "Don't go! I don't want to be here!"

HE LEAVES me in the dark with my bucket and cold Burger King.

I DON'T WANT to die.

. . .

LORD, I don't want to go out like this at all. *I have to do something.*

I STAND ON THE BUCKET, which only gives me a small boost. It's not enough to climb out of the hole on its own but... I'm not ready to give up. There has to be some *Shawshank Redemption* shit I can do to get out of this hole.

The smooth stone walls along the side have grooves in them that seem so tight it would be impossible to pry the stones apart. The five gallon bucket isn't the best tool, but I'm wearing a pair of short chelsea boots with a heel that's slightly harder than the flimsy plastic bucket. I take off one of my shoes and go to town on the stones, trying to loosen them up.

I don't know if it will work but I'm not going to die in this goddamn hole without putting up a fight.

THE BASTARD MUST HAVE BEEN FUCKING with me because he doesn't come back for two more days. No food and a fetid bucket for two days. I'm curled up in the corner in my sleeping bag when I hear the sheet of wood shift over the hole. *I'm pregnant. I need food. Without proper nutrition and self care, I could harm the baby. For all I know, this trauma has already done irreparable damage.*

The hacking cough and familiar bloated footsteps identify my primary captor but this time, I don't engage with him until he speaks.

"I'm sending down a rope for your shit bucket."

TWO DAYS and that's the first human contact I have. I don't move at first until he verbally prods me again. I groan and move slowly, securing the rope to my bucket. He pulls it up slowly so none of the contents spill over. I got used to the smell, but I still logically know how goddamn disgusting I must be down here.

ANNA

"I'll send down more food and a clean bucket," he says.

I WISH he could send a shower down into the hole.

I HEAR him take a few steps away from the hole and then... gunshots. Three gunshots. I slam my hand over my mouth to stop myself from screaming. *What the fuck? What the fuck?* I didn't hear any bikes or other vehicles, so whoever came here must have come on foot. Wherever the hell *here* is.

The footsteps outside the hole sound like they're much lighter than the heavyset man's footsteps.

"What the hell is that plywood doing over there?" The accent sounds like a weird mix of Midwestern and Southern, but I don't recognize the voice. *Not Southpaw.* I stay curled up in the sleeping bag as I hear more footsteps above. I don't have an exact count, but I suspect there are five or six people above ground. They might be here to help, or they might be here to kill me.

I don't know how the hell I'm supposed to tell from the hole in the ground. When you can't fight, you can at least hide. I have a better chance of escape if I don't get myself shot.

I CRAWL into the sleeping bag without another way to defend myself and try to calm myself as I hear the sound of men approaching the piece of wood and where my latest captors stashed me. Their voices sound lower now, so I can't exactly make out the accents.

"Shit. I see something down there!"

FUCK.

.   .   .

90

"REAPER! HAWK!"

REAPER!?

I THROW the sleeping bag over my head and expose myself to the men standing outside the hole. Reaper isn't the first person I see. It's Southpaw – the father of my child.

Chapter Thirteen
Southpaw

Owen and Ethan drag her out of the hole but once the woman is on solid ground, I shove them away from her and throw my arms around Anna myself. We've never had such an emotional embrace but after so many weeks apart from her, it feels right. Anna's stomach presses up against me as I hug her and I feel the taut flesh pulled over the slight bump protruding from her stomach. Maybe it's just my imagination. I don't know the workings of pregnancy very well. I suppose I'll find out...

Anna doesn't hug me back at first, but I can't blame her. She smells goddamn rancid which I can expect since she's spent a few days trapped in a hole in the ground somewhere in the middle of fucking nowhere Missouri. Following a tip from Lacey Hollingsworth, ten of us hiked up on this private land where the Blue Blood Knights have their clubhouse.

This makeshift prison is about a half mile away from the clubhouse, but our intelligence was mostly good. We found her. I press my nose into Anna's hair and quietly promise myself that I'll never let her go again. When I pull away from her, she just looks at me with gorgeous and wide brown eyes.

I touch her cheek.

"I'm sorry," I whisper. "I... I will never let you out of my sight again."

She swallows slowly, perhaps dreading the thought, but she doesn't slap me or show any signs of outrage, which I suspect I deserve. Anna glances over her shoulder and unfortunately, she gets a full view of her captor's body before Reaper can throw a blanket over him. I watch her face contort in anguish and pull her in for another deep hug.

"Did any of those men touch you?" I growl. "Because you tell me who to kill and I'll do it, Anna..."

She doesn't reply, but she slowly reaches her arms around me and finally hugs me back.

"I am so hungry," she whispers.

FAIR ENOUGH.

ANNA POUNDS BACK a double bacon cheeseburger from Wendy's before I have to stick her on the back of the bike and follow dad's instructions to move west with the group. After making this much trouble in Missouri, it's in our best interests for the majority of the barbarians to leave the state for at least a few weeks.

Everyone in the club agrees to the decision unanimously. Nobody wants to do anything to challenge the newly brokered peace. Anna isn't too thrilled about more riding, but she's too tired to put up a fight. I put her on the back of the bike with me.

"Hold on tight, woman. I'll get you to sleep soon."

Her body feels so small and precious sliding up against mine. Her tits press into my back, reminding me instantly of why I was willing to go so damn far for this woman. I love a good pair of tits. And a pretty smile. And soft thighs smacking against mine...

We get to Kansas in the evening. The Sinclair family owns a

motel just off the small patch of Route 66 that travels through Kansas. Hawk's mama runs the place and does a good job of it too. Before she was an old lady, Mrs. Sinclair did her fair share of gun running and enforcing for the club. You wouldn't know it from her petite figure and her Farah Fawcett hairstyle that she was anything more than a retired small town beauty, but she's like the rest of the Sinclair family – a force to contend with.

She welcomes us and gives us rooms in the furthest corner of the motel from the lobby in case we get rowdy when she has other customers. The summer road trip season hasn't started yet, so there are plenty of vacancies for us and very little chance we'll get into trouble, but her room assignments are as much of a warning as they are a request. Like I said, Mrs. Sinclair is a force to reckon with.

Most of the guys double up in rooms with each other but I take Anna into a small non-smoking room with a king sized bed. Mrs. Sinclair lets me have some of the motel breakfast food for free so I can give Anna something to eat. She sits on the edge of the bed quietly as she eats a plain bagel slathered in cream cheese.

My dice roll across my fingers as I stare at her, clearly making her uncomfortable. Anna clears her throat a couple times in an effort to stop my staring, but it doesn't work.

"You need a shower."

"I need to go home," she says, finishing up the bagel and glancing down at her thighs. "Please... I'm a nurse, Southpaw. A normal ass nurse. I don't belong in your world and quite frankly... you know that. So why am I here?"

Her eyes flash to mine.

"Because I want you here."

I don't have to think about the answer. Women have a way of overcomplicating things.

She can't possibly know about my conversation with my father, but Anna's intuition about the club is correct.

"It's a motorcycle club, not a cult. I can do what I want," I add defensively.

"No you can't," she says. "I'm not stupid, Southpaw. But it doesn't matter. I won't come after you for money or anything like that. I just... I want you to let me go."

"Too fucking bad."

I get up and grab Anna by the wrist, dragging her to the motel bathroom.

"Let me go!" she says. "Hey! Hey! What do you think you're doing!"

I guide Anna into the bathroom as she scratches me. Her nails tear skin away from my face and I wince, but otherwise barely react to her fighting me off. When I get her into the bathroom, I let go of her.

"What is wrong with you?" Anna says, taking a step back and pressing up against the shower's glass door. It wasn't a big bathroom to start with, but once I step inside it with Anna, there isn't much room for her to move around or create a fuss.

I'm sure that won't stop her from scratching and slapping me up. I touch the bloody scratch on my face but judging by the furious look on her face, she doesn't feel an ounce of regret about scratching me up.

"Nothing is wrong with me. Hit me again and I'll... punish you."

"By doing what?" she says. "I know you goddamn bikers like slapping a woman around but I'm pregnant and my ass will hit back."

I have no intentions of hitting Anna, but I find her threat amusing. I weigh at least a hundred pounds more than she does and I'm strong enough that she would have a hard time causing any damage, no matter how hard she hit me.

"I'm helping you take a shower. Clothes off," I command her.

"I don't need your help to take a shower," Anna says. She covers her body with her hands, desperate to keep me away from her like she could stop me even if she wanted to. I don't want to hurt her or scare her, so I don't take another step closer to her. She's small enough in comparison to me that I can more or less assess her visually from above.

Considering how long Anna spent away from me, her capture warrants a far deeper inspection. Her face turns mean under my gaze. Warm orange light from the motel bathroom bathes her dark brown skin in a warm, pretty glow. I know dad doesn't want me to keep her, but how the fuck does he expect me to let her go when her body has such a powerful effect on me?

Anna awakens every possessive instinct in me entirely against my will.

"I don't believe those men didn't hurt you. I need to check."

Rage flickers across her face again, but I hold steadfast in front of her. This woman will have to do a hell of a lot more than throw a tantrum to get me to leave her alone. All I want is to get closer to her. To touch her. Feel her. Naturally, Anna bristles with the fierce intensity of a porcupine.

"What the hell is your problem? I'm not your damn property. You don't need to check a damn thing. Get out of here."

"No. Take your clothes off."

"I'm not doing that in front of you."

"Why not? You're pregnant with my child. And if you don't take your clothes off... I'll do it for you."

"This is why your ass is always in trouble," she says to me, taking off her shirt and balling it up before throwing it at my head.

"Why is that?"

"You don't think a damn thing through."

"Maybe I think things through faster than other people.

"Right," she says, rolling her eyes before continuing with her brutal attack. "That's why you're a racist who knocked up a black woman in a truck stop bathroom."

"I'm not a racist."

"That's the part you focus on?" she says, taking her bra off and throwing it at my head. I catch the bra. Barely. Once Anna exposes her tits, I obviously can't focus on anything else. She has a gorgeous pair of titties that get me instantly hard. *Fuck.*

"Get the rest of your clothes off."

She glances down at my crotch and then frowns before covering her perfect dark brown breasts with her arms.

"No," she says. "Not while you're standing there like a pervert. Go outside."

I glare at her, halfway furious for her rejection but even angrier at the fact that our time apart apparently didn't impact her at all.

"Did you even want me to save your life or would you prefer I send you over to Reaper's bed. Because if that's what you want me to do, I'll fucking do it."

I can't tell if we're going to fuck or fight when our eyes meet.

"Jealous?" Anna taunts me, the glint in her eye driving me wild with fury. I can feel the heat spreading over my cheeks and her smug satisfaction while she tortures me pisses me the fuck off.

"Answer the question. If you want Reaper to rip you open with his dick, I'll send you over there. Fair warning, woman... He's not as nice as I am."

"You are downright delusional if you think you're nice," she says, her hands falling away from her breasts and balling up into tiny outraged fists by her sides. "And if I wanted to spend the night with Reaper, it would be my choice because you don't own me."

CHAPTER FOURTEEN
ANNA

If I ever thought Southpaw was stoic, or in smooth control of his emotions, I was completely wrong. He flares up like nothing I've ever seen before.

"If you want to fuck him, I'll call him," Southpaw responds icily.

"Did I say that? I simply pointed out that I have a choice."

"No," he says, taking a step towards me. "Executive decision. You no longer have a choice."

He grabs my wrist. I hoped exposing my boobs would distract him long enough for me to have a chance at escape but apparently, I read the situation all wrong and underestimated his lust for me. With my wrist in hand, he quickly backs me up a step and pins me against the bathroom door, holding both wrists over my head.

I wriggle in an effort to get out of his grasp, but Southpaw tightens his grasp easily and renders me immobile. He holds me against the door with one hand before slowly looking me up and down.

"Why are you trying to make me jealous, Anna?" he asks. "Do you like what type of person I become when I'm jealous?"

"I don't know what type of person you become."

"But you can guess. You saw what I've done to get you back."

He leans forward and kisses my neck slowly and possessively, in a way that I could never mistake for sweet. I whimper as he finds the most sensitive part of my flesh and then sucks on it hard enough to leave a bruise while his rough beard scratches the sensitive skin surrounding the spot he chooses to mark.

When he pulls away, he growls low in his throat. "Sweet fucking Anna, I missed you. Don't tell me you didn't think of me at least once..."

I close my eyes and try to separate myself from the intense pleasure I feel from Southpaw's lips on my neck and my confusion as he asks me to think about my emotions during the time apart from him.

"I didn't think about you."

"Good," he says, sucking on my neck again until I moan. "That means I didn't traumatize you..."

"Bastard..." I squeak out before I succumb to the pleasure Southpaw lavishes on my neck and moan again. The particularly lewd moan inspires another escape attempt since the very last thing that I want is to give in to his desire. It's bad enough we're enclosed in a small motel bathroom together and his natural male scent gets stronger the more time we spend in here.

He kisses my neck softly and then he pauses, looking at me for a very intense moment before his lips touch mine. I expect Southpaw's initial contact to be rough and demanding, but this is the softest kiss I've ever received. His free hand touches my cheek and his thumb runs slowly along my jawline before he returns to giving me the slowest kiss I have ever experienced.

Southpaw makes a low noise in his throat and pulls away again, stroking my hair before kissing the top of my head and making intense eye contact with me that sends a strange shiver straight down my spine.

"You are always going to be mine, Anna. So I will always be jealous. If another man so much as looks at you, I'll break his neck."

I watched him shoot someone in front of me over a similar crime. He isn't exaggerating.

"Don't talk like that."

"I mean it," he says. "When you have a good woman, you do everything you can to keep her safe."

"How the hell do you know I'm a good woman?"

He grins and kisses the top of my nose. "I just know."

Southpaw doesn't let his guard down as he kisses me, but I can't say the same. Our lips stay joined longer and longer. He touches my breasts with his free hand, then my cheek, lovingly exploring my body before he moves to take the rest of my clothes off.

When he reaches for the waistband of my pants, my instinct to protest Southpaw's demands resurges. I wriggle my hips away from him and try to keep us here – just kissing.

"I'm taking those off, Anna..."

"No..."

"Why?" he growls. "Did someone touch you? Because I'll find out... I swear I will..."

He lets go of my hands and grabs my cheeks, pulling me close to him and cupping my face like I'm precious. Like I'm his. Southpaw holds me so close to him I can feel the bulge tenting his pants pressing into me and shifting with excitement as he kisses me more intensely. Southpaw pulls away for a split second, giving me a moment to respond and lash out against him.

Except I don't. Our eyes meet again and we stop to examine each other's faces. He runs his tongue slowly over his lips. The desire written clearly all over his face scares me almost as much as my own emotions. The harder I try to push them back, the more they rise to the surface. I don't break eye contact with him or push him away.

The thoughts of running away vanish entirely. His body presses against mine and I could bury myself in the warmth of Southpaw's chest after all those nights trapped in a damp, wet hole in the ground. He shakes his head as I take the slightest step closer to him. I can feel him fighting his feelings for me.

I'm fighting my feelings too.

"You're just too fucking sexy. I can't help it," he says, offering up some explanation for why we can't keep our hands off each other when we should run in the opposite direction from each other.

"You should..." I whisper, trying to force myself to do the right thing, but already sure that I'll do the wrong thing.

"You should..." I whisper again, squeezing my eyes shut. I should tell him to go. But instead, I just shudder and wait for Southpaw to edge closer to me, pinning me to the door with his hips this time.

"I'll do what I please with my property, Anna," he says simply, then he kisses me with so much emotion that my hands drop to the waist of my pants and I slide them over my butt myself. I close my eyes as if that can help me pretend I'm not giving in to the crazy, violent biker who literally gambled my pussy away.

I don't have any self control. My pants and underwear hit the ground and I present my naked body to Southpaw again. This time, I'm willing to have him and I don't know what changed.

Is it because I know how hard he fought for me? Is it the baby? Maybe I've lost my damned mind...

CHAPTER FIFTEEN
SOUTHPAW

I flip her around to examine her naked body for bruises. I can't imagine bruising would show up easily on her skin tone, so I run my hand over her skin and look closer at any areas she shows sensitivity to. Even if she flinches plenty, I don't find any bruises on the exposed or sensitive areas of Anna's body.

After running the hot water for a few minutes, our motel room bathroom warms up enough that the mirror fogs up and she can't see how pretty she looks. I like the heat. She looks good in the heat and her hair looks like a halo of wildflowers around her head.

"You're showing already."

She glances down and shakes her head.

"This is not how I expected my life to turn out when I pulled into that rest stop."

"I'm sorry."

"Are you?"

I touch her stomach and she puts her hand on top of mine. Instead of pushing my hand away like I expect, her fingers curl around mine and her eyes meet mine.

"No," I answer honestly. "I'm not. But... you're right about me. I don't think things through and... the situation with my family concerns me."

The 'race thing' didn't matter when I only wanted to use Anna's body to pay a debt. Losing her so quickly after that only made me realize how badly I want her close and how badly I want to keep her for my own.

"This so-called club is more like a gang," she says. "I'm not an expert or anything, but I know crime. What kind of life is that for you, me, or a future kid?"

"We look after our own out here," I murmur, my hand traveling over her stomach in slow circles and then sliding down to Anna's mound. The tiny patch of hair she had over her pussy when I first had her has fleshed out into a full, thick bush of dark pubic hair.

There's something alluring and primal about the way the hair conceals her lower lips and my fingers want to explore more of Anna the longer I stroke her body.

"Does that keep you out of prison?"

"Not always," I whisper, sliding my finger between her lower lips and causing Anna to inhale sharply. "But I would keep you out of prison. And our child."

I kiss her neck again and then slowly part her lower lips with my finger, exploring her soft clit and the wet gooeyness between her legs. I'm not the only one aroused by our fighting or the tension between us. She bites her lower lip to stifle a moan and makes her best attempt to stick to the topic of our baby.

"Would you keep our child from getting lynched by your fellow bikers?" Anna asks as my index finger draws a smooth, slow circle around her clit. She presses her hand against my chest as I hit her sweet spot. Nails curl into my chest hair and then dig sharply into my muscles as she suppresses her honest reaction to my finger teasing her clit.

"Christ, Anna. We're not like that," I reply, warming her neck with my hot breath as I continue to stroke her clit in slow circles. I know if I make her cum she can forget about the race talk.

"Right," Anna says as she struggles to take each breath. "You're just regular racists."

I keep my finger on her clit and continue teasing her. If we're going to have this conversation, I want my hand surrounded by her soft pussy lips and I want to feel her moaning against my neck.

"Does it matter what I believe outside of this room?"

I squeeze her clit gently between two fingers and she can't hold back a loud moan which she obviously didn't want me to hear. Anna presses her face into my shoulder and inhales slowly, stifling another whimper as I keep working her clit.

"It matters," she moans and when I hit her sweet spot again, her teeth sink into my shoulder muscles. The gentle love bite sends energy flowing straight to my dick.

"It shouldn't," I whisper. "What matters is... I promise to keep you safe and to treat you right. Forget color. Forget my beliefs. Just let me touch you..."

She moans again, but then bites my shoulder even harder than before. She hates how I make her feel, but I can take it. Fuck, I hate how she makes me feel too. Does Anna really think I meant to end up here? I never expected to want a woman who looks like Anna. A nurse. A woman with some type of education and desire to have a life outside of a dive bar.

I don't know why I want her. Hell, I don't know that I have any right to have her at all. The way I want her feels different than any craving I've ever had. I want to blame her for the magnetic way I'm drawn to her. But it ain't her fault. I'm the one who can't keep my hands off her. I'm the one who doesn't want to let her go.

I DON'T FEEL like I can help this particular craving for something different.

"Does it matter what the club thinks if I like touching your soft black pussy?"

She moans again and then hits my chest with a fist. Nothing she does could hurt me so if it makes her feel better and cum harder to bite me and hit the fuck out of my chest, I'll let her do it. Juices gush from Anna's pussy and dribble down her thighs as I tease her flower open to touch more than just her clit.

I slide my fingers in a slow rhythm along her inner lips before focusing on her clit again. Anna emits a soft, quiet moan and instead of biting my shoulder, she grabs onto me and clings to me in some final surrender to the pleasure between her legs.

"You're so fucking wet, babe," I growl. "Are you gonna cum on my fingers for me?"

As she moans, I find her entrance with my finger and slide my index finger inside her. Her pussy tightens around my single finger as Anna moans. I enter her with every inch and stroke her spongy walls as I watch her squirm and moan in my arms. My chest surges with pride at the way I utterly destroyed her desire to resist me.

I kiss her neck again as I slide another finger inside Anna, desperate to make her cum all over me, not just leak juices on her thighs.

"Cum for me, woman," I growl. "I love feeling your tight black pussy wrapped around my fingers."

Her body arches against mine and she wraps her arm around me as she cums hard all over me. I can feel her pussy throbbing around my fingers and the only thing I crave more than anything is getting my dick inside her again.

I slowly withdraw my fingers from her tightness and suck Anna's juices off as she glances at her feet and gasps for breath.

"I missed that pussy."

Our eyes meet in another emotionally destructive moment of eye contact. Neither of us can look at each other like this for long before we have to break out of the moment and pretend the feelings between us don't exist.

. . .

I DON'T BLAME HER. The feelings between us don't make any sense. Outlaw bikers don't fall in love. You pick up an 'old lady' because she makes herself useful to you, lets you hit her, or for some other fucked up reason. I never had any reason to allow a woman that much power over my life but standing in front of Anna... I want to give her everything.

The worst part is that she isn't one of us and I don't know how the hell to reconcile that with my family or with the club. I've broken hearts before and I've had to patch things up with the Blackwoods and the Hollingsworths because of shit I've done as a kid.

Even the smaller families affiliated with the Rebel Barbarians either want me to take up with their daughters or they warn them to stay far away from the Shaw who gambles too much to ever settle down.

"THEY DIDN'T TOUCH YOU THERE."

"I told you they didn't," she says with all the hostility stripped from her voice. It might not be love, but at least it's progress.

"GET IN THE SHOWER. I'll get you clean before bed."

"I DON'T NEED your help to shower," Anna says. Damn right she doesn't. I might have my assurances that neither Reaper nor her pig captors put their hands on her but that doesn't mean I'm done with her.

For weeks without her body I didn't even look at another woman. I'm so wound up with desire for Anna that I desperately need release, and watching her unintentional sensual movements while she's pregnant with my child only makes my yearning for her stronger.

"You don't. But you will have it. I need to know what you know about the pigs."

"Which ones?"

She steps in the shower, more to get away from any potential reaction I might have to her obvious dig at me and the rest of the bikers. We might be bastards, but Reaper won her fair and square.

"I'm a worse pig than the bastard who stuffed you in a hole then?"

She steps into the hot water and lets out a gasp at the temperature. I reach over and adjust the nozzle to a slightly cooler temperature. Anna continues to resist the heat, waiting for the water to come to a more tolerable temperature.

"Maybe," she says. "I don't know what they wanted with me."

"I'm not the worst man you've ever met. I made you cum…"

She clearly needs a reminder of all the ways I've taken care of her, but my first reminder doesn't stop Anna from glaring at me wickedly.

"That makes forcing me fine, I suppose."

"I'm not a villain for giving you something you wanted, Anna."

She grabs the shower's glass door like she plans to close it on me, but I rest my hand on hers. I don't need to use any force to get Anna's obedience, but that doesn't stop her from testing me.

"You are demented, Southpaw. And I don't want you getting the wrong idea about me. I don't want you."

"Like fuck you do."

I grab the motel bar of soap and wet my hands. Time to ignore Anna and get her clean. Once she doesn't smell like a hole in the ground, I'll fuck some sense in her and remind her of the dick she has definitely been missing while we were apart.

"Don't you dare touch me," she says, giving me one of her fierce mean looks when she realizes she can't duck beneath my arms and sneak her way around me.

"I'll touch my property whenever I want to."

"I'm not your property," she says.

"Yes. You are."

I grab her wrist and begin cleaning her arm. Anna slaps me with her free hand, soaking my beard in water and dragging her nails into my cheek. What the hell is wrong with this woman?

Our eyes meet in the typical tense challenge that rises between us.

"Careful, Anna," I warn her in a low, serious voice.

"Or what?" she says. "I said I'm not your damn property."

"Why make a problem out of something you enjoy? For all your goddamn fussing, you haven't made any effort to escape. I just had my finger in your pussy and listened to you moan exactly like you wanted it."

Anna never backs off from a challenge and I'm beginning to see how much trouble I'm in allowing a woman like Anna into my life.

Maybe I am too goddamn impulsive.

"You touch me again, I'll smack the shit out of you," she says boldly. Her gaze never leaves mine. Anna's defiance sparks a deadly craving in me to make her submit. There's something very troubling about this woman that she can look a terrifying biker twice her size dead in the eye and threaten to hurt him.

"I wouldn't do that if I were you."

I continue cleaning her arm, expecting Anna to read my threatening tone and back off at least until she isn't naked and until I get her clean. Instead, she slaps me again. The noise reverberates through the bathroom. The damned woman hit me even harder.

We resume our tense, challenging eye contact. I grip the bar of soap so tightly, I expect it to shoot up into the ceiling and make a hole in it. All her defiance is tied to my use of the word 'property'. A word that perfectly describes women in our world offends her.

But it's just a word. A word for something you love. For something you protect. It's not like it used to be. Most men our age would never trade their woman for a bike.

I certainly wouldn't trade her. My grip on her wrist remains consistent as I caution her.

"Hit me again, Anna, and I'll have to teach you a lesson that you could learn without us making a mess."

"Don't you dare threaten me," she says as I soap up her stomach, running my hand purposefully over her slight baby bump. She shudders as I touch the physical representation of our permanent bond, but she doesn't hit me and she doesn't shy away from my touch.

"I'll threaten you if I think it will keep you safe."

"How the hell does calling me your property keep me safe?" she says. Her voice drips with disdain and she pulls her body away from mine slightly, testing my willingness to let her go. My hand grips her wrist a little tighter.

I don't need Anna testing my authority.

"It stops men from raping your cunt or asshole when I'm not looking."

"Charming."

"Believe me, Anna. There are worse men than me."

She allows me to clean her more, biting her lip and squirming uncomfortably as I rub my soapy hand over her lower lips and clean her flower and butt.

"Turn around."

She turns around obediently, giving me brief respite from her furious glaring. That ass of hers is too fucking perfect. I clean her back there too and Anna clearly doesn't like it. She turns around when I'm done, giving me more of her rage and less of her ass.

"You are so invasive," she says, making a futile effort to snatch the bar of soap from my hands.

"I told you, Anna. You are my property."

Our tense eye contact only lasts a second before Anna stumbles in her decision making and slaps me a third time. The second she does it, she can tell it's a mistake.

Chapter Sixteen
Anna

"Very well."

THE TWO WORDS terrify the shit out of me when Southpaw follows them up with silence. He roughly scrubs me clean and I can tell by the change in his demeanor that the man is goddamn serious about punishment.

Crap. I convince myself that because I'm pregnant, he won't have the capacity to hurt me, but I don't know if that's really true. I don't know this man or what he's capable of at all. For all I know, he could take particular demented pleasure in hurting me and there's nothing I could do about it.

When he finishes cleaning me off and exfoliating my skin within an inch of its life, he works to rinse me off meticulously with his brows pinched together and a stern, focused expression on his face.

I hate the way he talks to me and I definitely hate the way he talks about me, but I can't deny the care in the way he gets me clean and wants to look after my well-being. Even his rough scrubbing becomes more gentle seemingly against his will.

"Southpaw..."

"Don't speak."

I bite my lower lip. I'm in enough trouble already and know I shouldn't make it worse.

"I'm sorry."

He glares at me with the elite mixture of disdain and disapproval. Apology not accepted. Clearly.

"Doesn't change what's gonna happen to you, Anna. Don't worry. The fact that you're a stubborn woman doesn't bother me."

His unbothered stance only scares the fuck out of me more because I know for a fact this man is not "unbothered".

Once my body is clean, he washes my hair. I'm surprised I don't have to micromanage the way he touches my hair. I've always been the most tender-headed member of my family and my hair looks like a sheep on the last days of its life.

Southpaw doesn't mind. Standing outside of the shower fully clothed, he makes me turn around again and I expect him to tug at my hair or yank at my scalp unintentionally, but he works the knots out of my hair gently and washes it with the same amount of care I once watched Reaper clean his motorcycle outside of the motel.

Southpaw's tenderness as he helps me shower makes it easy to forget that not only is he less than perfect, he's downright dangerous and not necessarily less dangerous than the men who trapped me in a hole.

He said he wanted to ask questions about that, but I've been such a pain in the ass that he shifts his focus to punishing me instead.

"Step out of the shower," he commands. I obey him, scrutinizing him closely in case his demeanor changes and I really need to make a run for it. He wraps me in a bleached motel towel that smells like it just had a fresh run through the dryer.

The man won't even allow me to dry off on my own. Once he gets the water off my body, he squeezes the water from my curls and gently dries my hair before grabbing my hips and making me face him.

"I don't relish punishing you while you're pregnant," he says. "But a dick in the ass won't hurt our kid."

He leans forward and plants a soft, painfully warm kiss on my stomach. Terror surges through me and tightens an impossibly full knot in the back of my throat. I feel frozen in place.

"You knew disobedience would have consequences," he says. "Be thankful it's my dick going in your ass and not someone else's. Now go out there and get on the bed."

"South--

He interrupts me with a finger on my lips. Considering the brutality of his threat and the crude, domineering tone he just used with me, I find his touch surprisingly tender. Impossible warmth spreads through me. I have never found myself so easily manipulated by a man's touch.

"It's time you start calling me Wyatt in private."

"Who the hell is Wyatt?"

I know it's him. Obviously. But I can't connect the monster or the gangster to a man with a real and very normal name. Wyatt.

"Wyatt Shaw," he says. "Second son to Harlan 'Harley' Shaw, President of the Rebel Blood Barbarians Motorcycle Club."

Our eye contact is always intense. I never understood the depth of nonverbal communication possible between two people until I met him. Although now, it feels like I'm meeting him for the first time.

"Wyatt," I repeat. "What a normal name..."

I glance down at his hands. His left hand taps his thigh unconsciously. He holds his gun in his left hand. He always grabs me with his left hand... I never connected the dots. I was too busy surviving for word problems.

He smiles at my basic ass comment and shrugs.

"Don't give that name to anyone else," Wyatt says, his face taking on its stern, dark cast again. "Especially not the police."

I wrinkle my nose at the implication that I would have anything to say about officers of the law. As far as I know, I'm not too far off from where I went missing and none of those so-called officers have done anything to find me. If I believe Wyatt and Reaper, my second captors were also law enforcement. I shudder to think of what their badges enable them to do this far out from the cities.

"I don't have to be told not to talk to cops," I say truthfully. Wyatt's broad, muscular shoulders relax. His black hair sticks out from his head in wavy tufts because of the humidity. I don't know why I want to touch it.

"Good," he says, his hand wandering from my lips down the center line of my body all the way to my mound. He gives my pussy a gentle tap. Electricity travels from my pussy to my extremities. I fight back... everything.

"Do you understand why I told you my name?" he asks, slowly taking my hand in his, acting so tender that I forget he just smacked my mound.

"No."

"It's a promise. When I take you back to my dad, I'll have to fight the club to keep you. You have that name, you have my promise that I won't let anything happen to you."

The promise to keep me safe would make me feel a lot better if Wyatt didn't sound so certain that something bad would happen to me without it. He takes every inch of me in with his eyes again and then gives my mound another tap, this one harder than the last. Tingling spreads through me and I feel a small but hot gush between my thighs.

Why do I respond to him so easily? He makes a low growl in his throat once he touches me. I'm running out of time to avoid his promised punishment.

"Get that pussy in the bed," he says. "If you're good... I'll go easy on you."

I take my one chance to plead for mercy, hoping our new closeness might change my fate.

"If I could avoid having your giant dick in my ass, I would appreciate it."

"The only way to avoid that would have been listening to my instructions in the first place. There isn't another way to save your ass."

He leans forward and kisses the top of my mound. That frustrating shiver spreads through me again. I don't want to give in to his delusion that I want him as much as he wants me, but it's hard to deny the reaction I have whenever his lips touch my skin.

"I'll do anything," I plead with him weakly as he kisses the top of my mound again. Begging doesn't work. Wyatt pulls away, unmoved.

"Get in the bed, baby."

Wyatt watches me as I walk the short distance from the bathroom to the giant king-sized bed. As I lie back on to the giant king-sized bed, Wyatt moves to a standing position at the foot of the bed, maintaining his piercing stare, still fully dressed. Your first impression looking at him that he's both impossibly hot and terribly unhinged would be accurate.

Tattoos swirl across his visible skin and draw my attention to the definition in his muscles. I don't know how the hell he stays so goddamn shredded when he couldn't possibly have a spare minute to hit the gym with his busy life of crime.

"I like you naked," he says in a deep, patient voice as he stands at the foot of the bed. "Unfortunately, I have to endure a lot of trouble for the privilege of touching that pussy."

He doesn't struggle to mix up his outrage with either his amusement or his lust. I can't predict what he's going to do next. My punishment might involve my ass, but I don't know to what extent Wyatt intends on inflicting pain.

I watch his face turn red as he stares at me. The only thing he appears to want right now is to look at me for his pleasure and his pleasure alone.

"Touch yourself," he commands. "I want you nice and wet before I take your ass..."

Touching myself doesn't seem like much of a punishment, but I don't have any desire to touch myself in front of Wyatt either. It's easy to let myself go when he takes what he wants from me. Closing my eyes and allowing him to use my body for his pleasure is... terrifyingly easy.

Allowing myself to succumb to uncontrolled pleasure in Wyatt's presence forces me to lose control of just another thing. My hands move over my stomach slowly as I straddle the line between disobedience and putting my finger between my legs.

"Very good," he says. "Feel that soft stomach. The way it curves with my baby..."

I allow my hand to roam over my skin and it does feel good. It's not the type of pleasure he really wants me to feel right now, but I can't bring myself to fight against it.

"Keep moving your hand," he says.

The room smells like leather and Wyatt. Soap and conditioner aren't enough to drown out the pure smell of man that fills the room. Wyatt has a particularly strong fragrance that mixes with the scent of his cut and the grease from his bike that he can't seem to wash off.

My fingers sink into the fur surrounding my pussy as I allow myself to examine how much hair growth I've had down there since leaving Wyatt's custody. I explore the long curly hair surrounding my pussy and pull my lips apart slightly to expose very creamy wetness.

I avoid touching my clit, slowly massaging my outer lips and watching Wyatt's slow, heavy breathing as he stares at me. When I think he's too distracted to command me further, he barks at me, "Don't hold back. Touch your pussy, Anna."

I move my index finger between my lower lips and sink into an impossibly soft center. I'm so wet that it feels like dipping my finger into cake batter. The sound I make is unlike anything I've ever made before. Heat rushes to my cheeks as the humiliation of exposing myself like this in front of Wyatt feels like punishment enough.

"Fuck, that's hot," he says after I moan. "Don't stop. Touch yourself and think of how it felt to have my big white dick in your pussy."

My body shudders involuntarily as I react to his words and slide my finger in smooth circles throughout my wetness. My pleasure heightens with each passing second. I've never pushed myself to this point of arousal so quickly on my own before. Wyatt doesn't take his eyes off me and I am too horny to stop myself from touching myself like I mean it.

Every inch of my pussy tingles with arousal, so the slightest touch of my outer lips makes me moan and I nearly cum when I move back to running my finger in slow circles around my clit.

"Spread your legs wider," Wyatt commands. "I want to see you gush from that full bush."

I open my legs and give him the view he craves, splaying myself completely in front of Wyatt exactly as he demands. Touching myself has never felt this good and I don't want to stop.

CHAPTER SEVENTEEN
SOUTHPAW

I love watching her touch her pussy for me. Anna spreads those lower lips with shy hesitation at first, but then she loses herself in the pleasure of touching her own clit. The first soft moans Anna makes nearly make my dick split a hole through my pants.

"Don't stop, Anna."

She slowly moves her fingers in a smooth circle around her clit. Anna exposes the soft flesh between her furry lower lips and I watch clear juices coat her fingers as she touches herself. Anna moans again and adjusts her hips so she can massage her pussy at a better angle.

"Cum for me," I command her. "I need to watch you cum, Anna."

My dick wants her so bad it's almost sore for her. I can't please Anna tonight until I punish her despite how badly I want to feel her sweet ass pussy gripping my dick like a vice. She hesitates to obey my command initially, but her body fights off her rational thinking.

She shuts her eyes, visibly giving in to the pleasure.

"Put a finger in your cunt and fuck yourself for me," I tell her. "Spread those pussy lips and show me..."

Those words alone nearly make her burst. Her hands fly away from her body as she moans and catches her breath.

"I didn't say you could stop."

Her fingers obediently return to her entrance. I observe her with eager anticipation as she spreads her gooey center and pushes one finger deep between her legs. She's so damn hot. I nearly finish in my pants just watching that finger disappear between those gorgeous, swollen cunt lips.

"Deeper," I command her. "You're almost there. Add another finger."

There's nothing more beautiful than watching Anna give in to her pleasure completely. Her disobedience angers me even more because now instead of touching her, I have to watch her touch herself and then inflict more pain on her...

Anna's hips swirl and she moves with her hand as she touches her clit and fucks herself. The juices on her thighs and pussy create a wet spot on the bed that darkens the sheets.

I can tell she's getting closer from the way she moves.

"Cum for me, Anna..."

"Yes..." she moans. If Anna says the word 'yes' to me, she has lost her sense of control. I love it.

"Cum for me. Fuck yourself. Touch your soft ass pussy lips for your owner..."

I don't have to ask if she came. Anna cries out with pleasure and her juices squirt all over her thighs as she continues burying two fingers in her cunt with a slow, steady rhythm. She slowly descends from the high and removes both fingers from her pussy, shuddering and gasping for breath.

"Very fucking hot," I murmur, watching her as she lies there spread out for me. It would be so easy to forget my promise to punish her and take what I want from the soaked and spread pussy lips in front of me.

Slowing down from my impulses, I reach into my pocket for the dice, rolling them around my left hand a few times before putting them back in my pocket.

"Unfortunately, being the hottest piece of ass I've ever had the pleasure of taking to bed won't save you. Flip over."

Anna sits up, propping herself on her elbows as she scowls at me.

"Do you think you've done enough to earn mercy?"

"I shouldn't have to earn mercy," she says. "I don't need punishment."

"I would believe that if you ever displayed a shred of obedience. My world is dangerous, Anna."

"I spent several days in a hole in the ground," she says. "I'm aware of how dangerous your world is and I've never wanted any part in it."

"Too bad," I growl. "You're a part of it now."

And she always will be. I don't care what I have to do to secure the club's permission. I'm keeping her and I'm keeping that goddamn baby. They should all be happy that I squashed the beef with Reaper.

"I hate you," she says, purposefully spitting venom at me in hopes of what? Changing my mind?

"Flip over, Anna. Let me give you a reason to hate me first."

She exhales slowly, observing me carefully to see how serious I am about this punishment. Unflinchingly, I stare back at her. Anna's fire doesn't scare me. I don't mind a woman with a little fire. Hell, I wouldn't mind if she were a goddamn inferno.

Her hesitation is her only resistance. She flips onto her stomach, presenting that sexy black ass to me for punishment.

I WON'T DENY that it's damn tempting to lay a good smack on Anna's butt. She has a sexy bubble butt with two voluptuous ass cheeks that drew my attention like a goddamn magnet the first time I saw them.

Smacking that ass would be a treat.

. . .

BUT FUCKING IT would be better.

"Do you know what I'm going to do to you, Anna?" I ask her in a low, threatening voice. I'm not a monster. It's only right I prepare her for what's coming next.

She doesn't answer.

"That wasn't rhetorical."

"Yes," she says in a voice so low I wouldn't have heard it if I wasn't constantly attuned to Anna's voice. I could hear her talk in a crowded bar, I listen to her voice so closely.

"Good girl..."

I get to my knees and drag Anna to the edge of the bed. She shudders and braces herself against the bed in confusion. Poor woman. She makes an uncomfortable grunt as I spread her ass cheeks apart lewdly and get a good look at her tight, tender butthole.

SHE LOOKS WAY TOO small for my dick.

I GET straight to the point and run my flat tongue over her newly exposed back door. Anna lets out a strangled noise between a shriek and a moan. It's surprise, pleasure and humiliation wrapped into one cry before she yells my name out.

"Wyatt..."

Having her call me by my real name makes the bond between us feel realer and stronger. I push my tongue inside her asshole and taste one of the few parts of Anna I haven't yet touched. *If she has any doubt that she's mine, my tongue up her ass will be a step in the right direction towards changing that.*

She calls my name again, clearly protesting as I lavish attention on her asshole with my tongue. It doesn't take much to get her wet, but I don't just need her ass wet. I need her soaked and dripping enough to take a big dick all the way up her tight ass. I pull my tongue away from her ass, allowing Anna a chance to breathe through the overwhelming sensations.

"Do you want me to stop?"

"Yes."

"Too fucking bad."

I push my tongue deeper in her ass and she follows up with a satisfied moan. Her body doesn't want me to stop. Pulling my tongue out of her back door, I coat her ass in my spit with slow strokes and then push my tongue back in her tight hole to keep her nice and wet. When she nearly cums just from my tongue in her ass, I pull away and rise to my feet, giving Anna's bubble butt a hearty and well-deserved smack.

"That was... some punishment..." she whimpers, hopeful that I've forgotten. I know how she thinks so well. Unfortunately, she won't get off so easily.

Poor Anna.

"That wasn't your punishment, Anna. You know that."

She attempts to move but I stick my hand out quickly, using my palm to keep Anna pinned to the bed by her lower back. She emits a strangled grunt and wriggles in a futile effort to escape me.

"Where do you think you're going?"

She grunts again and squirms – without answering me. She hasn't lost her will to fight. Yet.

"Punishments don't typically feel good, Anna. But you will find that I am a very generous owner. So once I'm done shoving my dick in your ass, I promise... you will cum."

Anna makes another effort to escape my palm. This time, I give in to the urge to spank her bubble butt and hit one cheek. Hard. She yelps and stops her efforts to escape.

121

Continuing to hold her down with one hand, I free my dick from my pants with the other one. My cock is swollen with arousal and so red it looks angry. Enough precum oozes from the tip that it drips down the sides of my curved dick head.

While holding her still, I press the soft head against her freshly soaked back door. She shudders but holds incredibly still, instinctively sensing that sudden movements will hurt her more than they could ever hurt me. My dick is too big for her ass. I could barely get my tongue in her forbidden hole, she was so tight.

Anna's emotional resistance and the physical challenge of getting my big white dick in her tiny back door sends my arousal through the roof. I add my precum to the juices around her asshole and massage her entrance with the head of my dick to prepare both of us for what it will feel like when I enter her.

Both Anna's breathing and moans sound nervous.

"This will teach you not to disobey me," I growl as I make an initial effort to push the head of my dick into Anna's ass. Her tight sphincter resists my first effort, but I almost get in there. Anna yelps as she previews the pain she's about to experience. That's enough holding still for her.

Her legs thrash slightly as I pin her more tightly to the bed and move my hips forward again. This time, I spread her asshole with my dick just enough to get the head in. Anna makes a loud, anguished sound. I don't blame her. The surge rushing through me is just as intense. I bite down on my lower lip to keep from crying out.

That sweet, sexy black ass is even tighter than I expected.

"Real punishment would be giving you every inch of this dick in one thrust," I growl. "But I'm not a bad guy, Anna... Not at all..."

I wrap her hair around my wrist and tilt her neck back, continuing to use one hand to pin her to the bed as I slide the rest of my dick in her ass. Her back door was just wet enough for initial penetration not to make her bleed, but getting the rest of my cock in her ass will definitely hurt her.

"Please..." she begs as I slide another inch inside her.

"You lost your chance for mercy, Anna," I whisper, pushing her harder into the bed. "Now you have to feel the pain that comes with disobeying your owner."

I almost feel sorry for her when she cries out. But this is for her own good and once I have my dick in her ass... I know she'll feel better.

"Please..."

"Your sweet ass feels so good around my dick," I murmur. "So stop begging for mercy and beg for more... because that's all you're gonna get."

She lets out a moan that sounds halfway between a protest and like she's nearing the throes of pleasure again. Although I shouldn't ease her punishment, I reach around the front of her body to touch her clit. Anna gasps as I touch her pussy. I almost regret giving in to her pained moans when she pushes her hips back and voluntarily allows more of my dick to sink into her perfect ass.

I can't hold back and it's my turn to groan with absolute pleasure as I lose myself to how fucking good it feels to bury my dick in Anna's ass. I'm in fucking heaven and she almost feels too good for me to concern myself with punishment.

"Fuck, you're hot," I grunt.

"It hurts," Anna gasps. "Fuck, it hurts..."

I massage her clit in slower circles and touch her sweet spot as I keep sliding my wet dick into her ass. She cries out again and I thrust the last few inches inside her ass with one swift motion, pressing my crotch against those smooth, buttery brown butt cheeks. That ass is heaven. I have to breathe for a minute before I move. Her ass is so tight that the slightest movement along my shaft could easily make me cum.

"It's supposed to hurt," I grunt. "It's punishment..."

Anna thrusts her hips back instinctively as I keep massaging her clit. Her pussy and ass throb as she closes in on another orgasm. The fullness from my dick in her ass must make her body particularly sensitive and when I touch her clit, she explodes with screaming and moaning that make it even harder for me not to cum deep inside her smooth, tight ass.

"You like that, woman? Do you like when I touch your clit with my dick in your ass?"

She shouldn't like it – but she does. That seems to be the story of our entire goddamn relationship. Anna responds with a moan. She still has too much pride to confess how good it feels to have me dominating her ass with my dick while I control her orgasms.

I don't need her verbal response. Feeling her perfect ass throbbing around my dick is enough of a goddamn gift.

"You feel so good... Fuck..."

I keep massaging her clit as I work up an easy, romantic pace. Anna's body responds with surprising amounts of desire. She gasps and moans after a few short thrusts inside her tight back door and I can tell she's gonna cum again.

"Cum for me, woman... Cum with my dick in your ass..."

I keep her pinned to the bed just so I can feel her tight ass drawing my dick deeper as she cums. Her pussy throbs with her back door as she climaxes and juices drip down her thighs. I grunt and release inside her ass as I watch her cum. She's such a pretty goddamn sight that I can't help myself.

Thick ropes of cum erupt from the tip of my dick and I feel physically weak from the force of climaxing inside her. I release Anna from my grasp but neither of us move apart from each other as we catch our breath. What was punishment for her will become punishment for me as I have to move my body away from Anna's to lie back on the bed and catch my goddamn breath.

I groan as I slowly ease my dick out of her ass. I can't move further once I do and my body careens forward, crushing Anna as I fall into the bed. She squeaks and groans. I want to move but goddamn, she feels good. That soft ass pressing into my crotch just makes the pleasure from my orgasm feel better.

Moving her hair aside, I nibble Anna's ear. "I expect your obedience from now on. I believe I've made myself clear."

"You have," she says softly, the resistance completely ass-fucked out of her.

"Good," I reply, stroking the length of her spine. "Because if you or anyone else ever tries to take that sexy tight ass away from me, I will hunt you down and bring you back."

Her skin breaks out in goosebumps. I still scare her. *Good.*

"I'm not going anywhere," she says. "I'm in too deep, right?"

I press my nose into her neck and kiss her again. She sounds sad and after what I just experienced with Anna, I want to take all her pain and sadness away. I roll off her and pull her into my arms, surprised when she yields to my desire to cuddle. And thank fuck, she doesn't question my desire to have her snuggled in my arms.

I press my nose into Anna's hair and kiss her neck again. I didn't know if I would ever see her again and she's the first woman I've really wanted to see after the first time...

Her body just fits perfectly with mine even after we fuck. Instead of wanting her out of my bed, I never want her to leave. Anna sinks into the warmth of my arms. I enjoy how safe she seems to feel with me. This woman makes me feel stronger. More confident. The more I have her, the less I want to enter a heart-racing gut-wrenching bet that I know I can't afford to lose.

Anna moves her butt against my thigh and my cock nearly jerks awake again. Even if she's about to get me hard again, I'm more worried about her feelings than my dick. It's new to worry about a woman like that. I kiss her shoulder.

"Why don't you want to leave your life in Chicago?" I ask her. "Was there... someone?"

"No," she says, turning to face me with a strange expression on her face. "There's more to life than having a boyfriend. I have a career."

Had. The verbal slip up makes me want to hold onto her tighter out of fear that she'll go back. I don't think I could stand that.

"Nursing. It's a good career. You could do that with us."

I take her hand and slide my fingers through hers. Her resistance and surprise slowly fade once she realizes I'm just holding her hand. Anna's gaze flashes to mine briefly and I swear I catch the slightest hint of a smile on her face. I know it's wrong to find her features so fucking beautiful... but I just do.

I've seen so many country girls with the same blond hair and the same blue eyes. I've never seen a girl like Anna. She smells different from other women too... But she doesn't seem taken with my idea that she stay with us – voluntarily.

"Spend the rest of my life pulling bullets out of bikers covered in confederate and white supremacist tattoos? That sounds wonderful," Anna says sarcastically, dropping her gaze from mine long enough to send a pang of worry through my chest.

"You're having my baby. I want to take care of you. Is that wrong?"

"What you did wrong was getting me pregnant in the first place."

Does she want me to tell her this is a mistake? I don't feel that way. Nothing in this world happens by mistake.

"The only wrong I did was letting you out of my sight."

Chapter Eighteen
Anna

He talks about "us" like we make sense but there is no "us". There can't be a future between the two of us. Wyatt gazes at me with such intensity that it's like he's trying to burrow his way under his skin and join us more permanently than a child ever could.

"I guarantee I won't make the mistake of letting you out of my sight again," he says, running a firm, calloused hand over my cheek. The shiver goes straight to my pussy, despite every ounce of common sense I have willing me to resist his touch.

The heat between us ignited in the Flying J bathroom, and since it happened so long ago, at this point I could almost pretend that it happened to someone else instead of admitting to Wyatt or myself that he tapped into my primal and repressed sexual needs, giving me exactly what I wanted and needed.

But I have what I need in the "real" world. By that, I mean the world outside of the biker gang where people live normal lives and wake up in time for work and they get to the end of the block in time for the bus and they pay taxes. Wyatt doesn't look like he's filed a W-2 in his entire life -- if he even knows what it is. But damn... the way he looks at me.

Those fierce, demanding eyes seem more important than paying my rent or worrying about the latest bullshit nurse drama on shift. His thumb moves over my collarbone and shoulder.

"Your old life ended when we locked eyes in that gas station. That man who wouldn't leave you alone..."

The man he killed.

Wyatt trails off as if nothing more needs to be said. His eyes are empty and dark as he remembers what happened. Contrasting the man touching me now with the swift, emotionless killer from the gas station should cause my body to have some sort of instinctive revulsion to Wyatt.

But I shift closer to him and his hands move intentionally around my hips. I feel his desire mounting again and sense my punishment might not be complete yet.

He continues an entirely different train of thought, "I'll send guys back to your apartment to get the last of your things, make sure your identity is safe. But I'll need to do more..."

His finger slides across my collar bone, but it might as well have slid across my throat because finally, the instinctive terror I expect kicks in. Gooseflesh spreads across my skin and my hand thrusts out against Wyatt's chest. He grins.

"You are so intuitive," he says. "But you can't fight this, Anna. You can't fight any of this."

I squirm nervously, but as I open my mouth to beg Wyatt for an explanation, he sucks on my neck so hard it feels like he's piercing my skin. I moan in pain, but his hard kisses always end up stinging in a way that leaves a dull, pleasurable throbbing behind with the bruising on my neck.

It's fucked up how good it feels. Wyatt continues kissing my neck until I shove his chest much harder.

"What the hell are you planning?" I ask, my heart pounding

nervously. "I gave in to your punishment. I took your dick in my ass. I can't handle more..."

My pussy aches for him but I don't dare tell him that. I don't know what the hell he did to me when he put his dick in my back door, but I feel open, exhilarated and desperate for him to touch me more. Not like I can let him know that with all his arrogant talk about making me his property and never letting me go.

Wyatt's gaze snaps to mine again as he pauses his aggressive neck kisses. He runs his hand over my cheek again.

"I need to give you a tattoo so you're branded as my property."

I slap the shit out of him. It's stupid, impulsive and if he were another man, he might have broken my damn wrist for swinging on him like that. His beard absorbs most of the noise, but I can tell from the sting on my palm from his prickly hairs that I smacked him hard as fuck. His face turns back towards mine with his thick brows furrowed in anger.

"Hitting me again won't change the situation, but it will change how much I tie you up to get the job done."

I wriggle away from him, making an effort to scramble backwards on the bed, but there is no physical contest between me and Wyatt that I could possibly win. He easily positions his body on top of mine and pins my hands over my head, holding me there against the motel mattress.

THE LAST THING I should be thinking about is how fucking hot he is. Wyatt's looks hijack my sensibilities every time. Smelling his strong and goddamn delicious masculine odor only worsens my self control. Squirming for freedom only draws my hips closer to his dick, giving me an opportunity to feel his hardness. The man spends his time in a nearly constant state of arousal.

I don't even know how it's possible for him to stay in control of all his cruel plots against me and other people with his dick so hard all the damn time.

"Wyatt..." I grunt, making a futile effort to scramble backward as my back presses up against the shockingly fluffy motel pillows. "Can we at least–

"Discuss?" he interrupts. "No."

He kisses me on the lips. I fight the urge to bite his lips but luckily he's smart enough just to give me a peck and not shove his tongue down my throat right after threatening me. He kisses the top of my nose, giving me another opportunity to... what? Since we're not discussing anything, I suppose Wyatt just wants me to lie there beneath him and accept my fate.

"Why the hell do you need to give me a tattoo? Mental illness?"

He laughs. "Do I seem mentally ill?"

That must be a trick question, so I refuse to participate. I raise an eyebrow and wisely hold my tongue, making Wyatt laugh even harder.

"I'm not mentally ill," he says calmly. "You need a tattoo to keep you safe because if for some reason we're apart, everyone who sees the mark... will know..."

"Wyatt... This sounds like some crazy shit."

"You're already carrying my baby, Anna... what's crazier than that?"

He follows up by kissing me and although I resist him at first, I yearn for the warmth and softness. The baby hormones aren't helping the situation either. Every time Wyatt touches me, my body responds like he lit me on fire. I moan and squirm beneath him. I press my body into Wyatt's even when I should run away from him.

"Don't worry," he whispers. "I'll eat your pussy first so you have something else to remember about tonight."

I GUESS TAKING his giant dick in the ass wasn't enough...

. . .

130

HE KISSES his way down my bare stomach and spreads my legs apart with ease, like he was opening the pages of a very light magazine. I can't spring my thighs back together or push against his firm hands once Wyatt pries me open. He runs his tongue over my inner thighs possessively, tickling me with his beard and forcing me to make soft, pleasurable moans as his tongue inches closer to my wetness.

Wyatt pushes his tongue between my lower lips eagerly, getting straight to the point as he wraps his tongue around my clit and sucks my lower lips until I cum for him. He removes his tongue from my clit once I cum and runs it all the way down to my back door again. I cum instantly with the reminder of how much pleasure I got from Wyatt's tongue and dick in my ass.

With that climax and so much wetness coating my thighs, my yearning for Wyatt's dick goes into overdrive. I can't bear the thought of asking him for sex or yielding verbally in any way to his affection for me. He's crazy and I would be insane to return any of his feelings – even just his sexual feelings.

My hesitation doesn't stop Wyatt from planting kisses down the tops of my thighs and all the way down my shins until he gets to the top of my foot. I expect him to stop but Wyatt takes my big toe and sucks on it until I moan before he kisses the tops of my other toes and gives them particularly wet kisses. When he pulls away, he sits back and kisses the bottom of my feet.

"Good," he says with a smile. "Now that you're nice and calm... let's get to work."

"I never agreed to this tattoo."

"IT WILL BE MUCH EASIER if you do," he says.

"Can I at least know what magical tattoo will somehow signal to other bikers to stay away from me?"

He kisses the bottoms of my feet three times before answering.

. . .

ANNA

"PROPERTY OF SOUTHPAW."

Chapter Nineteen
Southpaw

I should have anticipated Anna flinging her damn foot at my face, but I didn't expect her to kick my nose and actually draw blood once she heard about the tattoo. I scream like a motherfucker once she kicks my face and the blood spurts everywhere. Her guilt instantly sets in.

"Oh shit! Shit!"

"Damn it, Anna…"

She quickly scrambles to a less compromising position and despite my best efforts to fight her off, she finds her way into my lap with a motel towel pressed to my face to soak up the blood. I hold the towel to my face and push Anna off. She comes running back and tilts my head back.

"Don't push me away, you idiot. I'm a nurse."

"You're going to break my neck."

"I'm tilting your neck back to help with the nose bleed," she says. "I'm the nurse, not you, so just listen."

"A nurse with a goddamn aggravated assault problem."

"Don't give me that shit, Wyatt."

I like how my name sounds on her tongue even if she's vicious with her fists and her feet. Hearing her say my name calms me down enough to let her close.

"Can I see if it's still bleeding?"

"Why? So you can make it bleed more?" I grunt, flinching as Anna takes the towel away from my face. She didn't get me that bad. I've had worse hits to the face. The damn woman just took me by surprise.

"We'll see."

"You have fucking problems, woman."

"Obviously," she says. "Otherwise I would have used this opportunity to escape."

"But?"

Anna scowls. "I have a duty as a nurse. That's all."

This damned woman.

"Do your duty, then. When you're done, I'll add sucking my cock to your list of tasks."

"Careful, Wyatt," Anna says. I don't want to be careful. Not with her. I grin and let her dab the blood off my face.

"Never," I respond, taking the opportunity to hold Anna's hips. I have always loved her figure. She has a plump ass and boobs to match – a perfect full-figured hourglass with extra weight in all the right places.

Her slim hips filled out during our weeks apart, which I find damn sexy. Everything about her is sexy. Even the way she fights me off with all the force she can muster and then crawls over to me to clean up her mess.

I push hair out of Anna's face as she pretends to closely examine my nose, which feels fine by this point. I don't mind her looking at my face. Fuck, if she wants to stare at me all night, I'll kneel right here and let her. But something tells me she won't let that happen.

"I can't let you tattoo that crazy shit on me," she says. "I know you think it's gonna keep me safe but... you're an outlaw, Wyatt.

134

Wouldn't it be safer to stuff me in some clubhouse back in Illinois and go... wherever you're going?"

"Not when you're carrying my child and not with ex-cops after us and a thousand fucking enemies on my tail. Sorry, woman. I protect what's mine..."

I kiss her until eventually... I give up. She clings to my t-shirt with desperate hands. I can't tell if she wants to pull me closer or push me away. This woman has me wrapped around her finger completely. *How the fuck does she have this much power over me?*

IF SHE DOESN'T WANT the tattoo, I've lost my will to give it to her.

I WOULD RATHER JUST HAVE Anna. I kiss her neck and lay her on her back. She touches my face, grabbing my cheeks with possessiveness I could mistake for my own as she kisses me and strokes my beard, awakening a fiery desire for her within me. I have no more patience for waiting. I need to feel Anna now.

I want her hands all over me as she strips me down to nothing.

"Take my clothes off," I murmur. "Fuck it. Just take it all off."

HER HANDS MOVE QUICKLY and urgently as if she wants this just as much as I do despite her squirming away from me and relentless protests against my advances. I know she wants this because a man just knows. She instinctively gives me the softest parts of her flesh as she strips me down to nothing.

And once I'm naked in bed with her, Anna's hands clutch at me desperately as she pulls me against her by my arms and back. Even as she uses most of her strength to pull me towards her desperately, I relish staying in complete control of the space between us.

Her heels hook behind my thighs in an attempt to draw me in. Tricky woman.

"If I didn't know better, I'd say you wanted me," I whisper as I rub the head of my dick along Anna's lower lips.

Teasing her tortures me just as much at this point, but I can't stop myself. I have to play this game with her body. Feel her. Yearn for her. Enjoy the point right before I take the biggest chance of a life-time – bringing a girl like Anna into the Amarillo club house. She moans as I rub her pussy with the head of my dick, making the urges to thrust into her all at once even harder to fight.

I kiss her neck and try to slow myself down by just focusing on how good she smells and tastes or how little she feels beneath me. I just want to protect her so fucking much. As our bodies slide together, the head of my dick slides just past her lower lips. Anna's moaning draws me into her deeper and my resistance fades.

"I want to fuck you so bad," I growl into her ear. Anna pulls me inside her deeper, digging her nails into my back. I almost cum just from entering her slowly. She feels too damn good for me to hold back. Fuck, she's soft. And her pussy is so goddamn tight.

She moans loudly again as the rest of my dick slides inside her. Every time our bodies join feels better than the last. Anna's close-ness, her warmth and the way she breathes between those soft, horny moans drives me fucking wild. After the way I treated her soft ass earlier, the last thing I want is to fuck her hard. I hold her face and kiss her slow and deep while I make love to her.

There's a difference between fucking and making love. Different situations call for different types of sex. After all our fussing, fight-ing, ass fucking and threats of violence, what Anna and I need is some slow, wet, disturbingly passionate love.

"Come here, baby," I whisper, hiking her thighs around me as I take her slow and deep. She looks bewildered as I hold her against me and slide into her pussy tenderly. Women are like bikes. The better you take care of them, the longer they last. Anna moans when I call her baby and every few strokes I hit her at such a sweet spot that she can't control herself.

Her nails dig into my muscles, soothing them while simultaneously lighting them ablaze with desire for her. The woman tortures my impulsive nature. She's perfect to make love to. Soft to the touch. Feisty when I need her to be. And goddamn, that skin is sweet like honey.

"I'm addicted to your tight ass pussy, baby..."

I DON'T KNOW what comes over me. I whisper the nastiest, filthiest things into this woman's ear and she cums all over my dick with each of the dirty phrases coming out of my mouth. I tell her how sexy she is, how I want to cum all over her face, her perfect dark brown tits, how I want to cum inside her again...

It's too much for Anna. I make love to her slowly as she cums, promising to never let anyone hurt her, promising to never let her out of my sight. Fuck, I've never promised so much to a woman as I promised Anna in the minutes before I feel my balls tighten against my body.

Our bodies pull even closer together as I thrust into her deeply one last time and fill her with my seed. I press my nose into her neck and draw her body against mine as I wait for the shuddering waves of pleasure to pass over me. I don't feel like a man, I feel like a fucking baby I'm so tired out from her pussy. It's the good kind of tired.

"Fuck, Anna. I think you're the best goddamn pussy I've ever had," I whisper once we're done. "I think I might be feeling something for you..."

"That feeling is horny," she replies, but when I pull out of her, she doesn't rush off to the bathroom or do anything to push me away. She doesn't even wait for me to drag her into my arms. Anna pushes her butt against me and seeks my body's warmth all on her own. I throw my arm around her and hold her close to me.

"No," I whisper. "It's something more than that, baby mama."

Her hair surrounds my face with a cloud of soft curls. I don't know if it's the pregnancy, the motel shower stuff or just Anna, but it's a new, magical smell. I feel like I'm high off her scent. My arms wrap more tightly around her.

"Not your baby mama," she says. "Your surrogate. That was your plan."

My cock shifts against her ass at the mention of the word surrogate. I like the idea of putting babies in her... regardless of the circumstances. I press my nose into her neck, my dick rising again. I want her so damn bad it hurts.

"Hm. I have a different plan now, baby mama."

"YOU ARE NOT KEEPING THAT NICKNAME," Anna protests.

"I'll be doing what I want with you, baby mama."

"I'd like to see you try doing whatever you want."

I kiss her neck, giving her the rough controlling kisses that Anna loves so damn much. She whimpers and pushes her body into mine. This damn woman. She's so tempting. So perfect. I push her onto her back and make love to Anna again. I can't stop myself and she doesn't stop me this time either.

When did I lose sight of my goal to pin her down and get her tatted up? I can't remember. I just feel so goddamn addicted to her pussy and I have a constant urge to cum inside this precious woman.

Everything I feel for her is so fucking different from anything I've felt for any other woman. She falls asleep easily in my arms and I love that I can make her feel safe. It's the least I can do for the woman in the cruel, fucked up world I've dragged her into.

LATE AT NIGHT, I'm still up. I walk outside with my dice rolling through my fingers and a half-empty flask of Hawk's moonshine. It's quiet out here... so goddamn quiet. My phone buzzes. My best friend has a sixth sense for when I can't sleep. Hawk and I have always been closer than me and any of my brothers.

Hawk: If you're like me, you can't sleep.

Me: Go to bed, fucker.

Hawk: Goddamn cops.

Me: We gotta handle this shit.

Hawk: Club house vote. You bringing the woman?

Me: Yes.

Hawk: Shit.

HE DOESN'T HAVE to say more than that. Anna can't enter the clubhouse. She can't be a part of our world. It's just the way things have always been. I shouldn't even want her in the first place. I just... got in too deep with a beautiful woman and now I can't imagine myself living a day without her.

BUT WHAT THE hell do I know about Anna? She's a nurse... I made her walk away from everything. She's carrying my child...

I NEED to know more about this woman because I think despite myself, I might be falling for her. Shit, I know I fell for her the second I laid eyes on her. The woman makes me so goddamn crazy.

. . .

SHE MAKES me feel like I'm crazy enough to gamble my position in the club by messing around with a woman of the wrong skin color.

I WOULD RISK it all for a chance at a life with her... a stranger.

IF THAT'S FALLING in love, I understand why they call it falling because I feel stupid, clumsy and totally fucking embarrassed that this woman makes me feel like this.

CHAPTER TWENTY
ANNA

Wyatt's wet lips and scratchy beard wake me up from a deep sleep that can only be achieved during pregnancy. I grumble and try to push him off of me. It must be five in the morning and the man needs to let me sleep.

"It's time to wake up, Anna," he whispers. "You and the baby need to eat something."

Great. It must not be five a.m. if it's breakfast time. I groan and try to push Wyatt off me. It doesn't work. He keeps planting the tenderest kisses on my cheek and neck. I pretend to stay asleep a little longer just to enjoy him kissing me. I swear I have him totally fooled when Wyatt's hand slides beneath the blankets and he teases my nipple with his fingers.

"I know you're awake, baby mama. Stop faking. I brought you some breakfast homemade special from the motel kitchen," he says. That means it must be after 6:30 a.m. when they bring out the motel breakfast.

His voice gets me instantly wet, and my stomach grumbles. I've learned not to get my hopes up about biker cuisine. Cold McDonalds. Pit food. Stale motel breakfast. These people act like they've never heard of regular home cooking. I don't even know if Wyatt has a home.

"Yum. Motel breakfast. I can't wait to have another bagel and warm yogurt," I grumble crankily, throwing the blanket over my head. I've been in survival mode for so long that I'm playing recklessly with Wyatt at this point. The threat of the tattoo still looms over me.

"I got you something special," he says. "Now get your ass up and come eat it before I finish it."

I throw the covers off. He's twice my size and he eats like a yeti. Wyatt chuckles as I scramble away from him towards the breakfast smell that finally takes over the entire motel room.

"It smells like pancakes."

I don't question the pancakes, but I thought we had to bust out of here early, so I'm skeptical about Wyatt's extravagant breakfast. Well, extravagant by biker standards. He just has his tattooed fingers wrapped around a steaming mug of hot coffee as he watches me dig in.

"Up all night?" I ask him, although I already know the answer. He has dark circles under his eyes. If you spend long enough in nursing, they're like tree rings. The bigger the dark circles, the longer you've been awake. Wyatt looks like he hasn't had proper sleep in almost two days.

"Doesn't matter," he responds in typical Wyatt fashion. "We're not going to Texas anymore. I'll have plenty of time to sleep soon."

"This is the first I'm hearing of Texas."

"Exactly," he says. "I needed to wait for a sign of what to do next and we aren't heading there anymore."

He acts like that makes his position less confusing, rather than more confusing. I fold my arms, hoping to prod a straight answer out of the giant biker.

"Where are we going?" I ask him, searching his handsome face as if I'll find answers there. Wyatt remains the stiff commander of our two-person army. I don't relish my role as second in command since I at least like to be the boss of myself but... this is the best night's sleep and breakfast I've had in ages. "And what the hell is in Texas?"

My tenderness and appreciation for Wyatt are at an all-time high. Making love last night definitely helped. Where was that sweetness in the Flying J bathroom? He kissed me with more enthusiasm than I had ever experienced from a man. *I loved it.* In the dark motel room, he was gentle and slow. He cupped my ass as he entered me the second and third time.

He called me such sweet names. For a few minutes I felt like I'd tamed a giant beast. This morning, the beast is back, determined to feed me and tell me what to do with my life like I'm his pet. *Not his pet, his property. That's how these crazy bikers think.*

The dice roll along the top of Wyatt's fingers. He doesn't have to look at the dice to keep the perfect rhythm going back and forth. His mindless habit makes me nervous. I try to use it to read his moods, but I don't have them all figured out yet. Wyatt is particularly good at keeping his thoughts from me when he wants to.

"To my house," he answers.

His response surprises me so much that I laugh. "Is it under a bridge?"

"No."

"Trailer park?"

"Careful," Wyatt says, raising a somewhat threatening eyebrow. I don't know what he wants me to say. I haven't seen any indication that these men have a home address.

"How would I know you have a house?"

Wyatt shrugs and says, "I have to live somewhere."

"From what I've seen, you live in every motel on Route 66. What's going on? Is this about the cops who kidnapped me or something?"

The dice stop moving across the top of his hand, one balanced between his middle and index finger, the other balanced between his middle and ring finger.

"No. But you're pregnant and Texas will be a goddamn mess if I go down there with a…"

Wyatt's lips flatten into a thin line and I'm grateful that he doesn't finish his sentence, because it doesn't sound like it was going anywhere good.

"Right. Your racism problem."

My ears warm up thinking about it. Whenever we're alone together – and especially in bed – I can forget Wyatt's racism problem. It's a lot harder when there's daylight, and impossible whenever he opens his mouth. I've heard how the bikers all talk to each other and while Wyatt tries his best to stay respectful around me… he clearly has a lot of foul shit on the tip of his tongue.

There's an element of confusing humiliation that I continue to entertain Wyatt. I know he technically dragged me along with him against my will but… I have found myself begging for Wyatt's dick when we're in bed together. I love cuddling in his arms. I've started to kiss him first.

I might have been an unwilling victim at first, but the longer I spend with Wyatt Shaw, the more confused I become about who or what I am. I'm pregnant. But that's more like a state of being than a permanent identity. I don't want to admit or even entertain the idea that my pregnancy makes Wyatt just a little bit correct about me. For now, I *am* his property. He won't let me out of his sight while I'm carrying his baby.

"It's not just that," Wyatt says, running his tongue along the inside of his mouth, stopping whatever snide remark he has on the tip of his tongue from recklessly falling out.

"At least you're admitting you have a racism problem," I mutter.

The dice begin moving back and forth again, so I'm getting under his skin, which I'm not sure is a good thing at this point. Detecting my satisfaction at the possibility of annoying him, Wyatt stuffs whatever argument he was about to conjure.

"I don't have a racism problem."

I roll my eyes.

"You are my problem, Anna," he says. I roll my eyes harder, but that doesn't stop Wyatt from staring at me. He puts the dice in his pocket and I start paying closer attention.

"I didn't choose to be your problem. Remember that."

"Yes. But you became my problem."

"I recall asking you to let me go several times. I can relieve you of that burden right now."

"No longer interested," Wyatt says. "I want to take you to my house so I can get to know you better, Anna. And so you can get to know me. Because when we go to Amarillo... neither of us can back out. That includes me."

He gets up and kisses me on the forehead.

"I have a nice place," he says. "Dad and Hawk think they can postpone the club meeting for another month."

"Okay..."

"We have quarterly club meetings to determine our affairs," he explains briefly. "I have to sort out my family business. Take care of personal matters pertaining to club membership and club leadership."

It sounds either boring or dangerous, depending on how much of the truth Wyatt is actually sharing with me right now.

"Great. So one month before you drive me into a den of racist outlaw bikers. I'll use that time to settle my affairs."

Wyatt laughs. "You're funny, Anna."

"I don't feel too funny."

He wraps his arms around me and kisses me again. "You don't mind it here, I think. Woman like you needs someone looking after you. Not the other way around."

I still don't feel comfortable on the back of Wyatt's bike. I take extra long in the shower before we leave the motel to postpone the inevitability of having to put my fragile human body on the back of that thing. Working as a nurse gave me a healthy disdain for motorcycles as being more trouble than they're worth. You see so many moms mourning young, reckless sons that it breaks your heart.

Wyatt is too carefree to give a crap about that, although he senses me getting more nervous as it comes time to ride.

"If only they invented vehicles that came with four walls to protect you from accidents," I grumble once we're outside in front of Wyatt's bike. The damn thing sounds like a rocket ship but on the back of it, I feel flimsy. Wyatt watches me put my helmet on with an impatient half-scowl on his face.

"I promise, I'll ride slow."

"The last time you said that, you were going 90 in a 55 the entire way."

"A man of his word," Wyatt says, throwing on his helmet and climbing on the bike expectantly. Wyatt doesn't tell me how long we're going to ride and I don't ask because knowing can make it worse and I don't want to spend every terrified minute counting down the miles on the flat, seemingly infinite Missouri highway.

WYATT STOPS every couple hours on the historic Route 66 highway back to Illinois. I'm grateful that he changed his mind about going to Texas.

WHEN WE FINALLY LEAVE THE historic Route 66, we travel for a few hours along a country highway with no significant landmarks unless you can tell the difference between ears of corn while zooming past at 65 mph.

I'm exhausted and hungry, and express my crankiness by purposefully digging into Wyatt to maximize his discomfort. He doesn't complain despite my best efforts to get under his skin, like he knows what to expect from my ass and it doesn't bother him.

We still have summertime sunlight when Wyatt veers sharply down a private drive and slows the bike to 30 mph for about a mile through rows and rows of cherry trees until he stops the bike in front of a large stone house with two white columns on the porch.

I leap off the bike first, partly due to nausea and partly out of habit. I didn't imagine Wyatt living in a house as big as this one — or as old. Or stone. I stare at every detail, trying to imagine this man living somewhere. I can imagine him on the bike. Naked in a motel shower. But I can't imagine this man living in a house.

"Welcome home, baby mama."

"It's not my home," I respond instinctively. Wyatt smacks me on the ass and walks ahead of me.

"Of course it is. Can't keep a baby on a Harley."

I don't know what to tell Wyatt off about first. I don't even know if I should tell him off first because I have so many questions.

"Do you have a job? I mean... how can you afford a house?"

"I'm a businessman," Wyatt says with the speed that only a man involved in several black market dealings could come up with. I might not know anything about bikers, but every nurse is an expert on shady people. It's the only way to survive the cutthroat hospital environment.

I know better than to ask Wyatt what kind of business, although I can play along.

"Right. This... cherry farm."

I don't know what the fuck to call it. Wyatt puts his arm around my shoulder and points me in the direction of the cherry threes.

"4-acres of cherries that way," he says before turning me to the right. "6-acres of Chambourcin grapes that way. My sister Tylee helps run the vineyard and the orchard. We make wine and keep all types of folks employed."

"I've never heard of your wine."

"And you won't be hearing of it since you're pregnant," Wyatt responds harshly. "Now come on. I need a shower."

He's right about that. The man is riper than the cherries outside. I follow Wyatt up the gravel driveway, still soaking in all the details of the immense property. It's gorgeous out here with a view of some pretty rolling hills that you don't normally see in flat ass Illinois.

The white covered porch has a giant porch swing on it with pillows. I can imagine drinking sweet tea on this porch.

Although maybe I shouldn't fantasize about a sunrise on that porch, since Wyatt is my captor and not the prince in a movie. A smart woman wouldn't let his genteel home distract her. But shit... maybe I'm not a smart woman. Maybe right now, I'm a tired, pregnant woman. Who just wants to sit on a porch and drink sweet tea.

Surprises continue when Wyatt opens the front door to his house and we step into another time. He takes his boots off and I follow suit. Wyatt shrugs his cut off and hangs it up right away. I'm gawking around so much that I don't notice Wyatt staring at me until he laughs at me.

"Like it?"

"I don't know," I answer truthfully. "I've never seen anything like it before except maybe in a movie."

"It's not a Chicago apartment."

"No," I answer, breathing in the fresh air and admiring how much space there is just in the foyer. "It's not."

"Is that where you grew up?"

"No."

Answering questions about my past shouldn't make me nervous. My past doesn't matter anymore, does it? The second I locked eyes with Wyatt Shaw, I set this magnetic, dangerous attraction in motion and by doing that, my past ceased to exist.

I don't feel like a biker. But I'm definitely not the same Anna he met in the gas station.

"Where did you grow up?" he asks. "I know you want to keep your secrets but... you know my secrets, Anna. It's time I know yours."

His fingers quickly find my hips. We're barely ten feet into his house and Wyatt can't keep his hands off me. I lean a little closer to him out of instinct. And maybe a little out of emotion because after all this time on the road, I'm excited to be in a real house — especially one that's way nicer than anywhere I ever lived.

"I grew up in a small town outside of Chicago. One of the only black families in a normal two bedroom, two bathroom house. Nothing fancy like this."

Wyatt laughs. His smile lines make his face look so damn handsome. I hate when he looks like a husband instead of like a criminal bastard. The man gets me all confused.

"Thank you," he says, planting a gentle kiss on my forehead. The soft touch of his full lips brings me immediate relief from the pent up tension and stress from the drive on the back of his demonic motorcycle. "Your family still around?"

"I don't need any of them involved in this."

"Answer the question, Anna."

I don't. Not until he puts his finger under my chin and forces me to look him in the eye.

"You will answer me," he says. "Trust me. That's all I want. Your trust. And your answer."

"So you want two things."

"Yes," Wyatt answers unflinchingly.

"My parents divorced halfway through my nursing program. My dad moved to Canada with his twenty-five year old Taiwanese mistress and my mom has been on one cruise after another with the alimony money."

"Siblings?"

"Two brothers. One in prison. The other's dead."

Wyatt furrows his brow. "I didn't know. I'm sorry."

"They had the same opportunities that I did," I answer. "But they got involved with the wrong people and made some fucked up choices."

"Hm," Wyatt says, kissing my forehead again. "Vague."

"If I'm not vague, that makes it more real, doesn't it? And now that they're gone, I just want to believe they were the good guys."

"I see," he says. I don't know if he actually does. It's weird but... I've never actually told anybody what happened to my brothers. I mean, people in the neighborhood knew but nobody in Chicago.

Nobody from my life as a nurse. Wyatt doesn't sound like he judges me though. He's not like the girls I went to college with who were always quick to call things ghetto and then say "no offense" to me specifically... constantly reminding me that I was on the outside without knowing a damn thing about my life.

Wyatt pushes hair away from my face and then sighs.

"Come upstairs, baby mama. Let me give you a tour of the place so I can get in the damn shower. I smell like a skunk and I need a drink."

CHAPTER TWENTY-ONE
SOUTHPAW

One month later...

I wake up before Anna and make her breakfast downstairs. One month with her has deepened my attachment to her in a way that terrifies me. I haven't had a girlfriend in a long time and I haven't wanted one. Part of it is self-preservation and another part of it is the profound fear that a woman from my world would stifle my independence with her demands.

Anna might be the wrong woman to set myself up with if I want to avoid demands, but Anna feels different. I have this desire to please and impress Anna that transcends common sense, and our month together has been one effort after another to please her. The more time I spend with her, the harder it becomes to imagine a life without her.

Whenever I return to Missouri, I want to see her smiling on that front porch.

I spend every second of my month away from riding with

spoiling Anna completely, and ignoring the fact that eventually I'll have to leave. For now, I give Anna everything she wants – except her freedom and an opportunity to meet my family.

I've kept her away from mom and Tylee while we've been here, but I can't avoid her meeting the rest of the family forever... especially not with the news of her pregnancy spreading thanks to Tylee forgetting that our mom has hearing like a fox.

Mom might be an old lady, but she didn't make any of the promises I did to keep our bloodline racially pure. She doesn't disapprove of Anna's skin color in the slightest and insists that I allow her to meet the mother of her grandchild.

"And you'd better marry her..." mom adds.

Crazy woman. Anna would never agree to marry me. I push open the door to our bedroom and listen to her snoring for a few seconds in the doorway before I walk in with her breakfast tray. She barely has an appetite or any energy from the pregnancy without me feeding her. And she sounds cute when she snores.

When I set Anna's tray on her bedside table and slowly tap her shoulder to wake her up, she opens one cute, sleepy dark brown eye with impossibly long lashes.

"Is it morning already? No..."

"Breakfast time, baby mama."

She sits up and smiles at me. Anna has a pretty smile and I like that she's taken to smiling at me. Women don't normally stay smiling at me very long. Even Anna took a while before I could bring it out of her.

"This smells incredible. How did you know I was craving pancakes?"

"Everyone craves pancakes. It's common sense."

"Did you eat already?"

"I brought myself coffee."

Anna sits up and I watch her baby bump with awe and admiration. She's growing a life in there. A baby. Little hands. A small beating heart. That baby is a little piece of me growing in someone else and there's something goddamn beautiful and strange about that.

It's something that the two of us share and always will. The more I watch the two of them grow together, the more obsessed I become with the idea of us being a family. Which might become a problem when I have to leave for the clubhouse...

Once Anna sets up her tray -- she refuses my help violently every morning -- she digs into her pancakes with enthusiasm. She can fit almost a whole pancake in her mouth and it's hot as fuck. I pretend like I'm not watching her as I sip my coffee. Maple syrup and cherry compote stain Anna's lips and I wish I could lick the syrup off.

It's one of those mornings.

"WHEN ARE YOU LEAVING FOR TEXAS?"

I wish I brought a bigger mug of coffee because I don't want to think about Texas. The club has a new meeting date on the horizon, thanks to dad pulling some strings. Everyone agrees we need more time to prepare for the meeting. Hawk is out tracking the cop gang with Ethan and Owen.

As dad and the rest of the original club members age out of their hardcore outlaw years, the dispute over the club's future puts more pressure on the quarterly club meetings. When we were kids, nobody cared about anything other than drinking, gambling, drugs and fucking.

It's all different now and maybe what we need is for this club to go back to its origins. Brotherhood. Freedom. Making money just to blow it all. The American fucking dream.

BUT THEN THERE'S ANNA.

. . .

AND AS MUCH as I yearn for Route 66 and the road that connects all the towns and people affiliated with the Rebel Barbarians, I enjoy being home with Anna. She just feels like... mine. My old lady. Although, she doesn't like the idea of anyone calling her old. Ever.

"We have four more weeks," I say to Anna. She doesn't stop eating. I don't know why I expect her to have an emotional reaction to the thought of me leaving.

"Will you be back when the baby is due?"

I can't make her any promises. I don't know what will happen when I head out there. For all I know, the club meeting could turn into a bender or a gunfight or an assignment from my father to run guns or drugs out to California or Arizona.

"Yes," I say to her. Because that's what you say to your old lady. You give her the reassurance she needs and then find a way to make it work. Anna's too sharp for her own good.

She drops her fork.

"You can't possibly know that, can you? I pay attention, Wyatt. If we're going to be together, there's no point in you lying to me."

My heart skips a beat.

"I didn't know we had a chance of being together."

"Well now you know," Anna says softly. Then she keeps eating and I drink coffee and I don't know why everything with her is so twisted up. It's both complicated and simple at the same time.

THE FUSS over Anna meeting the women of the family proves to be unnecessary. Tylee insists on bringing over a cherry pie, mom stops for homemade ice-cream from one of the creameries along the highway, and I give Anna as much mental preparation as I think she can handle before my mother and sister come careening through the front door.

I can hear Tylee's truck crashing down the dirt road about twenty miles faster than she ought to travel with mom in the front seat.

Anna gets up nervously from her seat in the living room and smooths her clothes out.

"How do I look?"

"Pregnant."

I don't think that's the right answer, but it's too late because mom and Tylee knock on the front door like they think I'm hiding pumpkin spice lattes in here.

"Calm down, calm down, I'm coming."

"Hurry up, Wyatt," Tylee yells with her country accent leaning into her *r's*. "We want to meet this woman and set her free if necessary."

Anna stands behind me as I open the door and allow hell to descend into my home. Tylee and my mom look similar. Tylee has copper hair which she wears in a thick messy braid. Mom wears her auburn hair – a Hollingsworth family trait – in a shoulder-length bob, the way she has since 1999.

Tylee races over to Anna, but Mom and I haven't seen each other since Christmas and I can tell she's mad about it.

"You... are a terrible son," she says, before wrapping her arms around me and sinking into my chest with a mixture of joy and relief. There's nothing like a hug from your mama, even if you're a grown man. Even a man who can unflinchingly end another man's life becomes absolutely weak in his mother's arms.

"I know, mama. I know."

Tylee distracts me from my mother-son moment.

"I don't know where my brother found you but my God, you have an ass like an Instagram model!"

"Tylee!" I growl, pulling away from mom and dragging Tylee's wrist away from Anna's ass before she can grope her inappropriately.

"I swear she looks familiar," Tylee says. "Is she..."

"Stay out of my business, Tylee. Mom, this is Anna."

.   .   .

MY MOTHER LOOKS at me like I have two heads and she scrutinizes Anna like a supermarket grapefruit.

"You've never brought a girl home before," she says to me before continuing her examination of Anna. I warned her about the pregnancy, so that Anna's baby bump doesn't draw any raised eyebrows or embarrassing statements. Yet. "Anna. I'm Deb Shaw."

"Nice to meet you."

Deb gives me a critical look. "She's too good for you."

"MAMA..."

"I can tell," she continues, without taking her eyes off Anna. "Nice teeth. And her hands... were you a nurse?"

Anna looks at me like my mom's ability to read people is somehow my fault.

"Yes," Anna says. "How can you tell from my hands?"

My mom laughs. "It's not your hands, sweetheart. It's... everything. You would have to be a saint to put up with Wyatt this long and not kill him."

"I haven't known him very long," Anna says.

Mom glances at her stomach. "Long enough that my statement applies."

"Thank you, mom. I'm glad you think so highly of me."

She shrugs. "You're better off than Ethan ever will be. I doubt this one sleeps with her own cousins."

Anna bites her lower lip to stifle a laugh. Tylee doesn't bother.

"Savage, Deb," Tylee says, leaning on our mother's shoulder. Tylee has Hollingsworth hair, but she's taller than most of the Hollingsworth women, an Amazonian six-feet tall. Mom purses her lips and then lets go of Anna's hand.

"Tylee, get the pie and ice cream. I like her. You win this time."

"I told you she wasn't a tramp," Tylee says.

"No offense," mom says to Anna quickly. "You get to know the men in our world and your expectations will sink into the floor."

"I know what you mean," Anna says, giving me a nervous look. Considering the way Tylee and mom are talking to her, I don't dare disagree with her. I mumble something about getting the pie for them and let the women sit around and talk about babies, women stuff...

MOM AND TYLEE LIKE HER. I'd still keep her if they didn't, but I can't act like it doesn't make a difference to me. Our club has always been about family. It's what drew me to stay here and buy this place. Family. I always wanted one, but never met a woman who I wanted it with. I might have given Anna our baby in the throes of a gambling-related high but...

The storm is gone and she's here, pregnant. And I still want her.

I FIND myself slicing cherry pie at the kitchen counter for her and the women in the living room. With most women, I'm Southpaw. With her, with my family, I get to be Wyatt. And with the hell out there on the highway, it feels so goddamn right to come home to something good and sweet – like Anna and cherry pie.

CHAPTER TWENTY-TWO
ANNA

Another month later...

I don't want Wyatt to leave for Texas. I can barely admit it to myself, but it's the truth. No one can hear my thoughts, right? That makes it completely safe to admit. I'm at the phase of pregnancy where I want to blame everything on the baby. Fart too loud? The baby made me do it. Sleep too much? The baby needed sleep. Binge-eat Wyatt's leftovers that he specifically asked me not to eat and hid beneath the gallon of milk? The baby guided my hand to the leftovers.

But I can't stop him. In four days, he's driving out to Amarillo, Texas to the Rebel Barbarians clubhouse for the quarterly meeting. Judging by his change in habits the past week, he's nervous.

This man unflinchingly bet me and my pussy on a game of pool. If anything makes him nervous, I want to know what it is. Club business. That's Wyatt's answer for everything and it becomes a more unsatisfying answer the closer he gets to leaving.

Will he survive? Will he come back? What if he goes to prison? I don't want to know. The baby wants to know.

"YOUR THOUGHTS ARE TOO LOUD," Wyatt groans, acting like someone is asking him to snuggle me this closely. I love this bed, and I don't want to get out of it, especially not with racing thoughts. The last thing I want is Wyatt calling me out about it.

"Are you going to die?"

Wyatt groans. "Do women ever relax?"

"No," I answer, turning to face him and getting ready to smack him if he makes another smart ass comment about women while his baby's foot is pressing against my kidney. Or I just need to fart again.

"Okay," Wyatt whispers. "Yes. I'm going to die."

My stomach drops.

"Is that funny to you?"

"No. But it's true. We're all going to die. Right now, I'm here. With you. And I would much prefer you wake me up for sex."

"Really? You would prefer sex to a deep conversation. Who would have suspected that?"

Wyatt's fingers curl around my shoulder and then he traces down the length of my arm and my hips.

"What do you want, Anna?" he murmurs. "Because if I had to guess... I would think you wanted me to die. Or that you were only here because you were too scared to leave."

He makes the question worse by following it up with intense, piercing eye contact. His eyes swallow me whole and like most men, he has unfairly pretty eyes with gorgeous lashes that contrast against his harsh, manly face.

"I want to have a baby. Our baby. I know how we met was a mess and this has been... crazy but... since we came to this house, whatever the hell we have here feels real. I want to feel that... for a while."

Wyatt is so goddamn handsome when he smiles. I only get a moment to appreciate his smile before he kisses me. Not like I really mind getting an intense, deep kiss. He rolls me onto my back and carefully positions himself on top not to hurt the baby.

"Then stay," Wyatt says. "Don't worry about my death. Just be mine, Anna. Because... because..."

He looks downright terrified and then the words just fall out of Wyatt's mouth.

"I LOVE YOU, Anna. Fuck, I love you."

I don't know what to say. This is so sudden. The past couple months of playing house have been the most intimate I have been with a man, but that doesn't mean...

I gaze up at Wyatt in surprise, wondering when he decided to fall in love with me in between the dishes and the laundry. He spent so much time working on his bike that I thought he wanted to get back on the highway more than he wanted to come to bed with me.

"Are you sure?"

He laughs. "Haven't you been here the past two months?"

"Yes. You have sex with me every night. You eat what I cook for you. But you don't say much."

"Do I have to say much to love you?" He whispers, leaning forward and kissing my neck, grazing the softest part of my flesh with his rough beard.

Confusing palpitations in my chest make thinking straight impossible. His hand strokes my cheek, and I remember him bringing me tea every morning, holding my hair back while I had morning sickness, and cuddling me every night.

"This is random," I whisper.

"No," he says. "It's love at first sight. Except... now I'm sure that I'm not just high off of how goddamn hot you are..."

He doesn't give me a chance to answer. He just kisses me and presses his hips forward against my thighs so I can feel his hardness against my leg. His back tenses as I touch him and draw him against me. Love. What the hell does a man like Wyatt mean by the word love?

"I love you," he repeats, kissing my neck and then my collar bone and then... I don't even try to figure out what he means.

"Okay," I whisper. "Okay, I believe you."

"No," Wyatt growls. "Say it back, Anna..."

He leans forward, pressing his dick into me and forcing me to feel just how much I arouse him. This man has always had a strange way of drawing out my hidden desires. I don't know what it is about Wyatt. Maybe it's knowing that he could obliterate me with a single look or with one touch from his rough, masculine hands.

Instead of destroying me, his hands only seek to pleasure me. He knows how to touch me like we were made for each other. I never thought I would meet a man who knows exactly how to handle me. He grabs my hips and rearranges my body before lowering his head between my thighs to start me off with a deep slow tongue-fucking before we make love. Wyatt's tongue finds my juicy center quickly and even if I want him to eat me out until I release all over his face, the initial contact is so damn intense.

My body knows what to expect and if I want to enjoy this tender, easy love-making, I need to slow him down. Electricity spreads through me as Wyatt struggles to slow down kissing my outer lips and sliding his tongue in slow, wet circles around my clit. It doesn't help that I start moaning like crazy the second his tongue touches my clit.

I mess up his hair with my hands and spread the scent of Wyatt's sexy ass black hair all over my hands as he kisses me slower and deeper. I lose control of my moans as Wyatt's tongue slides past my entrance and he tastes my inner walls, massaging me with a surprisingly flexible tongue. As he plays with my pussy and teases my inner walls, he stimulates my clit with his fingers.

The mixture of intense sensations from Wyatt's soft tongue and the firm pressure from this thumb around my clit push me over the edge. He doesn't stop sucking my lower lips when I cum. My juices spill all over my thighs, onto Wyatt's lips, onto his cheeks and all over the bed. He gets my pussy so wet that it's like the sex I had before Wyatt wasn't even real.

I DIDN'T KNOW a white guy could throw down some dick and pussy eating like this but I feel like I was missing out before Wyatt.

HE IS SO DAMN good in bed that I can forget he's an evil motherfucker who would kill a man without a second thought if he just... wanted to. Maybe his inability to give a fuck makes him better in bed. I don't have an explanation for why he feels so good.

When I lose count of how many wet orgasms I have all over Wyatt's face, I use my feet to push his shoulders and give my swollen pussy a break from the stimulation. He keeps me moaning by focusing his attention on kissing and licking my thighs.

He grabs hold of my feet and kisses the tops of them before sucking on my toes again until I moan and call out his name. Naturally, he likes hearing his name. He stops, chuckles and gives the bottoms of my feet one last kiss.

"All fours, baby. Let me take your sweet pussy from behind..."

I EAGERLY ROLL over onto all fours and arch my back, giving Wyatt a complete view of the sloppy mess he made between my legs. From this angle, his big thick cock hits me so deep that I instinctively shake with anticipation before Wyatt even positions his enormous body behind me.

There's something so goddamn primal about being manhandled and tossed around by a guy the size of Wyatt Shaw. He's by far the biggest man I've ever been with and from the time I feel his large hands cupping my ass, my body trembles in suspense of the painful mixture I'm about to experience.

He starts off by pressing his wet index finger between my lower lips and exploring my pussy again slowly. He does this for his enjoyment, not mine, allowing his finger to touch my spongy inner walls for the sake of knowing every inch of the body he believes belongs to him on some deep, animalistic level.

Wyatt kneels on the bed and spreads warmth through me as our thighs touch and he positions himself to enter me. The soft head of Wyatt's immense cock pushes my elastic entrance. My body resists him, sending his dick back out of my pussy with a gush of juices.

He's already oozing with desire for me. Wyatt grips my hips with determined possessiveness and then makes another effort to push inside me. I whimper as his fingers sink into my fleshy thighs and he thrusts into me again with greater force.

This time, his dick easily splits me open and he presses the first few inches inside me. Raw pleasure surges through me. I arch my back more, drawing him in deeper. Wanting more of him. Tonight, I know he won't hurt me. Or the baby. The more pregnant I get, the tamer the beast gets.

I can almost forget that he's a gangster. Or a killer. I don't want to remember, anyway.

"Fuck, that pussy feels so good..."

He grunts one last time before bottoming out between my legs. Our hips join together as incredible fullness sends pleasurable tingles from my core throughout all my limbs. I grip the bed sheets to keep from sliding forward from the size of this beast taking me from behind. Wyatt cups my ass and grabs my hips to slide my pussy up and down the length of his shaft.

Wyatt's dick moving just one inch inside me sends crazy pleasure throughout my body. I moan and push my hips back, pulling him in deeper and teasing him with my jiggly butt and the warmth of my body. My pussy wants him deeper. Harder...

But he just moves his hips with a painfully slow rhythm that just teases me with pleasure. He has a smooth, sensual rhythm that's so easy to yield to. I lose myself in Wyatt's deep, slow thrusts. When our hips meet and I moan so loudly that I stop myself from breathing, he goes even slower.

He's so tender. So loving. He leans over and kisses me as he takes me from behind. I cum hard with his large body hovering so closely over mine and Wyatt's thrusts pushing into me deeper, teasing my depths with more pleasure than I can handle. He touches my clit as I cum, making it easier for the waves of pleasure to crash into me.

I love how he makes me cum and I love how easy it is to access that part of myself with him. I don't care how I look. I don't care about pleasing him. He's happy just to be with me -- he doesn't need me to do any tricks or anything.

"I fucking love you," Wyatt grunts, pulling out of me and flipping me onto my back. I think he's planning to enter me again, but he pushes his head between my legs and eats my pussy to three more orgasms before he flips me onto my side without asking and enters me from behind.

His dick surprises me with how deeply he enters me and the untouched parts of my pussy now stimulated by Wyatt's big cock. I bounce my hips back to meet his dick and feel another more intense orgasm building in my core. The tight pressure between my legs only worsens as Wyatt reaches around to rub my clit.

I'm on the edge of an explosion and I need to get there. I want to cum so badly that I press my feet against Wyatt's legs to get a better angle on thrusting my hips back to meet him. His fingers slide between my lower lips as he touches me all over and fucks me slow.

"Let go, baby mama," Wyatt croons into my ear. Fuck, his voice sounds so smooth. "Cum all over daddy's dick. I want to feel you, baby. I want to feel you..."

It's too much for me to handle. I thrust back against him one last time and cum hard. The intensity only makes me take Wyatt's dick deeper. He grabs my hips to hold me close, forcing me to feel my pussy convulsing around his dick.

"I'm close," he whispers, moving his hips even slower. It's too much. I want to fight him off. The pleasure is too damn intense for me to handle and damn, I need to breathe. But I can't fight him off. Not when he's close. Bigger than me. Thrusting into me.

"Cum inside me," I gasp weakly, struggling to take in any air at all. Wyatt groans and with one arm wrapped around me, nearly cutting me off from any oxygen at all, he climaxes inside me forcefully.

I DON'T KNOW what comes over me. He finishes and pulls out of me. Then, Wyatt does what he always does. He pulls me in for a slow kiss. And then... I say it.

"I LOVE YOU, WYATT."

What the fuck? It's like he can read my mind. Because Wyatt sees the panic on my face and instead of having a normal reaction, he smiles. Then he laughs a little bit, like there's something hilarious about my distress.

"I know," he whispers. "I know, baby mama. I know..."

CHAPTER TWENTY-THREE
SOUTHPAW

I f she were any other woman, I would have snuck out without saying goodbye. Hell, I was tempted to leave without saying goodbye anyway. I don't want to say goodbye to Anna. If she weren't pregnant, I would throw her on the back of my bike, ignore her damn complaints and drag her ass to Amarillo with me. She's my woman to do whatever I please with – including bringing to Texas.

It's just not safe. With questions of the club's future, word spreading around that I've taken up with a black woman, and a possible resurgence of my conflict with Reaper, it's best I keep her well out of trouble. But that doesn't make saying goodbye any easier.

She stands in the doorway wearing my 2XL t-shirt from our last charity bike ride and no pants. I gave her a kiss goodbye that relieved her of those pants about half an hour before leaving. Her thighs are brown, thicker than ever because of pregnancy weight gain, and plastered together with her juices. I can't stop staring at them.

"I'll be back in a week," I say to her, knowing damn well I can't promise that. I'll meet up with Hawk in Springfield, Missouri, and after that we plan on taking a straight shot down to Amarillo, but anything can happen during biker nights in Springfield.

166

Big shots need Vegas gambling to get their rocks off, but good old boys that grew up in shitty redneck dive bars know that Missouri is the real Vegas. You can't bet pussy or bike parts in Vegas without having the gaming commission, the FBI or the goddamn mob so far up your ass they're in your stomach.

"Can I call you?" she asks. "I know you have a house phone. I plan on calling my mom once you're gone. "

My eyes flutter nervously to hers. I've never asked Anna if she plans on leaving once I'm gone and I've never said that I would stop her. I just assumed things were different because... well, because we love each other now. I hope it doesn't make me a goddamn idiot to believe that Anna would stay with me. That she wants to now.

"You can't call me," I say, even if I want her to call me while I'm gone. "But I don't mind you calling... anyone else. Tylee and mom will come over to check on you."

"You mean to make sure I don't run away?"

I don't like when she jokes about that, and she can tell because Anna immediately apologizes. I wrap my fingers around her hips. It's the first time I haven't wanted to hop on my bike and race out of here from laying low for so long. It's the first time I look forward to winter months when it's too cold to ride anywhere but the Southwest, so when I'm home, I just have to be... *home.*

She makes me want to be at home. And she feels like home. I've never felt like I had a home to leave. Even when I was a kid, all the people I loved were always spread out across the highway. Home was Grandma Hollingsworths and it was Grandpa Shaws and cousin Sinclairs... and the clubhouse.

I press my forehead to hers and kiss her again. Just one last kiss before I hit the highway. She smells good. It's pregnancy and that t-shirt she's wearing and the fact that I don't want to leave this woman. *I'm gonna miss her.*

"If you run, I will get on the back of that bike and find you, baby mama. Doesn't matter where you go. Doesn't matter if you cross the goddamn ocean. You're mine so... if you run, I'll bring you back."

"So that's it, then. I left my life as a nurse to wait for you?"

"Put your feet up. I'll tell Tylee to give you the information to that Amazon shopping account she's so obsessed with. It's one week, Anna. Not your whole life. I'll be back."

She seems skeptical.

"What if you die out there?"

"Can you quit with all the dying talk?"

"I've seen your lifestyle, Wyatt. And I know you can't resist a pool table. I'd hate to see you around blackjack or poker."

"I'll come home, Anna. I promise. And not just for you."

THE LAST KISS goodbye hurts the worst. She grabs onto my face so fiercely and kisses me so hard it's like she wants to crawl inside me. I fucking wish she could. I don't look back when I put my helmet on and drive away. Seeing her one last time will make leaving ten times harder. It's already painful enough to say goodbye.

I DIDN'T REALIZE how much I would miss her body on the back of my bike. Or her warmth in general. After the first hour ride towards Saint Louis, I want to call the house just to hear her voice or her breathing. It's not safe to call your landline – same rule applies to outlaw bikers as it does to the mob. If you want your people safe, you leave them alone when you're on the road. No real names, nothing that ties you to the life you want to protect.

Hearing nothing from Hawk at my first stop for gas, I pick up and call him. Since we're meeting outside of Springfield and I'm drawing closer, I need to know when I can expect him to get there. It's not like him to be radio silent like this. He doesn't pick up immediately, so I head into the gas station for coffee. The dude working behind the counter laughs and jokes around with his friend until he sees my cut.

He stiffens up and offers me Zyns over the counter free of charge along with the coffee I order. By the time I bring the shitty black coffee out to my bike, Hawk calls back.

"I'm trying to get my shit together," he says. "Sorry for the silence. I've been up to my ears in bullshit."

"What kind of bullshit?"

"I don't know if I can make it to Springfield."

"What the fuck? What are you talking about?"

I hear him yelling in the background. "You be QUIET!"

I rip the phone away from my ear, my ear drum ringing from his yell. Hawk clears his throat and comes back to the call.

"I'm not alone," he says. "I'm very much not alone and this is... fuck..."

"Come to Springfield," I say to him sternly. "If I don't see you at *The Fire Spot* tonight, I'll send Owen out."

"Did you leave Anna behind?"

"Of course I left her behind. We're going to Amarillo, dipshit. We can't bring people like her down there. Finally came to my senses and realized... it's too risky."

"Fuck!" Hawk yells. "I'll see you in Springfield. Then you can tell me what the fuck I'm supposed to do about this fucked up situation."

He hangs up before I can ask him what the hell he's talking about. It takes a lot to rattle Hawk, which makes me wonder what he's gotten himself into. Was he stupid enough to quit drinking? It's been a couple months since I've last seen him, except this attitude normally follows a couple days off the bottle. Not a month.

Hawk hasn't made it a month without liquor since high school. No way to find out what shit he's gotten himself into until I meet him in Springfield. I message Ethan and Owen before getting back on my bike to see if they have any idea what the hell has Hawk so uptight.

IT'S JUST NOT like him.

· · ·

I GET to The Fire Spot first. Dad's second cousin who died in Afghanistan opened it, now his daughters run the place. They're mean, country, and both married to normal men who don't even ride. But they don't mind us using their place for business and at the end of the day, a Shaw is a Shaw.

Out front sits a stop sign riddled with bullet holes and painted with *ABANDON HOPE ALL YE WHO ENTER* to fit the theme. I see two bikes parked out front – neither of them Hawk's. It's still a couple hours before happy hour, so I walk up to the bar and see if any of those Shaws are working.

The girl behind the counter looks Indian. I don't know all the particulars about the tribes or anything, but she's dark with those slightly slanted eyes and thick black hair in two braids. She glances at my cut, and doesn't outwardly react, but she talks to me with proper manners and quickly adds that I don't have to pay for my drinks.

"I know you're family," she says.

"Am I now?"

BEFORE I CAN INVESTIGATE her peculiar statement, Hawk bursts in the door swearing his motherfucking head off. I hear a loud female scream following his litany of swear words, and that grabs my attention because the last person I expect to bring a woman to The Fire Spot is Hawk.

He doesn't keep women around him for longer than one night and he prefers spending most of his nights at the bottom of the bottle of tequila. We all have our vices and I've never judged him for his. But this is worse than a vice. This is a turn in the wrong direction down a road that I've never seen Hawk travel down before.

A very short woman breaks free of Hawk's grasp and instead of running towards the door, she runs straight towards the bar and leaps over it, hiding behind the Indian girl who looks both terrified and confused.

Hawk doesn't budge.

"You get your ass back here!" he yells at the woman.

"She's black!" I yell at him. I instantly regret my comment given my own desires, but what the hell is going on in this damn bar? Where the fuck did he find this woman? I leave him alone for two months and he finds himself in worse trouble than me. The woman grabs a full bottle of Tito's and throws it at Hawk's head.

"You will never take me alive!" she screams.

"Damn right, I won't!"

Hawk reaches for his pistol. That doesn't stop the crazy woman behind the counter from grabbing a giant bottle of vodka and whipping it around her head before throwing it at Hawk. And missing. The vodka bottle crashes into a mirror and the explosion is epic. I couldn't have caused so much destruction if I was three beers deep myself.

I duck so the next bottle doesn't come flying at my head, but perhaps I ought not to be so self-centered. The Indian girl behind the counter seemingly comes out of nowhere with a shotgun that looks like it could knock that little woman into Oklahoma.

"HEY!" I yell at both of them. "Put the guns down!"

The Indian woman points her shotgun at Hawk.

"You put your gun down," the Indian woman says, looking through the sight and putting her finger over the trigger. She means business. Hawk glances at me, as if I were stupid enough to reach for my weapon with a little girl like that holding a shotgun within a couple feet of my head.

I nod at him and Hawk slowly lowers his weapon. The black woman behind the counter seizes her opportunity to throw a knife at him. Hawk ducks and the knife sticks into the wooden beam behind his head. The Indian girl lowers the muzzle of her shotgun and turns to the black woman behind her with fury.

"Stop throwing things! I don't know what the hell is going on here but if any of you and I mean any of you take another step, I will blow all your goddamn brains out."

"Don't you dare talk to her like that," Hawk says to the woman with the shotgun, protecting the disobedient hell-hound he just unleashed on the property. I don't take my eye off that damn gun.

"Shut up, Hawk. Listen, there's gonna be no more fighting. Hawk has this clearly mentally ill woman in his gentle custody and once he calms her down, I'll pay for the broken shit and there won't be any more misbehavior."

"You already owe $200 on the liquor and that mirror was a $2,000 antique from the Muscogee Nation art festival," the Indian girl says. "You don't look like you can afford that but I see both of you have pretty nice bikes out front."

I COULD KILL my best friend.

"WE'RE GOOD FOR THE MONEY," I tell her. " Hand over the mentally ill woman and we'll take her outside and get her calm."

"I am *not* mentally ill!" the woman shrieks. "He kidnapped me! That biker kidnapped me! I need you to call the police."

The Indian girl looks at her sympathetically, but then she looks back at me and Hawk. I hear more motorcycles arriving in the parking lot outside. *Thank God we have back up, but that doesn't explain what the hell Hawk has gotten himself into.*

"Okay, I believe you. Not mentally ill. What's your name, ma'am and how did you meet Hawk?"

"I'm not telling you my name," the woman says, balling up her fists and making a face at me like she's about to be Muhammad Ali. *This woman must be out of her goddamn mind.* I throw Hawk a sharp look. Where the hell did he find this creature? She looks crazy. Her nostrils are flared out like an angry little piglet's and she is far too short for her rage levels. And far too plump for her height.

She's black, like Anna, but with a pale terracotta skin tone. The bronze undertones highlight her eyes, which are brown but again, not as dark as Anna's. She's fat – no offense, it's just the truth – but that might work to this little creature's advantage.

"You'd better talk or I'll let Hawk have his way with you. Listen to me and... I might just set you free."

Hawk throws me a dirty look, but once he sees how I'm eyeing the woman, he realizes there isn't a chance in hell I'm letting her go. She looks like the type to run straight to the cops and squeal. Hell. She looks like just about anything would make her squeal.

"I'm not telling you shit!"

"Listen, piggie. You talk or I'll gut you and make the Indian watch. You think she gives a crap what happens to you because you got the same skin tone? This is outlaw biker territory. Whatever you think you know... Whatever life you had before this... it's fucking over. So talk."

Her lower lip trembles. She looks like she's going to cry.

"She's only nineteen, Southpaw," Hawk says. It's too late for any intervention. I don't plan on going easy.

"Name," I snarl at her. "Or I'll give you a new name and tattoo it right on your sweet brown neck."

"IT'S JULIETTE!" she says. Her eyes well with tears, but her voice stiffens as she musters up all the strength she can. I watch her pull herself to her full height, which couldn't be more than four-eleven. "I don't care if you kill me because I'm going to escape you bastards or die trying."

Hawk's shoulders relax and he repeats her name like it's the first time he's heard it. "Juliette."

I GIVE HIM A SHARP LOOK. Where the hell did he find this goddamn woman?

CHAPTER TWENTY-FOUR
ANNA

I miss him. When I call my mom to tell her that I left Chicago and I'm pregnant, she barely had any reaction. She says that she'll believe me when I post it to Instagram. Funny how the parents who told us to stay off our phones end up more addicted to the damn technology than we ever could be. I built up my family's reaction to my pregnancy so much in my head that my mom's placid response underwhelms me.

"I'm honestly just happy you're with a man and not with a woman," she says at the end of the call. "It's about time you give me a grandchild."

"Did you miss the part where I told you the baby daddy is a criminal?"

"You said he was six-four and muscular. He sounds very good-looking."

I knew she wanted a grand baby, but I didn't know she was that desperate for me to settle down with just about anyone. I guess Wyatt isn't just anyone. He's... a walking red flag.

.   .   .

SO WHY DO I miss him so damn much?

WHEN WYATT LEFT, he promised that his sister Tylee would drop by to check on me and keep me company. She's chatty, country, and I have a million questions to ask her about Wyatt, including what he looks like without a thick beard. I bet he looks like a jackal. A sexy one... but still.

I hear an engine up the road and assume it's Tylee, except it doesn't sound like the truck. I'm not expecting anyone else. Wyatt promised me I wouldn't have to worry about any intruders, but he left me with an emergency plan for that too. Crazy ass motherfucker. I'm not shooting anybody.

I couldn't do that. But the motorcycle outside concerns me. I creep up to the window slowly, staying out of view as I peer outside. It's not Tylee. My heart drops into my stomach as I watch a tall figure dismount a Harley-Davidson. I recognize the bike before the man but when he removes his helmet, I confirm my suspicions. Reaper.

I pieced together his real name – Gideon Blackwood – but I get the gut sense I should stick to the club nickname if I want to stay on his good side. He's not the biker I fear the most, so even if I don't expect him and I'm wary of that, I open the door and meet him on the front porch.

Reaper is pink. He's been riding all day or possibly the past two days. His lips are chapped and his eyes bloodshot. He reaches into his pocket for his vape and sets himself up with it.

"I ain't slept in days," he says, puffing slowly. I watch the relief settle in his chest. He can't be here for a good reason.

"Does Southpaw know where you are?"

"No. Don't mean anything. I'm here to keep you safe. Pigs want you back. I'm disobeying my father's direct orders because... well... I took a liking to you in the motel."

His eyes meet mine and a nervous shiver goes straight through me.

"I'm pregnant with Wyatt's baby."

Reaper turns bright red.

"Shit, I didn't mean it like that. You tell Wyatt I came onto you, he'll shoot me. I just mean... I just meant I appreciate all you did for me and I couldn't put politics first."

Reaper glances around furtively and takes a step forward. I find his nerves contagious. "Is Tylee around?" he asks.

"No. She's supposed to come by later today."

"Okay. Good. She'll know what to do."

"Can I offer you some water? Time out of the sun?"

"Am I that red?"

"Yes."

"I'll take you up on your offer, ma'am. And if I could remind you to tell Southpaw I respect his old lady–

"I'm not his old lady," I answer defensively. Internally, the title makes my stomach flip. I don't want to admit the sense of pride and belonging I feel.

Reaper laughs. "Sure you are. He got you pregnant. I've known that boy his whole life and he ain't ever taken a chance like that. He must like you."

"It doesn't matter. I'm not a biker and I'm not white."

"Right. I noticed," Reaper says, following me into the house. He removes a pistol from his pocket and sets it on the counter. I try to act like it doesn't make me nervous but he seems blissfully unaware and makes himself at home, sitting at the kitchen counter. I pour Reaper a glass of water and hand it to him.

He doesn't take his eyes off me the whole time and I find it unnerving.

"DID the pigs say anything about why they took you? Did they mention what problems they have with the Shaw family?"

He's clever. From the questions he asks to the fact that he's sitting here instead of in Amarillo, everything seems calculated. I don't know if I trust him completely. I know Reaper won't hurt me, but that doesn't mean he won't hurt Wyatt. Or someone else. He's an outlaw, just like the rest of them.

"No."

I lean on the counter across from Reaper, looking right back at him, giving him equal consideration. He might be smart, but I'm no fool. You don't make it through nursing school or forty-eight hour shifts without being keen. I might not be Wyatt's old lady, but I understand enough about the bikers to know that carrying Wyatt's baby offers me enough protection not to give everything up to Reaper without getting something in return.

"Southpaw has a way of getting into trouble. My father, some of the older generation... they think that means he ain't suitable to lead. They want me in that position. Or a Sinclair. But Wyatt has a way of drawing people in. You understand that."

Reaper gestures towards my baby bump with his chin. I can't explain why I love Wyatt, but maybe Reaper has a point. I nod and let him continue. Best to keep quiet and let the man's thoughts run their course.

He continues, keeping those creepy blue eyes on my face. "He needs strong people behind him, that's all. He belongs in this role. He's just like Harley. A people person. I'm not like that."

Harley is Wyatt's dad. Hard to keep track of all the names, nicknames, and faces, but it's also hard to learn the names of muscles, neurotransmitters and synapses. It's all information. Right now, biker politics are the most important information relevant to my survival, so I pay attention.

"What are you getting at, Reaper?"

"If I find out why the pigs want you, I'll handle them myself. Going against my dad makes me nervous but... it's the right thing to do. I need to know everything that happened while you were with the pigs."

"It wasn't exciting or informative. I spent most of the time in a deep ditch."

"Did you count 'em?" Reaper asks, slowly sipping his water.

"Three to seven. Maybe more. I was asleep most of the time. They argued a lot."

He frowns, polishes off the water and wipes the bottom of the glass before setting it on the counter. Reaper taps nervously on the counter once he sets the glass down. Nicotine is a helluva drug – underrated in how quickly you start going through withdrawals. Thinking makes most smokers crave it even more.

"What's your instinct?" Reaper asks.

I haven't thought about the cops since I reunited with Wyatt. I feel safe out here and thinking about that stupid ditch doesn't make me feel safe. My bed still smells like Wyatt. I have reminders of him everywhere and a collection of 2XL t-shirts soaked with his scent. My instincts about the ditch are to forget about it and enjoy my life.

"I don't have instincts about this. I'm a nurse, not an outlaw."

"Sure you do," he says. "If you didn't... I think you would have left him. You're a smart woman. You understand we might live on the edge of the law but... we ain't all bad."

"I saw him kill someone."

I don't want to betray Southpaw, but Reaper doesn't flinch, so I can't have said anything he considers news. He stops smiling right away.

"You ain't repeat that to anybody?"

"No. Obviously."

"Smart girl."

"Doesn't that concern you?"

"I see it concerns you?" Reaper asks. I can't believe I'm having a heart to heart with a biker. This is the most pregnant behavior I've exhibited in weeks. But it's the first time I've had a chance to ask anyone about Wyatt. The women in this family make it clear that they don't want to talk about "club business". Tylee prefers discussing her *Hobby Lobby* finds from the location a couple towns over, or interesting customers she ran into at the gas station, or orchard business.

I can't ignore the opportunity presented by Reaper's presence.

"Do you have sisters?" I ask him. "Wouldn't it concern you if they ended up with Southpaw?"

"Damn straight. But not because he's a killer."

"Right. But if he's violent maybe he... I don't know. Slaps women around."

"You're his property. If he wants to slap you around, he can," Reaper says with coldness that sends a chill straight through me. He genuinely believes that. *You're his property.* I'm too close to answers about Wyatt to argue with him, but every fiber of my internal being fights that claim. Reaper continues before I can argue back. "He ain't the type to slap his women. He's dangerous because that's the nature of being the club president. Or the president hopeful."

"But how can he just take a man's life like that?"

"He never kills without a reason. He wouldn't. Others... but not him."

Again, there's something chilling about the way he says it. I wonder about Reaper. There are flashes in conversation where I get this deep, gut-wrenching sense that he's faking his emotions. Just as soon as I get the instinct, he flashes me a good old boy smile and I tell myself that I'm just nervous, pregnant and crazy.

"Good to know I can trust Wyatt, I guess."

"Yes," he says. "And you can trust me too. I want him to lead the club. But I suspect there's something going on with the pigs. I just don't know what it is."

He pauses for a beat and then we both turn our heads to the sound of Tylee's truck coming up the road. Reaper gets up and shoves his hands in his pockets.

"She hates my guts," he says. "Fair warning. If she puts a bullet through me, make sure Doc gets my bike."

Doc is his father, but I don't think Reaper has to be that dramatic. I walk to the front door to head Tylee off and alert her to Reaper's presence. He hangs back, genuinely nervous. I don't understand men. I can hear *Mean* by Taylor Swift getting louder as Tylee's truck approaches the parking spot next to Reaper's bike. The music cuts off as I step out onto the porch. Tylee bounds up with a pistol in her hand that makes me jump out of my skin.

"Tylee! Why do you have a gun?"

"I'd recognize a Blackwood bike anywhere. Is he holding you hostage? Did he rape you? Which one of them is it? I'll blow his brains out, I swear. Wyatt didn't tell me anything about letting any damn Blackwood in here–

She waves the gun around in an incredibly frightening manner. This woman knows damn well how to handle a gun, so her unhinged behavior makes my heart leap into my throat.

"Tylee, calm down!" I scream, hoping to break through her hysterical response. I shouldn't have doubted Reaper. I have to yell at her a few more times to calm her down, but it works and she lowers the gun. "It's Reaper."

"It's not loaded," she says. "What the fuck does he want? You don't seem hurt."

Tylee puts her hands on her hips and glares at the door like she can see Reaper standing on the other side.

"He's worried about me and he wants to help Southpaw. I trust him. He had every opportunity to hurt me and he didn't."

"You don't know bikers like I do," Tylee says, her voice tightening. I've seen her go through several different emotional states, but I've never seen her filled with hatred and distrust.

"Do you have a personal history with him? I wouldn't blame you if it's something like that."

"No," she says. "I'm married. But I've seen that man do depraved things. He ain't right in the head. I don't trust him."

"Why isn't he in Amarillo then?"

"I don't know. Maybe he's waiting for you to fall asleep so he can cut your baby out of you."

"Tylee," I hiss. "Don't you think that's a little paranoid? He's been here for almost an hour and he hasn't so much as reached for a butter knife."

"I'll come inside and scare him off."

"Hear him out first," I suggest. Tylee's lips purse with skepticism. She shakes her head.

"You're damn naive for a nurse," she says, pushing the door open and entering ahead of me. Reaper stands a few feet away from the door. He doesn't hide that he was listening in. Tylee shoves him back.

"Get back, you nosy bastard. What do you want? Why are you here? I'm not Anna, so I won't buy your bullshit lies."

"You look nice today, Tylee," Reaper says. "Hair looks like fire."

"Fuck you, Giddy."

"What is your problem?"

"You're sick in the head. That's my problem."

"Pigs are coming to kill your brother's old lady. I'd bet on it."

"Excuse me if I don't have much respect for gamblers," Tylee throws back. "If you goddamn idiots wouldn't burn all your money on liquor and gambling, maybe some of our kids could go to college."

"I'm not here to argue with you, Tylee. I told you. Pigs are coming. And they want blood."

"I'd like to see proof of that."

"I doubt that," he says. "I need you to do me a favor and find out why they're looking for Anna. What mess your brother got us into."

Tylee's eyes flash angrily to Reaper's, but then her anger fades quickly. We all know if there's trouble to get into, Southpaw will find it. I don't know him as well as they do, but by now, I've realized his tendency to rocket launch himself into trouble.

"Do you know he did something?" Tylee asks more gently. "Because fuck you and fuck Wyatt but... I've taken a liking to his old lady."

There it is again. The two words cause a strange throbbing sensation between my legs. I'm not proud of my body's weird response to the words, but I can safely blame Wyatt for the situation. I wrap my arms around my body, wishing I could talk to him or better yet, wishing I had a sense I wouldn't have to use the gun he taught me how to use before he left.

Reaper smiles at Tylee, trying to keep the easier mood between them. She doesn't smile back, but she isn't fighting or attacking him, which feels like a step up to me. They act like two house cats fighting for the warmest spot on the couch. I just hope they don't actually hurt each other.

"I don't have proof Southpaw did anything," Reaper says. "I heard he got the money for his gambling debts from some Jew but... far as I know, nothing to do with the pigs who took Anna."

Tylee frowns. "How did the pigs find Anna?"

"Tricked me."

"I see," Tylee says, her face easing up. "That explains why you're so invested. It's a personal slight. Has nothing to do with Wyatt's baby mama."

Baby mama. Ugh. Those two words hit me even harder than 'old lady'. I fight Wyatt's urge to refer to me as his old lady, but he always makes me instantly wet when he calls me his 'baby mama'. My pussy doesn't give a damn how fucked up and wrong it is to let him into my head like that.

"It's not just personal," Reaper says as his cheeks turn red again. "Those pigs felt so brave as to just walk up to a Rebel Barbarian and snatch something away from us. You grew up in this world just like me, Tylee. That would have never happened a decade ago."

"World is a different place now," Tylee says, her brow furrowing over Reaper's words as she tosses out the mindless addition to the conversation. She runs her tongue over her lips slowly, lost in her thoughts for a few painfully quiet moments before she answers. "What are you saying, Reaper? They're dirty cops? So what? We don't bother them, they won't bother us. Everybody knows Route 66 belongs to the club."

"No empire lasts forever, Tylee. Not even ours."

Tylee finally smiles. "You're fucking paranoid. But if you're staying the night, I'm staying too. Wyatt won't want you alone with his old lady."

"I planned to sleep outside on the porch swing," Reaper says.

"Bullshit," Tylee says. "I'll call Isaac, tell him to send some back up. In case you're right."

HER OFFER TO send for backup does nothing to ease Reaper's visible discomfort. Remembering my time in that stupid ditch is enough to make me uneasy. The threat of going back there will make it downright impossible to sleep.

AND THERE ARE STILL several more days before Wyatt gets back.

I'LL BE safe with the bikers. I know that. Wyatt promised I would be safe...

CHAPTER TWENTY-FIVE
SOUTHPAW

I get the unpleasant task of dragging Hawk's captive – Juliette Rawlings – onto the back of his motorcycle while she kicks and screams. She might be short but due to the size of her body at that height, the little demon can pack a mean fucking punch. Anna might have hit me, but she didn't hit me with the force of bloodlust.

We don't have much time for discussion. The Indian girl threatens to do worse than blow our heads off. The last thing this situation needs is more attention. We have to get our asses to Amarillo. Now. Meetings can't start without this fancy latin word called "quorum". That means we need more than half the club members in the room before we vote on anything.

Our presence can swing a vote. Our club has four big families – the Shaws, the Sinclairs, the Hollingsworths and the Blackwoods. Right now, dad is the president, Hawk's father the Vice President. The two of us have been raised our entire lives for this moment. Dad hasn't confirmed it, but he's dropped his little hints at retirement.

· · ·

THE CLUB WILL NEED a new president soon. Doc Blackwood clearly suspects that, or he wouldn't have pushed his family's only half-decent prospect into the limelight. Reaper... Maybe he would do better at this job than I would. No clue where the idiot is right now. My guess is, he's already in Amarillo. Waiting. Drinking. Winning folks over.

Can't worry about it now, can I?

IT'S NOT like I've ever seen much point in leading the club. With great responsibility comes a great absence of freedom. That's the part they don't tell you.

WE ONLY DRIVE west for ninety minutes before Hawk signals our need to pull over. The farther west we travel, the more the country seems to clear out. I hated riding in Chicago, but now that we're out West on the less populated portions of the old Route 66 highway, we're on the long stretches of road made and kept just for riding. I feel just the right temperature in my cut and as the wind whips around the bike, adrenaline courses through me. The machine's raw power vibrates through my body and for every minute of that ride, I become united with the machine.

It feels fucking awesome. I'd rather not pull over so soon, but Hawk signals again frantically, like there's an emergency. His bike looks fine from my vantage point behind him and we're still in a damn hurry, but he's adamant and if I don't follow his lead, I'll lose him.

Out here, the gas stations are more spread out between small towns and tourist traps. They're all simple, kitschy reminders of an older America. Hawk's cousin runs this gas station. She's on the slower side and spent five years in prison for marijuana possession, which she never recovered from.

I park my bike next to Hawk's and hop off. Hawk's bike wobbles and nearly falls over as Juliette launches herself off it, takes her helmet off and throws it before taking off in the direction of the main road leading towards the highway at her version of a dead sprint. I give Hawk a glare and take off after her as he works to extricate himself from the bike.

Why the hell did he pull over and give this crazy woman a chance to escape?

We're blessed not to have any witnesses. The only vehicle parked outside the gas station is a small camper van with the window shades pulled shut. Bikers don't have problems with folks living in vans and RVs. And they don't have problems with us.

"HELP!" Juliette screams as she bounces with each step. She ain't a bad looking woman, but she looks like she might get out of breath climbing a flight of stairs. She slows down as she approaches the road, looking frantically from left to right. This escape ain't too thought out. I dart left, she darts right. She tries to dash past me, but underestimates the length of my limbs and my desire to get her ass back on Hawk's bike.

The next shriek out of Juliette's mouth nearly deafens me as I wrap my arms around her waist to get a good grip on her to subdue her.

"Be careful!" Hawk yells at me. Careful?! I ought to throw this creature into the gas station bathroom and call someone to pick her ass up and take her back to Missouri.

Despite her aggressive fighting, I get my arm around Juliette easily enough and whip around, ready to launch her at Hawk for the goddamn audacity of him telling me how to handle the problem he solved.

"Careful? You're lucky I don't take her behind the gas station and put a fucking bullet in her head."

I'm only exaggerating my position, but this comment sends Juliette into a goddamn fit and she fights me even harder than before.

With her wiggling and the size of her waist, it's hard for me to get a good grip on her and I can tell I don't have long before she wriggles free. *Fucking damn it.*

"Calm down, Southpaw!" Hawk says.

"Why the fuck did you pull over?"

He sets his helmet down and pulls off his cut and shirt. I have to fight the vicious beast of a woman over my shoulder into submission throughout this entire process. I'll have this motherfucker buying drinks for me every minute of our time in Amarillo. When he gets his chest bare, I let out a series of expletives.

The bitch bit him and where she couldn't bite him, she dug her nails in so hard she drew blood.

"You goddamn idiot," I snarl. "I'll handle her."

"NO!" she screams. "Hawk, don't you DARE!"

This is beyond Hawk. I've never seen him act all soft like this and it's pissing me off. We wasted plenty of time because of his acquisition and every minute I spend dealing with his shit, I have to spend away from Anna. I miss my damn baby mama. I want to hear her voice. I would give *anything* to have her with me right now instead of this chubby and over excited Werther's Original.

"Listen," I snap, setting her down firmly. "One more sound out of you, one more attempt at escape and I'll whoop you so hard with my belt that I'll bruise your pretty light skin."

Hawk looks like he wants to kill me. But it shuts Juliette right up and he's too afraid to break the peaceful silence. *Finally.* She glares at me and that pretty light skin, such a pale shade of caramel that you can see freckles across her nose, turns dark purple.

"I'm not Hawk," I say sternly. "You try that shit with me, I'll leave your ass in a ditch. I have a baby mama to get back to and important business in Texas and you, little miss, are a pain in my fucking ass."

Wisely, she doesn't answer. But unwisely, she's moving her mouth the way someone does when they're about to spit on you. I've been in enough bar fights to read the signs. I raise one eyebrow slowly, warning her without words. She's smart enough to take one good look at my face and know I'm not fucking around.

Hawk still hasn't explained how the fuck he ended up in possession of this woman. She's not like Anna. Her spirit isn't gentle or magnetic. She's like a damn wolverine and with her erratic attitude, she's begging to be abandoned.

"You apologize for biting him," I snap at her. We can't have this happen again before Texas.

Juliette's lip curls in disgust and those piggy little nostrils flare out again. It occurs to me that Hawk might find this woman attractive. *Woman.* She's far too young for him by the looks of her and by her attitude, far more trouble than she could be worth. I give her another second to come to terms with her fate, but she still doesn't apologize. Juliette just glares.

"I said *apologize.*"

It's so quiet, you could hear a clap from the next town over. But we're out on the highway, in Barbarian territory. So there's nothing – just us.

"No," she says with a terrified, trembling voice. My impatience rises and I feel my dark tendencies rising again. I've spent too much time away from Anna. She draws a certain softness out of me that makes me feel like a whole human being. But when I'm away from her, I can't help the fierce draw my darker habits have on my entire spirit.

"This is your last chance," I say the words slowly, so the little miss knows I'm serious. "You apologize to him, Juliette Rawlings. Or we'll have problems."

Hawk gives me a worried look. He doesn't dare cross me in front of her, but he's my best friend, so I know what he's thinking. And he might suspect I'm pissed off but... he doesn't know what I'm thinking.

· · ·

188

"I AM NOT sorry for biting him up like that," she says. "So I won't apologize."

THERE'S something about her smug face that makes me want to smack the shit out of her. I might have to do it if she keeps this up but for now... no need to whoop her.

"FINE. Hawk, take Juliette into the gas station and fuck this attitude out of her. Now."

SILENCE. Again. He doesn't move. But neither does she. I don't think she can believe the words that came out of my mouth.

BELIEVE THAT SHIT, princess.

"I'm not asking you again. I'm tired of this shit and I don't want your fresh pussy acting up again. If you don't do it, I will."

I'm bluffing about the last part. I doubt I could get my dick hard for another woman. Anna has a complete hold on my soul. But this ain't about Anna, and Hawk knows club rules. If a girl isn't his old lady, she's fair game. If I want her, I could have her.

Juliette finally breaks the silence by emitting a strangled sob. I don't like the way Hawk is looking at me and I swear I'm gonna smack the shit out of that sappy motherfucker if he doesn't drag her back there and do what I say...

"I can't do that," he says.

"I told you, if you don't do it, I will. Anna's not here and you won't tell. We don't have time."

"No pressure then," he says bitterly, glaring at me with pure venom.

"What? Did you want it to be special? It's not your first fucking time. Get her out of here before I rethink shooting her and leaving her on the side of the highway."

"CHRIST, SOUTHPAW," Hawk mutters, gazing at me from beneath dark, angry brows.

THE EMOTIONAL STORM moving across his face doesn't affect me.

"JUST DO IT."

JULIETTE SOBS MORE LOUDLY. "PLEASE," she says. "Let me go."

HAWK'S HAND snaps around her wrist. She screams and makes an effort to break away from him. I hit her, but I don't do it hard enough to leave a mark even if I want her to remember the fuck out of this lesson. Hawk might make me pay for the slap later, but it subdues her enough that he can take her inside and do what I asked.

EIGHTEEN MINUTES LATER, I step in there ready to break down the bathroom door. I don't even look behind the counter to see who we have working. Before I can pound on the door, it creaks open and Juliette emerges red-faced, but subdued.

"We won't be having any more problems, will we?" I ask, grabbing her cheeks forcefully. She flinches when I touch her. *Good. No more problems.*

"No," she says, her gaze fluttering away from mine.

Hawk barely looks at me.

"Go wait by the bike, Juliette."

She walks away from him and I don't question his authority. Once she's out of earshot, I get an earful from Hawk.

"You didn't have to scare her like that."

"What the fuck is her problem?"

"She's scared. That's all."

"It's gonna get a lot worse when we get to Amarillo."

I thought better than to bring Anna down to Texas. I might have power and respect within the club, but it's a bad time to subject my personal life to scrutiny. It's not safe. If dad announces his retirement like I suspect, and if I gain a stronger position within the club... maybe that will change.

For now, Anna will be safe in Missouri and she can raise a family back East without concerning herself with any of this shit. She sure as fuck wouldn't have approved of the way I handled Juliette. I keep staring at Hawk, waiting for some acknowledgment of the bullshit he's gonna go through in Amarillo.

No way he rides into town with a black person on the back of his bike and nobody notices.

"I know," he says. "Fuck... I know. I'm in over my head, Southpaw. It's fucked up."

I've never seen him this bent out of shape. Part of me wants to ask what happened and another part of me can't afford to give a damn. I don't like this delay and I don't like this troublemaking woman much either.

"I'm supposed to be the fuck up," I growl at him. "The one who can't fill his father's shoes. But as far as I can tell, I'm the only one who gives a shit about us getting to Texas so we can secure the club's future."

I thought I could avoid following in my father's footsteps. I always wanted to carve my own path. Never quite worked out that way. I thought I would leave the Midwest and give up riding, but I ended up in my hometown working under my father with no plans to leave.

I never thought I would care this much about the club. But

everyone in that goddamn club is my family. Even Reaper. Even the annoying motherfucker in front of me who might drag us into the worst kind of trouble.

"You have never been the fuck up," Hawk says, partly to calm my temper, I'm sure.

I raise an eyebrow, waiting for him to continue.

Hawk sighs, raking his fingers through his hair before he adds on to his compliment. "Impulsive, yes. Stupid, sure. But you've always been Harley's son. You care about the club. More than I do."

"Don't fucking say that shit."

"It's true. If I cared as much as you did, I would have left Juliette behind. But she has to come with us. No two ways about it."

"Screwing up once doesn't mean shit," I tell him. "If that were the case, my gambling problem would have screwed me out of my role in the club a long time ago."

"You were always going to be the next president," Hawk says. "Always."

I wish I had his conviction that I belonged in this role.

"What if it comes down to a vote?" I ask him.

Hawk shakes his head. "If your dad planned on retiring, you would find out. Harley still has five, ten years left in him."

"Fine. Let's say you're right. But if it came down to a vote, it would be between me and Reaper. Not me and you. I can handle you leading the club but…"

There's no need for me to finish that sentence in public. We all know why Gideon Blackwood doesn't belong anywhere in a position of power. He's family, in the larger sense, but just because he's family doesn't mean I have the freedom to deny the truth about him.

HE'S the type of man you want to keep loyal to your cause, let's say.

.   .   .

"THERE WON'T BE A VOTE," Hawk says. "And if it came to you and Reaper, you would win. Like I said, you're Harley's son."

"What does that mean?"

"It means you're born for this shit, Southpaw."

IT DOESN'T FUCKING feel that way. But it helps to have him on my side. To feel like he's loyal. Because the more I think about Texas, the less I like the thought.

CHAPTER TWENTY-SIX
ANNA

Reaper's concerns about an attack fade away by late evening. Tylee has a way of making me forget my problems temporarily, so I spend most of the afternoon with her as Reaper paces nervously until it gets later and quieter and nothing happens.

Tylee puts on *Real Housewives of Salt Lake City* and gives me a detailed personal history of all the characters. This is her third time seeing it. I can barely tell these women apart, but I nod and desperately try to follow along as Tylee intersperses her retelling of random events that happened to her throughout the week with her description of the show's characters, backstory and the current drama.

Reaper interrupts us after a few episodes, insisting I get a refresher course on using a shotgun. I prefer sitting on my ass to handling a dangerous weapon, but he promises that if I pay attention to the lesson, he will calm down for at least an hour.

The show runs on mute in the background while Reaper demonstrates how to load the weapon, and all the things I shouldn't do. Most of them seem obvious to me, but I nod patiently because he means well and he scares me into thinking I'll really need this knowledge. You never know. Wyatt clearly gets mixed up in trouble more times than I would like to admit.

Tylee complains throughout Reaper's lesson in an effort to either piss him off or lighten the mood. Most likely both. She makes fun of Reaper for having large ears, sunburnt skin, no ass and no girlfriend. She leaves no stone unturned and it's hard not to burst into laughter at some of her more aggressive jabs.

He doesn't respond to Tylee except when she interrupts his lesson on how to use a lever-action shotgun that looks like an old movie prop until Reaper makes me hold it and feel the weight.

"Sleep with this near your bed," he says earnestly. His eyes are cold and every part of his face deadly serious. "Be ready to use it. Aim straight for the chest. Don't worry about aiming too well as long as you control the muzzle."

Tylee makes a sound like an annoyed horse and rolls her eyes.

"My Lord, men are dramatic. Don't you think if anyone were going to attack us, they would've come by now? Isaac has people watching the highway. We're fine."

"I know you're Isaac's old lady, Tylee, but this is club business and I recommend you stay out of it."

"Club business. What the fuck do you know about club business?" she snaps, but then she wanders away to the kitchen, for a glass of milk. I don't know if Wyatt expects me to be like that. Then again, I don't know when the fuck I started caring what Wyatt thinks.

Hm.

I HEAD to bed first when the pregnancy exhaustion hits me like a train. My ass nearly falls asleep on the couch, but Reaper gets me up and helps me set up the shotgun and ammunition near my bed. I get under the covers and he all but tucks me in.

"Sorry," he says when I swat his hand away from tucking me in. "I want Southpaw to know I took good care of you."

"I'll put in a good word. Get lost."

I hear him and Tylee arguing outside for a few minutes and they either stop arguing, or I fall asleep. I don't know what happens first. The sleep that hits me is next level. The power of pregnancy hormones, stress hormones and missing the fuck out of Wyatt sends me into the deepest, most delicious sleep.

THE ONLY NATURAL thing to happen next when you sleep that deeply is that some bullshit wakes you up. I think it's Tylee arguing with Reaper when I wake up. I'm too groggy to make sense of anything happening and any instincts I might have about waking up in the middle of the night from my nursing days are lost in the mental fog of my pregnancy.

"Shut up..." I grumble with all the energy of a zombie who hasn't had his daily serving of human flesh. Or whatever zombies eat. I hope I don't dream about zombies...

MY EYES FLUTTER closed for a few more peaceful seconds before three loud pops snap my ass awake immediately. *Gunshots.* I hear a bloodcurdling scream dangerously close to my door. Adrenaline floods every inch of me, causing me to sit up straight in bed. I hear three more pops in quick succession.

Fuck.

I swing my legs out of bed, my heart beating so loud I can feel it expanding in my throat with each painful pulse. Reaper's lecture must have been good enough for me to learn from it because I easily load a shell into the chamber. My hands shake as I think of turning off the safety. I don't know if I can shoot someone. I'm a nurse – not a murderer.

But I also know if it comes down to killing someone or protecting my unborn child, I'll cope. Somehow. Wyatt gets through life without letting his past hold him back. I'll lean on him if I have to blow a motherfucker's brains out. I hold the gun as safely as I can when I approach the bedroom door and slip into some slippers in case I need to escape.

A full minute passes before I hear another noise. No gunshots. Time slows down so much that I generate a million different worst case scenarios in my head. I don't hear footsteps before I feel someone push their weight against the door.

"Don't shoot," Reaper says as he opens the door and quickly enters my room, shutting the door behind him quietly. I don't know how the hell a man so big moves so quietly, but I'm glad he's the one in here and I'm glad that I didn't shoot him.

"Where's Tylee?" I whisper.

"She can handle herself. Or her husband can handle her. I'm not worried about him, I'm worried about the pigs."

"I heard gunshots. I woke right up... do we need to leave?"

"Yes, ma'am," Reaper says. "We need to climb out that window. I parked my bike outside after I put you to bed. I still can't get a hold of your man."

"I can't leave here without telling him."

I don't need to elaborate for Reaper to know that Wyatt could kill us both for disobeying him. He won't ask questions if he perceives any betrayal. The man is not all the way right in the head.

If Wyatt returns and finds me gone, I struggle to imagine us talking sense into him.

"We don't have time to come up with a better idea. I need to get your pregnant ass out the window without damaging the precious cargo. Now move."

"Who got shot?"

"Nobody worth concerning yourself with."

Reaper fired the shots. That's good to know, but judging by his hushed tones, we aren't out of the woods yet. I hope he's telling the truth about Tylee but I'm not in a position to argue. Reaper ushers me to the window and I peer out of it. My stomach turns the second

I look out the window and I feel like I'm looking out the window of an airplane.

Logically, I know it's not that high but considering I have to jump, a fear of heights grasps me in a chokehold. What if I land on my stomach?

"I'll climb down if you hold onto my back. But you cannot tell Wyatt how I got you down there."

"Is that your main worry right now?"

"Come on, get on my back," Reaper responds hurriedly. "The quicker we get this over with..."

"What about the shotgun?"

"Shit, keep a hold of it. You might need to shoot."

"That had better be a joke."

"Don't blow my fucking head off. Now come on..."

Reaper is out of his goddamn mind if he thinks I would *ever* tell this story to Wyatt. I still barely even know how I hold the shotgun without causing a major accident, but I climb onto Reaper's back and he hikes my thighs up so I can wrap my legs around his torso and one arm around his neck. I hold the shotgun with my right hand, but I still don't trust myself to take all the necessary steps to actually fire it.

Reaper edges towards the window and glances down, considering his path. The loud sound of boots pound down the hallway. The floor shakes and my body is so sweaty I nearly fall off Reaper's back. A thick Ozark accent bellows, "Check the rooms! I know he's got a bitch in here somewhere."

He throws one leg over the windowsill. I grab onto him tighter. The bedroom door swings open. Reaper keeps climbing down.

"Shoot if you have to!"

I'll blow his fucking hearing out if I shoot. But I'm suddenly face to face with the a man who has the same tattoo as the guy who threw food into the pit after me. He must be from the same cop/outlaw biker gang. I still don't know which one it was...

My heart pounds like crazy, I aim the shotgun at him and it gives

Reaper enough time to lower us to the ground. Reaper nearly drops me and the gun jerks back, hitting my jaw. The shockwaves of pain surging through me make it hard to get my bearings. I reach out for stability and find Reaper's hand.

He grabs me and drags me toward the bike. I normally fuss and fight a lot more before getting on the back of those things. I don't have a helmet. Or time.

"Don't let go," Reaper says, although I don't need to be told twice. I scream loudly as a gunshot fires out from the window above us and blows up a planter pot outside Southpaw's house that previously possessed a large hydrangea bush. Petals and leaves explode everywhere as Reaper revs the engine. I rest my head against his back in an instinctive attempt to protect myself, although obviously the action would be useless against bullets.

He swerves the bike around and accelerates so quickly, I feel my heart drop into my ass. It's worse than riding on a roller coaster. I have nothing keeping me clinging to Reaper's back except my sheer will. I have to ride every curve and sharp turn without knowing where we're headed. I've never done that with anyone before. Wyatt didn't ever have to ride as fast as this.

I have to trust him.

WE LOSE them after twenty miles. Reaper does his best not to scare the crap out of me but my fingers slip against his cut several times during the high speed chase. I recognize the place we end up, although I'm not convinced this is the safest place for us. Reaper's family owns the motel, so I understand why he's here but... couldn't the cops (or ex-cops) track us here?

I'm just happy to be alive by the time we get there and too tired to ask too many questions.

"You okay?" Reaper asks with genuine concern. He wasn't wearing a helmet either but he's unbothered.

"Yes."

"We're getting separate rooms tonight. You're not a prisoner, but you don't open the door unless I knock. Hungry?"

"If I wasn't scared of my damn mind, I would be."

"I'll send someone to McDonalds for you," Reaper offers. My stomach turns. I can't imagine having more McDonalds. Even if my pregnancy hormones weren't controlling every aspect of my appetite, after moving into Wyatt's house, I haven't been able to tolerate the thought of McDonalds.

"Can I *please* get Taco Bell instead? I need something spicy."

Reaper's lips purse in a thin, frustrated line. "What's wrong with McDonalds?"

I don't mean to be trouble because he's clearly tired from the ride, but if I so much as smell a McDonalds french fry, I will throw up. Everywhere.

"I didn't say anything was wrong with McDonalds. I'm pregnant, Reaper. I have cravings."

He sighs.

"Okay. But after that ride, you can call me Gideon. My family calls me Giddy. I fucking hate that, so never call me that. Just... Gideon."

There's something oddly sentimental about the request. But I feel deeply uncomfortable thinking of this man as anything other than Reaper. His name sounds religious. Strong. Masculine. But Reaper sounds like the man who kept me in the motel room all those weeks.

"I don't know if I can get used to calling you something new at this point."

"Please," he says. "You're Wyatt's old lady. You're family."

"I'm not Wyatt's old lady."

Reaper grins. "Not yet. But you will be."

"That sounds like it would be Wyatt's decision, not mine."

"He made that decision when he knocked you up. Stupid motherfucker."

"Thanks."

"Not what I meant," Reaper grumbles awkwardly, turning so red that he reminds me more of a school boy than a terrifying biker. "Let me get you that damn Taco Bell before I screw up more..."

When he notices me staring at his face too closely, his grin drops away into a more stern, tight-lipped expression. He leaves me alone in the motel room and I sit on the bed, letting all the crazy shit that just happened play out in my head.

I WISH I knew what Wyatt would want me to do. I can handle myself and keep the baby alive... but then what? I don't even know how to find Wyatt or where to go next. I just have to trust that Gideon means it when he calls me family.

CHAPTER TWENTY-SEVEN
SOUTHPAW

My burner phone rings and wakes me up in the middle of the night. I wouldn't mind if it weren't the third fucking time some damn noise has roused me from my necessary rest. Hawk and Juliette won't keep it down. I answer my phone with a furious snarl.

"We need enforcers back East and I need you to get a hold of Harley. Shit hit the fan, Southpaw. Shit hit the fan."

It's Reaper.

"Aren't you in Texas?"

"No," he says. "I'm not in Texas. I have Anna. She's safe. I haven't heard from Tylee, but I had to promise Anna she was fine to get her out of the house."

"Slow down. Slow the fuck down. What the hell is going on?"

I STEP OUTSIDE of the motel room to smoke. Reaper updates me on everything that happened on the phone. He killed two of the pigs, but they're still in my house and he doesn't know if the *real* cops have gone out there yet. Shit.

It's the middle of the night and he still hasn't heard from Tylee, but he promises me that Anna came out of the situation completely unharmed. She ate Taco Bell and immediately fell asleep. That sounds like Anna, so I assume he's telling me the truth.

Reaper called my dad first, but couldn't get through to him. Normally, I would wait for dad's instructions but considering the situation, I have to make a judgment call.

I WISH I could go back East right away but right now... I just can't. We're scheduled to meet dad in Amarillo tonight with a full day of driving ahead of us. Reaper can handle the shit on the East Coast for the next three days. His job is simple – keep my old lady alive, find my sister and get all the information he can off the dead bodies in my house.

Then burn them.

I FINISH three cigarettes before I wake Hawk from the room next door. I don't think he's really asleep, but when I glance over his shoulder, I see the chubby, troublesome woman sleeping ass up on the bed and fully nude. I pretend like I don't see her because at this point, I'm willing to accept anything that keeps that hellcat under control.

"Get her up. We need to get to Texas now."

"Feels like you're punishing me?"

"That's how I felt when you had that goddamn woman squealing for an hour straight."

"I'll get her up," Hawk says awkwardly. "Don't talk to her. You scare the crap out of her and I can keep her well behaved."

Scare her? I can't imagine a goddamn thing scaring that unruly woman.

"If only you could change her skin color too," I mutter, giving another glance at the woman's exposed ass. Hawk is a crazy mother-fucker for this one.

"Like you're one to talk," Hawk says. "Get a headstart. I know the way."

"Don't wait too long."

"I won't. I'll need a minute to get her dressed."

"Hurry."

I ride out the first twenty miles at a smooth, easy pace. Hawk joins me in my rearview mirror around the twenty-fifth mile out. We still have a long drive along the highway. During our first stop for gas, I buy more Zyns. No time to smoke and I shouldn't have had those cigarettes in the first place.

Hawk's prize leans on the edge of his motorcycle with her arms crossed. She ignores my existence and I ignore hers to keep the peace.

I normally enjoy riding across Oklahoma but this time, my agitation makes it hard to enjoy the ride. We stop again in Shamrock, Texas. Juliette and Hawk have a loud argument that I ought to pay attention to. Instead, I buy three donuts from the gas station and eat them while talking to the girl behind the counter. She's a half-Indian cousin of Doc Blackwood.

I can't keep track of all the family trees, but I've never met her before. Once I finish the donuts, I head outside to find Hawk tipping his flask down his throat while Juliette glares at him.

"Y'all had enough rest?"

"I'm not getting on the back of his bike after he's had alcohol," Juliette says. "I'm riding with you."

Hawk turns purple. "Damn fucking right you are. If you so much as touch her, Southpaw, I'll shoot you."

It's his woman. Once she stopped making any trouble for me, she belonged to Hawk. I don't touch her. She gives me a pleading look, but I can't help her.

TWO MILES away from the clubhouse, the air thickens with black clouds of smoke that engulf the entire stretch of the highway. Hawk rides alongside me with Juliette clinging to his back and signals. It's an unofficial "what the fuck"? I can't tell him what's going on with the smoke, but I don't like it.

Texas is known for deserts, not wildfires. Last I checked, folks came here to escape the wildfires. The closer we get to the club-house, the thicker the smoke. I signal to Hawk for us to pull over. Hawk parks his bike next to mine on the shoulder. The highway out here is notoriously desolate, but right now, it feels too empty.

We haven't seen a single biker in over a hundred miles of highway.

"This doesn't feel right," Hawk says.

I nod. "We should be careful."

"I'll hang back, watch your backs and see what's coming."

I NOD. Hawk takes off the direction we came from so he can loop around and get the advantage of surprise. I don't like riding into uncertainty alone, but I can only hope that we're both paranoid assholes and the thick plumes of smoke mean nothing.

Over time, you develop a gut instinct about danger. The air tastes different. Hawk felt the shift the closer we got to the clubhouse. Before I head down the highway towards some inevitable bullshit, I try calling dad again. Nothing.

Fuck.

TWO MORE MINUTES of riding and I can see the fire before I get to the parking lot entrance. I expect a flood of adrenaline but instead, everything slows down. I stop my bike before the entrance as an eerie chill travels up my arm and seems to pass through me and the bike like we're one and the same organism.

I get off the bike and I don't think. Flames engulf the clubhouse. There are bikes out front. No fire trucks. Nobody on the scene. Just me...

WITHOUT LOADING MY PISTOL, I race for the clubhouse door. When I open it – fucking pandemonium.

AND IT'S a hell of a lot worse than I thought.

SWEAT COVERS every inch of my bare skin within seconds and I can't step more than a few feet into the building. There's too much fire and I can't put it out alone. I can smell blood. Bodies. Burnt wood. A rush of smoke chokes my lungs. *I have to leave.*

I RUN BACK outside the clubhouse. It takes a lot to knock me off my saddle but the bloodbath in the clubhouse gets my hand shaking. They're all dead. I don't have to count the bodies. I can see their bikes outside and use that to tally up the bodies.

Law enforcement has to come here. Shit. There are no two ways around it.

HOLY FUCKING SHIT.

HAWK SHOWS up a few minutes before the firetrucks and the cops. The scene before is is downright horrific. I steel myself off from any emotion. The smell is the worst part of it, but the thick smoke makes it hard to breathe and even harder to keep the contents of my stomach down.

This shit is a goddamn nightmare. Hawk and I argue about whether we should enter the building, but we can't even if we want to. The heat emanates from the fiery clubhouse and there's no doubt we need law enforcement and firefighters.

"I'll call," Hawk says. "If there was any contraband in there, it's burned up."

We don't have time to come up with a good story for the cops or explain this shit. Hawk just has to call and we have to hope that we get some good old boys willing to take our side in this situation. I watch the flames as I wait for the sirens.

All I know is this shit is gonna cost us. When the firefights put the fire out, they start dragging out bodies with the help of the EMTs and the cops. We won't make final identifications until after they get the bodies to the coroner's office, but I can already tell who we've lost.

Hawk stands with his arm around Juliette, who stares in abject horror at everything unfolded. I watch as they bring out Doc Blackwood's body, Randall Sinclair, Don Hollingsworth, and then the hardest one to watch.

MY FATHER. I don't care what the EMTs say, I have to see him. I fight my way past and they let me stand over his body once Hawk tells them he's my father. I throw the sheet back without thinking.

I don't want to believe it's my father. My brain replaces the image with something else, but I have to face it.

My brain tries to protect me from what I'm seeing but after a few seconds, the image grows more clear and I recognize my father's features beneath the blackened and charred portions of his face. It's him. It's dad. Half his face is burned black. He looks mangled and gory...

. . .

LIKE HE DIDN'T DIE in peace. His body is riddled with bullet holes. *Goddamn.*

"THEY SHOT HIM."

My voice comes out stiff and emotionless, although I feel a storm brewing inside me I don't know if I can contain. I hear Juliette sobbing softly, but I don't cry. I can't. Her sobbing makes me think of Tylee. And mom.

THIS IS GONNA BREAK my mother.

"MR. SHAW, we're gonna ask you to come down to the station if that's alright. We just want to talk to you about the fire."

Who could have done this? My first suspects would have been the pigs who kidnapped Anna but according to Reaper, the pigs are all back east.

"Yes, sir."

CHAPTER TWENTY-EIGHT
ANNA

I never expected to end up back at my mom's house. It's better than getting sent off to Canada with my dad and his mistress, but my mom gets under my skin like no one else can. I love her to death, but she treats me like I'm thirteen and not a grown ass pregnant woman.

Wyatt won't tell me what happened in Texas, but I found out from Tylee that her father passed away, which means that Wyatt lost his dad and he hasn't said a word about it. All the news hits me like a freight train. I'm happy Tylee is safe, but the incident in Texas seems serious and I can't get any information – from anyone.

Tylee won't tell me what happened either but when I asked her if her father was sick, she turned red and I felt guilty as I watched her fight back tears.

I'm trying to be sensitive, but it's hard to be patient. If I didn't have the baby, I would have already rented a car and hunted Wyatt down. Instead, I listen to Reaper's instructions and let him take me back to my teenage years. My mom never changed the wall color I picked out when I was fifteen. My mid-00s taste was tacky as hell. I can't believe my mother didn't question her daughter painting her bedroom magenta.

The color gives me a headache and the posters of Chris Brown make me cringe. My friends would have roasted me for having any white boys up on my bedroom wall, but I remember desperately wanting to pin up my collection of bags from Abercrombie & Fitch with hot California tanned models printed all over them.

I pretend I'm going to bed early to stop my mom from asking me too many questions. She hates that I quit my job – Wyatt didn't give me a choice – and nothing calms her down. Reaper gave her $3,000 to "earn her trust" and that just made her more suspicious. Obviously. I understand why Wyatt calls the other members of his motorcycle club idiots sometimes...

Lying in my Twin XL bed from high school, complete with the itchiest zebra print sheets in existence, I'm pregnant with an outlaw biker's baby and I wonder what the hell I did to get to this point. The last time I had to question my life choices like this was after I passed my licensing exam and went out to celebrate with my friends.

Sigh. One of the worst hangovers of my life and now, lying in bed like this, I think it might have been the happiest time of my life.

Those friends moved away from Chicago and I never met anyone else who I clicked with. Nursing shifts aren't exactly conducive to making friends. I hear my mom blasting the television downstairs as she watches the most random shit ever on YouTube TV. What is it about parents and their ability to end up in the strangest corners of the internet? Why does my mother need to learn how to bake a cake shaped like Tiana from *Princess And The Frog*?

I CLOSE my eyes and remember the days of listening to my iPod with those long white headphones plugged into a giant brick that contained my favorite bedtime anthems – Ms. New Booty by Bubba Sparxx and Run It by Chris Brown – hoping the nostalgia will help me drift to sleep.

. . .

ANOTHER EQUALLY NOSTALGIC event prevents me from sleeping.

"ANNA! OH MY GOD! OH MY GOD!"

Sigh. My eyes snap open and I stare right into the eyes of Kobe Bryant, the star of the peeling poster taped to the ceiling.

MY MOTHER SCREAMS "OH MY GOD" for *everything* ranging from a dramatic moment on television to a death in the family with absolutely no variation in her intonation. I learned over the years to let her feel her feelings and react later. But she keeps screaming and hollering my name. This had better not be a cake related emergency.

"DAMN IT MOM, I'M COMING!"

No matter how much you want to practice love and light, your parents can drag the goddamn demons out of you. It's like she forgets that I'm pregnant. My mother keeps screaming while I hobble downstairs. Once I get past the hallway to the top of the stairs, I can't see a damn thing.

"Why are all the lights off?" I ask her in a normal voice once I make it down the stairs without breaking my neck. The only switch is downstairs, or I would have flicked the light on myself. I can't even see my mom down there.

"SHH!!!"

I guess we're done screaming.

"Mom. Where are you? What are you doing?"

"There is a terrifying man wearing leather on the porch. I saw him on the secret camera I installed on Kayla Walker's pine tree–

"You put a camera on the neighbor's property?"

"It's pointed towards the street so I can see all angles," she hisses defensively. "Now quiet down before that man hears you. I'm calling the police."

"Are you sure it's not the man who dropped me off?"

He was *Gideon* when he dropped me off and he came in without his cut. My mom might be paranoid, but she spent so much time staring mesmerized at Reaper, I would think she would remember him.

"I remember blondie," she says. Her voice sounds like it's coming from behind a curtain. "This man looks very sinister and evil... like he would choke a baby."

"Mom!"

Even if I haven't lived here in years, I can still navigate my mom's house in the dark. Playing along slightly, I crouch as I peel back the curtain.

"Give me your phone," I hiss. "You're acting crazy."

"I'm saving your life!"

I look at the crisp video feed on my mother's phone. She's right. It's not Gideon. I drop my mom's phone back in her hand and run towards the front door.

"ANNA!"

It's more of a waddle than a run, but my mom doesn't follow me. She's standing within earshot, but she's clearly too afraid to chase after me. It doesn't matter. I fling the front door open and without giving Wyatt time to react, I jump into his arms.

I KNOW he'll catch me. I trust him.

MY ARMS WRAP around his neck as my body slams into his chest. He wraps me in a warm hug as his protective instincts override his surprise.

"Anna," he whispers, his voice shaky and choked up. My thighs wrap around Wyatt's torso to help me balance and he hoists me effortlessly in his arms in the warmest, tightest embrace we've ever had.

. . .

HE'S HOME.

I PRESS my nose into the crook of Wyatt's neck, inhaling his scent. I missed that smell and my sensitive pregnant nose responds immediately to him. The powerful magnetism as our eyes meet remains just as strong as the first time we met. I feel my breath catch. He breaths out with slow relief and the corners of his lips curve upwards slightly before his lips purse in a thin line again.

"Anna," he says again, running his tongue over those perfect, dark purple lips that I so thoroughly miss kissing and sucking on. "Fuck, I missed you."

I HONESTLY FORGET my mom's presence inside and intertwine my body with Wyatt's as he holds me up. Our eyes meet again for another moment of deep, intense, longing eye contact before Wyatt kisses me.

I part his lips first to press my tongue into his mouth. The familiar taste of peppermint spreads more warmth and desire for him through me. I hold onto Wyatt's flexed bicep and the size of his giant muscles sends a ripple of desire straight between my legs.

Damn. My pussy could at least wait for him to walk through the door first. Wyatt has the annoying ability to tell exactly how badly I want him and he pulls away from our kiss with a cocky grin on his face. Much better than the half-smile he had when he first saw me.

"That kiss makes me feel better," he says. "I'm glad you're okay..."

My heart skips a beat. It still surprises me when Wyatt behaves better than the brute who dragged me into a Flying J bathroom to knock me up. Wyatt's fingers gently stroke my hair, careful not to catch in the curls and create tangles. The light touch sends another one of those thirsty ass ripples of desire between my legs. I clutch his biceps tighter.

Wyatt breaks eye contact with me and clears his throat after making a funny expression on his face.

"What?"

He clears his throat again and sets me on the ground. I'm ready to tell him off when I remember... my mama. I turn around, ready to get a mouthful from my mom and I see her staring slack-jawed at Wyatt. Even if my heart is beating out of control, I try to act as calm as possible.

IF I JUST ACT LIKE my thuggish, white biker boyfriend is normal, my overprotective black mother will have a totally normal reaction.

"MOM, THIS IS WYATT."

"Is that who got you pregnant?" she asks without taking her eyes off Wyatt. The response isn't entirely rude, I guess, because she sticks out her hand for him to shake it.

I expect Wyatt to at least turn red, but he just shakes her hand.

"Yes, ma'am. I'm the one. Wyatt Shaw. I'm a businessman who fixes up bikes on the side. I own a winery and I have every intention of making an honest woman out of your daughter."

I look at Wyatt like he has two heads. Is this the same man who put his dick inside me within a couple hours of meeting me? Most of his sentences end with grunts or disgruntled looks. The man in front of me just spoke like a goddamn gentleman.

An honest woman? What is he even talking about?

"You're getting married?!" my mom says, looking at me with disapproval like I could somehow keep a secret from her that I just found out. Wyatt can't seriously expect this to count as a wedding proposal, right? I glare at him, ready to give him a good punch in the shoulder, but he just keeps grinning.

"Once I officially propose, it's up to Anna."

My heart skips a beat again. I know some serious shit happened in Texas and that he's back here under the worst circumstances. What I don't know is how Wyatt can smile and act like everything is fine. And charm the pants off my mom. But that's what he does for the next two hours. She serves him beer and he answers all her questions with polish, even her questions about me quitting my job.

"Anna will have all the money she needs and more. I don't want her exposed to the sorts of people that end up in an inner city emergency room."

That answer satisfies my mom well enough and after a while, Wyatt kindly asks her if he can take me up to my room to spend some time with me and give me rest for the baby. She gushes over him more and agrees. I finally get some peace of mind when she heads to her room and I take Wyatt up to my teenage bedroom.

He glances around with a bemused expression on his face and I pretend to play it cool while he chuckles at my Chris Brown poster. I don't even want to know what type of posters Wyatt had hanging up in his teenage bedroom. I'm sure there were boobs involved.

I close the door behind me and frown at him.

"I feel like a high schooler and that feels wrong."

"Cute bed."

"Shut up."

Wyatt puts his hands on my hips and cuts to the chase. Kissing. Very hot kissing. His lips spread mine open again and I yield to him without hesitation or complaint. His tongue takes control of mine, teasing it around my mouth until he sucks on my tongue possessively and moves to sucking on my lower lips.

We stumble backwards onto my "cute bed" and it squeaks aggressively. I cringe internally and try to push Wyatt off me. He doesn't stop touching me and kissing me.

"I'll be quiet," he whispers and then moves slightly, causing the bed to creak again. He chuckles and runs his hand slowly under my shirt, distracting me from my efforts to push him off me again. I shiver and fight back a moan as his fingers touch my nipples. I haven't felt his hands in such a long time that I forgot what it was like.

My nipples feel entirely new as Wyatt rubs them in slow circles. My boobs have grown so much during my pregnancy and feel so sensitive to his touch that I have to bite down on my lower lip to stifle a moan. Wyatt chuckles and eases my shirt off. *Oh no...*

"Do you really want my mom to hear us having sex?" I whisper, raking my fingers through Wyatt's beard as I wrap my legs around him and feel the common sense beginning to drain from my body. I can feel his dick pressing against me through his pants and I drag Wyatt's face closer to mine so I can kiss him the way he kissed me.

He's careful not to press his weight into my baby bump but I miss how it feels to have his body on mine.

"I said I would be quiet," Wyatt whispers. "You're the one with the screaming problem."

"Shut up," I whisper, raking my fingers through Wyatt's hair. "We have to just... be quiet...and stop this..."

I DON'T KNOW if I can stop. I've never been able to stop myself with Wyatt Shaw. *The worst part is that being with Wyatt has stopped scaring the crap out of me.*

Chapter Twenty-Nine
Southpaw

I want to put my dick in her so fucking bad it hurts. I want to respect Anna's mother but I also want to feel my old lady's pussy after all the bullshit I went through in Amarillo. Dad is dead. The club scattered to the winds. We don't know what the future holds and all we can expect is pure anarchy ahead. I just want to feel my woman and forget the bullshit going on in my world.

"I'll fuck you on the floor," I whisper. "I'll take you from behind and touch your clit until you cum. All you have to do is push your face into a pillow and try not to scream."

She pushes her hips up to meet me instinctively even if her face scrunches up disagreeably at my command.

"This is a terrible idea."

I grab her and slowly roll off the low barely-off-the-ground bed onto the floor with Anna in my arms, careful to protect her baby bump from the impact. We land with a soft thud, not loud enough for her mother to hear. Her eyes widen as she clings to me fiercely, sinking her fingers into my arms. I missed feeling her grabbing onto me. The whole way back from Amarillo I couldn't stop myself from yearning for Anna on the back of my bike.

It doesn't feel right to ride that long without her. Once she has the baby, I'll have to come home more. I've never felt that urge before. On the floor, I keep kissing Anna and work her shirt off so I can see her breasts up close. Those perfect dark brown tits are even prettier and bigger than I remember. Her nipples doubled in size and they look thicker and longer.

I just have to run my tongue over her sexy nipples and Anna squirms beneath me as she struggles to stifle a moan. Licking on her nipples turns to sucking on them and I get her boobs really wet with spit while Anna wriggles beneath me.

"Don't worry baby," I whisper. "I'll get my tongue in your pussy soon enough."

Her pussy must be so fucking wet right now. I can't wait to get my tongue between her legs.

"I can't..." she gasps as I suck harder on her tits and she has to cut herself off to stop a moan from escaping her lips.

"Turn around baby," I murmur as I lick her ears and pull away from her. My dick is gonna burst if I don't get it inside Anna soon. She flips onto all fours and I peel her sexy black flared leggings away from her ass. Her pussy must be soaked because I have to work hard to get the leggings and her thong out of Anna's ass crack.

Fuck... Anna is even wetter than I expected. Her pussy drips juices down her thighs and both her thong and leggings are soaked with her arousal. My dick officially hurts. I want her so goddamn bad.

"I missed that sweet ass pussy," I whisper, running my tongue over her butt cheek and wishing I could drive my tongue straight into her asshole without preparation. But first, I kiss her ass cheeks, just enjoying the soft flesh and the alluring shape of Anna's perfect butt.

She grabs a pillow from the bed as I press my tongue into her soft pussy lips. Anna buries her face in the pillow. I don't have to hear her moans to know how she feels with my lips down there. She's so fucking wet. I love it.

"You taste so fucking good," I murmur before attacking Anna's pussy with my tongue again. She whimpers and pushes her hips back to meet me after a few seconds of me kissing her pussy and tongue fucking her tight little hole. I grab Anna's thighs and fixate my attention on her clit as I hold her still.

She clutches the pillow tightly and pushes her hips back more, forcing me to bury my face between her thick bubbly ass cheeks. Air struggles to get into my lungs as I drive my tongue deeper. I can feel her getting close. Her body shifts and I hear her moans despite her best efforts to silence them in the pillow.

I tease Anna's clit until I drive her over the edge. Her pussy gushes like a waterfall as she finishes all over my face. I love how goddamn hot she is when she cums. If I didn't need to breathe, I would keep my face buried in her perfect pussy. Instead, I lick the juices off Anna's outer lips and give myself a breather.

Anna climaxes again just from me licking juices away from her pussy lips and when she cums a second time, I give in to the temptation I tried so desperately to ignore earlier and slide my tongue over her tight backdoor. She has a deliciously salty, tangy taste that makes me want to push my tongue in deeper. Anna edges her hips forward away from my tongue when she feels my tongue graze her back door.

I can't tell if she's afraid or just too sensitive.

"Don't move."

I spit on her asshole and Anna flinches. The glob of spit slides into her back door and I question my goddamn sanity. My dick is already so hard and heavy with blood that it feels like I'm gonna pass out. Watching my spit slide into Anna's sexy black ass is almost more than I can tolerate.

She turns her cheek to the side as she arches her back and keeps her face obediently pressed into the pillow.

Fuck, her ass looks so hot.

"Wyatt..." Anna protests in a soft, breathy voice that just makes her situation worse.

. . .

I ONLY WANT to fuck her more.

"YOU HAVE A NICE BUTT," I grunt, using the fresh spit to slide my thumb into Anna's ass. She gasps as I push my finger into her ass but I can tell it doesn't hurt her. The way her asshole clamps down on my finger makes me want to put something bigger in there.

I tease Anna's back door with my finger, rubbing her inner walls as gently as I can while I get her lubricated. Her body reacts despite her soft verbal grunts in protest. She can't help herself. I like making her feel good, even if Anna fights me a little. I kiss her butt cheeks and keep fingering her ass until she lets out a soft, squeaky moan.

I pull my finger out of her ass and wipe it off on her soft, fluffy butt cheek.

"Don't worry, baby. I'll give you my dick now..."

SHE DOESN'T MENTION her mama hearing us again.

THE LAST TIME I remember taking my clothes off that quickly, I was a teenager about to do a polar bear plunge in some girl's backyard pond to impress her. I don't know if I'm any less goddamn stupid, but I know I'm more in love with Anna than I ever was with anyone else. She stirred something in me the first time I laid eyes on her.

I haven't been the same ever since and I don't want to go back to the person I was.

THERE'S no need for me to spit on my dick or lube it up with Anna's pussy gushing like a waterfall. I guide the soft, dripping head of my cock to her entrance without missing another beat once I have my clothes off.

Everything Anna does turns me on so goddamn much.

HER SOFT ENTRANCE gives easily to my first thrust. The head of my cock stretches her out so much that she has to bury her head in the pillow. Her pussy grips my cock so goddamn hard I swear I'm gonna cum before I get every inch inside her. Veins burst along the side of my cock as arousal pulses through me.

I push another inch inside her. Anna shudders in a mixture of pain and pleasure. Her tight, smooth asshole practically begs for me to slide my finger inside it again as I take her from behind. I need to remind this woman that every goddamn hole in her body belongs to me. She arches her back and stifles another moan as I spit on her ass again.

My spit drips all over her tight puckered hole and my dick, getting Anna's sweet asshole nice and wet for my finger. I ease about half of my dick inside her pussy and grip her smooth butt cheeks, yearning for a closer connection. With her large baby bump, I have to be careful of how I handle her.

I hold her hips and slide the rest of my dick inside her, feeling her body rub closer to mine as I drive the rest of my cock inside her from behind. She buries her face in the pillow again and tries her best to stifle her moaning but this moan is damn loud.

"I like how you take my dick baby," I whisper, teasing Anna's curls more and kissing her shoulders. "Your pregnant pussy feels so fucking good wrapped around daddy's dick."

She moans when I say that, so I drive my dick inside her soft ass pussy even deeper. I love the way she grips my dick. Pushing my thumb into her ass while I thrust into her with a steady rhythm drives Anna crazy. She thrusts her hips back instinctively, forgetting my finger in her ass, causing her to take both my finger and dick deep inside her at the same time.

Anna has to force her face into the pillow to silence the heavenly noises that escape her lips. My finger in her ass forces her pussy to grip my dick tighter and I can feel her sweet entrance drawing an orgasm out of me. *I have no goddamn control here.*

I cum so hard that I have to draw blood from my lower lip to stop a groan of pleasure from escaping my lips. Goddamn. This woman's pussy is so fucking sweet. I bury my finger in her ass as my cock twitches in Anna's sopping wet pregnant pussy. She feels so fucking tight and as I thrust my finger in her ass, she cums around my cock again.

I ease my finger out of Anna's ass reluctantly. I wish I could stay buried in that perfect tight back door, but now that I'm spent, I just want to hold my woman and never let her go.

Once I pull out of her, she shudders and I hold her body against mine as I pull my dick out of her and turn Anna around on her knees so she's facing me, kneeling together on the floor of her childhood bedroom. I have never been more grateful for shag carpet. I interlace our fingers as Anna looks up at me with those sexy ass brown eyes.

She's so fucking pretty.

"What happened in Texas, Wyatt?"

My heart broke. That's what happened. Tylee's heart. Mom's heart. It's not just losing dad but the men I considered cousins and uncles too. Half the fucking club went up in flames and the only reason we aren't sitting in jail or dead is sheer dumb luck. My life is so fucking fragile and I don't want Anna to know that.

I always want this woman to be safe, even in the arms of a goddamn demon.

"I don't want to bring that shit home."

She runs her finger slowly over my lips. I can't take my eyes off her.

"I know," she says. "But your dad died and I know it's deeper than that. I know you, Wyatt. And if you want me to be fully yours, you have to be fully mine."

I hate how right she is.

"They were dead before the fire. Coroner's report suspects four shooters based on the ballistics. Each of them had three or four bullets…"

She doesn't beg me to start from the beginning or ask me to make sense of anything. Anna just lets me speak. I tell her everything about the clubhouse, the quarterly meeting, how we were late because of Hawk and some woman, and the condition we found the clubhouse in.

I tell her about seeing dad dead and before I know it, she has me in her arms and I feel like a little boy again. That feeling lasts for about a second because her tits press into me and that little boy feeling disappears because my dick is hard as fuck just from the way she touches me.

"I need you again," I whisper as she holds me.

"Men," she mutters disapprovingly. "Does everything have to be about sex for you?"

I grab her cheeks and tilt Anna's face so her eyes meet mine.

"I love you. That's why your slightest touch gets me hard as fuck. And after all the death I've seen, you make me feel alive."

She shudders and moves her body even closer to mine. Those sexy, thick nipples graze against my chest. My dick is ready to burst again.

"Touch my cock," I whisper. "I want to feel your hands…"

ANNA and I fall asleep in her teenage bedroom together. Once she falls asleep, I roll onto the floor because there's no way in hell my giant ass can make it a full night with Anna in a bed that small. It's painful to pry her off me, but I don't mind the floor.

In the morning, her mother cooks us breakfast and gives no indication that she heard anything the previous night. Anna packs her things up and she doesn't even ask where I'm taking her, which is a first. She still hesitates when she approaches the bike and gives me a disapproving look.

"You're gonna need to get a mom van."

"I will *never* have a mom van."

"Fine. I need a mom van then," Anna replies calmly, eyeing my bike with even more disgust than normal. I thought she was getting used to the bike.

"Fine. I'll get you a mom van. Get your helmet on."

She folds her arms and glares at my bike even harder. "This is not a suitable vehicle for a pregnant woman or a baby."

"Can you hop on just this once without making a scene?"

"No."

"Will I have to drag you on?"

"No," Anna says huffily, taking the spare helmet I brought for her. "I can handle it. I'm just pointing out the truth. This isn't safe for a baby. Family means responsibility."

Don't I know it. She doesn't intend to provoke intense, wounding guilt inside me but that's what her comment does. The club is in fucking shambles right now and scattered across the country. I don't know what the future holds for any of us and aside from Anna, I feel like I've failed my family.

WE STILL DON'T KNOW who did this. All we know is that four men walked into a clubhouse full of armed bikers and left without a goddamn scratch. I find that suspicious. Hawk and Reaper find it suspicious. I bet anyone with half a brain finds it suspicious. But what we do next is up to us.

Reaper believes the attack on Wyatt's house from the pigs and Anna's kidnapping both have some connection to the clubhouse fire. I want to believe him, but there's no real way of knowing yet. Hawk thinks it's easier to imagine us only having one enemy, but what if that weren't the case.

I don't know the right thing to do and hell, I don't know if it's even my job to come up with the right thing to do. I'm Harley's son, but there was never a vote and every piece of original memorabilia pertaining to the club went up in flames. The four original founding families have various artifacts at home and we kept everyone's bikes but... everything else is gone.

The clubhouse burned along with every last one of the original members. We have no leader, no set date for the next quarterly meeting and no one telling us what to do about the unsolved murders.

The "biker gang murders" are trending and that means even more bullshit is headed our way.

I want to look after my family. Both families. Anna and the club.

IF DAD HANDLED a family and the club, so can I. But I can't guarantee the future and I can't guarantee that I'll be in charge of the club. All I can do is take my old lady home and keep her ass out of trouble.

THE FUTURE HAS a funny way of working itself out.

MY PHONE BUZZES in my pocket. It's Hawk... but I'll answer once I get Anna home. Right now, I want every last thing to be about her. My old lady. *My future wife.*

CHAPTER THIRTY
ANNA

I will never get tired of watching him walk around in just his boxer briefs. His dick curls up in a nice thick bulge between his legs and every part of his body is so sexy that I can pick a new one to focus on every day. I am too pregnant to move – according to Wyatt. If I threaten to leave the bed too long, he lures me back by giving me the most back breaking, panty-soaking oral sex.

I'm weak.

I'M ALSO SUSPICIOUS. Wyatt's proposal wasn't a surprise, but the engagement ring definitely was. I know he has various "income sources" but I didn't expect a 24 karat yellow gold half-pave halo engagement ring with a giant emerald cut diamond at the center. It's so much fancier than anything I could have dreamed of.

"You are mine to spoil," Wyatt says. "Don't question it."

THAT DOESN'T MAKE me less suspicious. Wyatt might be a quiet, brooding pillar of muscle but I'm close to popping, which means we have known each other almost a year. Sure, our path to "knowing each other" has been unconventional, but I know Wyatt's habits and I'm sensitive to his movements.

HE'S PLANNING to leave again. He fixed up the bike. Washed a bunch of plain white t-shirts. He shined his boots. The man even got a haircut. I don't know who told him to get a low-top fade, but that's what he shows up with along with a beard trim. *He looks so goddamn hot.* Wyatt's hotness doesn't distract me from reading the signs.

I'm two weeks away from the due date, so I don't know where the hell he thinks he's going...

"WHY ARE you looking at me like you want to eat me?" Wyatt grumbles as he returns to bed from our master bathroom.

"You're acting suspicious."

"I can't take a piss now? It's like we're already married."

"Yes, you're the victim here," I grumble sarcastically.

Wyatt chuckles and leans over to kiss my cheek. His beard tickles and his warm lips almost distract me from getting to the truth. When he kisses me like that, I always want sex. Wyatt is a damn good kisser.

"I'm not suspicious," he whispers. "You're anxious because of the baby."

"That's gaslighting, Wyatt."

"I don't smoke anymore, I swear..."

He keeps kissing his way down my neck and I don't think he knows or cares what the word gaslight means. I try to push him away, but he just keeps kissing me with the persistence of an excited puppy.

"You're fixing the bike and acting weird. I know you're going to leave so stop lying to me or I will take your baby and run."

Wyatt pulls away from me and he's no longer laughing and

smiling around. I fold my arms over my chest and glare at him defiantly.

"The only reason I haven't tatted your ass with my name is because you're pregnant. The second you have my baby, I will ink you up good so that anyone you meet will know who the fuck you belong to."

He has the cold, serious voice he uses when he isn't fucking around. Yeah, yeah, white boy. Wyatt runs his finger over my lips and shakes his head with obvious frustration. My heart sinks into my stomach. I knew it.

"You're right," he says. "You would have enjoyed our time together more if you didn't know what was coming."

"Wyatt..."

The guilty look on his face doesn't make me feel better. He touches me gently and I move closer to him even if I should want to slap him. Instead of pushing him away this time, I want to make him stay. I like our life together. I knew he would have to attend another meeting eventually, but I at least thought he would wait until I had the baby.

"I didn't want to hurt you," Wyatt says as he kisses the top of my nose gently.

I don't want to imagine a night without him in my bed or what it would be like to give birth without Wyatt by my side. "You can't leave right now."

"I have to."

"Why?!"

"Because my father died and my future is up in the air and so is yours. If I don't go now, anything could happen. *Anything.* I can't put you in danger anymore."

"You can't be in danger either. I can't be a part of your world without you."

I can't keep Wyatt's kid away from his grandparents and uncles forever, but the thought of spending time with his family without him is too much to handle. Wyatt smiles and kisses me. I wish his kisses made me feel better but they don't. Not yet.

"You could," he says. "You can do anything alone, Anna. If you can have me wrapped around your finger after the life of brutality I've had... you can do anything."

"I don't want to, then. I want to be with you."

"I'll come back," he says. "I swear. I didn't tell you because I knew I would come back to you."

"I need to know everything, Wyatt."

"Hawk, Reaper, Rage, and I are meeting. One representative from each family."

I've only heard Southpaw mention the name *Rage* in passing once. He's a member of the Hollingsworth family, but I've never met him. I don't care about the other folks meeting. Why does Wyatt have to be the one to leave? He's the only one with a baby on the way.

"Why not your older brother?"

I can tell from the way he's looking at me that nothing I say could change his mind and stop him from going.

"We voted," he says simply.

I DON'T KNOW what else I can do or say to keep Wyatt out of trouble. I throw my arms around him and press my nose into his neck. I intentionally press my baby bump into him, hoping to send him a little reminder of exactly why he should stay here.

"Okay. Who else knows about this meeting?" I whisper, kissing Wyatt's neck. He's so goddamn warm. *I want him here.*

"No one. I trust these men with my life, Anna."

"Where are you meeting?"

"I shouldn't tell you. For your safety. It's a two day's ride."

"That could be as far as Oklahoma."

"I'll be back, sweetheart. I promise."

"How can I know you're gonna be safe? All I know is the last time you left, there was a massacre."

ANNA

"I came back, didn't I? I might not be a lucky gambler, but I'm lucky in other ways."

He pulls me close and kisses me gently before he adds. "I'm lucky I met you."

"You didn't meet me. You grabbed me in a gas station and had your way with me."

"I went after what I wanted," he whispers. "And I'm not sorry because when I get back here, I'll have you, our baby and a life together. But whoever murdered our families won't get away with this."

"That doesn't make me think you plan on staying out of trouble."

"I do. This time. I promise you, Anna Shaw, I'll be here when you give birth to the baby."

"PROMISE?"

"I promise."

HE CALLS me Anna Shaw because he "likes the sound of it" even if we aren't married yet. *Ugh, stupid Wyatt.* It's so hard to fight him when he holds me like this and when he stares at me like I'm the center of his goddamn universe. Like nothing could make him take his eyes off me.

"I love you, Anna," he says. "When I come back to you, we will have our happily ever after. I promise."

"I want it right now."

"Then let's enjoy right now. Don't think about how I'm leaving. Just stay right here. With me."

I curl up on his hairy chest and enjoy the sexy man smell he leaves everywhere. Any time he leaves I cling to his t-shirts and hoodies, even his pillow just to have his scent. I find it comforting. Wyatt's large arms wrap around me and I sink into his broad, muscular chest as my breath matches up with his.

. . .

I CAN BE HAPPY NOW.

I FEEL the baby kicking and since I have my bump pressed to Wyatt's body, he can feel the movement. He turns to look at me with bemusement. He *loves* feeling the baby kick.

"Can I?"

I nod and he moves his hand between us, curving it around my baby bump. I fall asleep against his chest just like that.

I KNOW he'll come back.

I TRUST HIM. I love him. We just feel right together...

CHAPTER THIRTY-ONE
HAWK

I can't bring Juliette to the meeting in Oklahoma, no matter how much she might want me to. Looking at her asleep in that bed makes it harder to leave her behind. After all the bullshit that went down, I called in a favor with my brother Magnum and dragged Juliette kicking and screaming to his apartment complex in downtown Santa Fe.

We haven't left since I brought her down here, which has been great for me and not so great for Juliette who has tried everything in her power to get away from me. Unfortunately for her, I can't let her go. Not after what I found out. She thought she could hide it from me, but I'm keeping such a close watch that it couldn't escape me.

SHE MISSED HER PERIOD.

SOUTHPAW WAS out of his goddamn mind when he had me drag her into that bathroom. I thought I had been careful enough. But what the hell do I remember? I had to down enough liquor to kill a horse to get hard enough to get inside her with all her fussing and fighting.

I never touched a girl that dark or that big before. Nothing against her. Hell, nothing against her? *I fucking love how big she is.* Everything I touched on Juliette's body was soft and I could lose my hands in every part of her, especially those thighs.

My cock gets semi-hard just thinking about her body. I make her sleep naked every night because of it. She doesn't like that too much, but she liked the tattoo even less.

I DON'T KNOW how Wyatt runs around with his woman unmarked. I couldn't do the same, quite frankly. Even if I have to let her go in the end, I won't want another man touching her ever again.

ONCE THAT WOMAN has my baby, she belongs to me forever. Her pussy belongs to me forever.

I HAD to tie her up to finish the tattoo and when she wasn't aiming wads of spit at my head she called me every name in the book. *You dirty fucking horse-faced dog-assed cock sucking nutjob cracker!*

NEVER IN MY life have I heard a woman speak like that. I turned her ass purple for all those cuss words. If she swore like that around my dad, he would slap the shit out of her. *But dad's dead. So it's my job to keep my woman in line...*

I'VE DONE things to calm down that fussing and fighting a little since we got to Santa Fe, but Juliette has this bizarre desire to never calm the fuck down or to shut up about the various things she doesn't like about me.

Doesn't matter what she doesn't like about me anymore. Sweet Juliette will have to find a way to adjust to my good habits and vices because she won't be getting too far out of my sight from now on – except for the next couple of days.

My cousin Isaac and his wife Tylee are out east keeping an eye on Anna and ready to send Southpaw an emergency message if the baby comes. If my twin brother Ryder weren't in jail, I would have him keeping watch of Juliette but he still has six months and a couple weeks before his release date.

I wrote him a letter about dad but he stopped responding. He's been in solitary confinement for about eight weeks. Ryder barely had his wits about him in the first place. I can't imagine what this will do to him.

IT'S AS good a time as any to get the bad part over with.

"I KNOW YOU'RE AWAKE JULIETTE."

I FUCK her every night to make sure she doesn't go to extreme lengths to slit my throat in my sleep.

She doesn't move, but I can tell from the way her chest moves that she's awake.

"WOULD you like me to punish you again?"

HER ASS IS COMPLETELY red from her last punishment. Nothing teaches her to stop screwing with me. I don't know what could possibly change her mind about me. I did her a goddamn favor and she treats me like a monster.

Worse, she still doesn't answer me.

"GET UP, Juliette or I'll put my dick so far up your ass, I'll fuck you awake."

She rolls over and deftly throws a pillow at my face. I catch it and toss it aside. I knew she was awake. Her braids hang in tangled lengths over her shoulders, grazing the large nipples on Juliette's enormous breasts as she sits up halfway in bed, propping her weight up on one hand.

I don't care if she looks at me with absolute loathing like this as long as she looks at me.

"You are sick in the head," she says. "Do you think that's any way to talk to the mother of your child?"

"If the mother of my child had any goddamn decency, I would talk to her with respect."

"Fuck you."

"IS THAT WHAT YOU WANT?" I say, lowering my voice and knowing it's going to scare the fuck out of her. "You want me to fuck you?"

"I never said that."

"You cum every time I do it."

"FUCK YOU, HUNTER."

I SCOWL.

"How do you know my name?"

Juliette glares at me stubbornly. This goddamn woman... She

might be beautiful, but Wyatt is right to question my sanity. I don't mess around with women who don't share my heritage and background. I don't care to learn about anyone else's culture or to have a so-called open mind.

My life right here in America is great the way it is. I drink. I fuck. I ride my bike. I make money when I need to and burn through it when I get the great urge to self immolate.

I could tell just from looking at her she would be trouble. But I just couldn't stop myself. I had to get involved in some family affair and now I have blood on my hands and a bitch who won't stop scratching at me like a mountain lion.

"I asked you a goddamn question, Juliette," I growl.

She has been the hardest woman to train that I've ever met. Most women leap at my every command, but Juliette needs me to tell her two or three times to answer any fucking question. She tests my patience by glaring right back, continuing to ignore me.

She must have gone through my wallet. Goddamn it... She's right. I drink too much.

"IT DOESN'T MATTER. I'm leaving tonight and I need you to stay out of trouble. I'll be back in three days and you have plenty of food to make it that long without me," I say to her as she continues her sassy glaring session.

When she realizes I'm serious, she finally opens her goddamn mouth to do something other than hurl an insult in my direction. This time, she complains.

"You're leaving me alone for three days?" she says.

"Yes."

She smiles gleefully and I let her enjoy whatever smug victory she thinks she's about to enjoy. Juliette replies, "That's plenty of time away from you to find a way to escape."

"Except if you escape, my brother is gonna beat the shit out of you and fuck your pussy every chance he gets until I get back. I made a deal with him that you wouldn't escape. I said I trusted you."

"Well that was stupid," she says, although I can tell from the change in her tone that she's taking my threat seriously. As she should.

"They call him Condom because he doesn't use them," I caution Anna. "But he does share his bitches with his friends. Do you really want ten sketchy bikers cumming inside you?"

"Shut up," she says. "Just stop being a pig for one second."

"I'm not being a pig. I'm letting you know what awaits you outside this apartment. You have everything you need."

"Except my freedom."

"DIDN'T you see what happened in Amarillo?" I growl at her. "Everyone I looked up to is dead. Just by being with me, you could end up shot or worse."

"What the hell could be worse than this?"

"I could think of a few thousand things, Juliette. Don't tempt me to describe them to you while I fuck your ass."

She gets out of bed naked and comes right up to me like she's going to hit me. I don't budge. This woman has lost her mind if she thinks she can step up to me and make me back down. I'm taller than her. Stronger than her.

AND SHE'S MY PROPERTY.

"HOW DARE you talk to me like that? I'm *pregnant.* Doesn't that mean anything to you, or are you actually a goddamn sociopath?"

"I'm a man sick of repeating himself."

"You're worse than Chiron," she hisses before she slaps me across the face. I don't move, but that doesn't mean her fierce little hands don't sting. They feel like what I imagine getting slapped by raccoon paws would feel like.

When she pulls her hands away, she gasps like she knows how badly she fucked up. Every ounce of emotion vanishes from my body. I turn into a cold, drunken, unfeeling version of myself.

"GET ON THE BED."

"I didn't mean that," Juliette says quickly. Her chest heaves anxiously. Yeah, you fucked up big time, didn't you...

"I think you did. Now get on the bed."

"You're not–

"Get on the fucking bed, Juliette."

HER EYES WELL WITH TEARS. "NO."

"IS THIS HOW YOU REPAY ME?"

"I never..."

"I'm done arguing with you," I growl at her. "Get your ass on the bed or I'll drag you there myself."

She whimpers and sits on the edge of the bed naked, her light brown thighs pressed together. Everything about this woman's naked body is sheer perfection. The second I laid eyes on her, I developed a deep, dark and powerful obsession with her.

The hold she had on me was immediate. I knew I would kill for her the second I saw her. It helps that she has the perfect body and lips that look goddamn immaculate wrapped around my cock.

THE ONLY UNFORTUNATE thing about Juliette is that her voluptuous physique and dark alluring skin comes with a smart ass mouth that constantly tempts me to beat her into submission.

I told myself I would never hurt a woman like that... turn her into a shell of herself... but Juliette tests every ounce of my patience.

IT'S TOO late for Juliette's act of submission via her averted gaze.

"WHAT DID I say would happen if you hit me again?"
She doesn't answer. She knows how much that shit pisses me off.
"Answer me, Juliette."
"I can't say anything good right now," Juliette says.
"You could answer my question."

THERE SHE IS. Juliette, the woman who doesn't know when to test me and when to sit her ass down and obey.

"I SAID I would spank your ass so hard I would turn your pretty light brown skin fifteen shades of purple. Since I plan on leaving your ass here for three days, I don't give a damn if you can't walk. So turn around."

"I'M NOT DOING THAT."

I GRAB her arm and turn her around as screams and makes every effort to fight me off. Juliette's butt is large enough to easily throw off her center of gravity and despite her kicking, screaming, hollering, and calling me several anti-white racial slurs, I get her pinned to the bed ass up where I can deliver the spanking she deserves.

"You are my woman," I whisper, rubbing my hand over the soft flesh of Juliette's ass cheek. "I don't care if you think you can handle yourself out there alone. I will *never* let you be alone."

She shudders and opens her mouth to say something, but I hit her ass so hard that she lets out a loud scream instead. Her ass jiggles and a reddish-brown handprint forms right where I hit her. She's sensitive from the first time and given her attitude, Juliette hasn't gone too many days in a row without getting a hard ass spanking.

"I WISH one was enough to learn your lesson," I mutter. "But we both know that ain't the truth. You, Juliette Rawlings, have earned nine more lashes on your pretty black ass..."

🌾

THE END

Click here to order Book #2
https://bit.ly/barbarians2

Character Glossary

The Four Families

The Sinclairs
The Shaws
The Blackwoods
The Hollingsworths

The Shaw Family

Harlan Shaw, HARLEY, Club President – married to Renée, who he had two daughters with until Renée died in 1994. Harlan's daughters from his first marriage are Kelsey and Tylee. Harlan remarried Deborah Hollingsworth, who became his old lady and they had four children together: Ethan, Wyatt, Stacy, & Owen.

Renée Shaw, Harley's first old lady – Tylee & Kelsey's mother who died in 1994.

Deborah Hollingsworth Shaw, Harley's Old Lady – married to Harlan Shaw. She had two children with Harley while he was married to Renée Shaw (Ethan and Wyatt). After Renée's passing, Deborah and Harley married.

Tylee Shaw Sinclair, b. 1990 – Harlan and Renée's daughter. Works for the family, fell in love with Isaac Sinclair.

Kelsey Shaw, b. 1993 – Harlan and Renée's daughter. She works for the club and lives on her own in a small trailer ten miles off Route 66 in a small Missouri town.

Ethan Shaw, BEAR, b. 1989, Officer – Harley's eldest son. The angry one.

Wyatt Shaw, SOUTHPAW, b. 1991, Jr. Officer – Harley's second son, ready to make Anna his old lady.

Owen Shaw, SCRAP, b. 1996, Officer – Harley's youngest son. The patient one.

Stacy Shaw, b. 2000 – The youngest of the Shaw daughters, she still lives with Deborah Hollingsworth.

Claude Shaw, ROTTIE, *club member* – Harley's brother.

Michael Shaw, KEY, *club member* – Harley's brother.

The Sinclair Family

Randall Sinclair, RANDY, Club Vice President, b. 1956 – Club Vice President and patriarch of the Sinclair family. He is Harley's best friend who served in Afghanistan in 1991. He had twin boys, Ryder and Hunter after his service in the first Gulf War. He served along with Lyle Blackwood.

Karen H. Sinclair, b. 1979 – Karen Hollingsworth married Randy when they were very young and she had twin boys after his service in the first Gulf War.

The twins...

Ryder Sinclair, STEEL, Officer, b. 1992 – Hawk's twin brother is currently serving time in *Lansing Correctional Facility* in Kansas.

Hunter Sinclair, HAWK, Jr. Officer, b. 1992 – main character of *Biker's Servant,* Wyatt's best friend from high school and his right hand man. He possibly has a problem with alcohol.

Barrett Sinclair, BENCH, Officer, b. 1967 – Randall's brother and fellow club member. He has one divorce under his belt from Selma Sinclair, but remains in a contentious marriage with his second wife, Caitlin Sinclair.

Selma Sinclair, b. 1969 – divorced from Barrett Sinclair. Isaac Sinclair's mother. Tylee's mother-in-law (who hates Tylee's red hair). She was Barrett's high school sweetheart and remains bitter about their divorce. She hates Caitlin for stealing her man.

Isaac Sinclair, GHOST, b. 1986 – married to Tylee Shaw Sinclair.

Caitlin Sinclair, Barrett's old lady, b. 1975 – Magnum's mother and Barrett's old lady and current wife. He marries Caitlin after divorcing Selma when Isaac was 10-years-old.

Magnum Sinclair, CONDOM, Officer, b. 1992 – Caitlin and Barrett's son. Hawk's cousin. He owns an apartment building in Santa Fe.

The Blackwood Family

Lyle Blackwood, DOC, Enforcer, b. 1958 – Religious Gulf War veteran who distrusts Wyatt Shaw.

Brexlynn Shaw Blackwood, Doc's old lady, b. 1968 – Claude Shaw's sister, Harley's cousin. She is bitter and doesn't like Harley very much. Religious. She is currently in prison for conspiracy to commit murder.

The twins

Jairus Blackwood, BISHOP, Officer b. 1992

Jotham Blackwood, PINS, Officer b. 1992

The other siblings

Gideon Blackwood, REAPER, Jr. Officer, b. 1994 – Religious and violent contender for the throne of the Rebel Barbarians motorcycle club. Ex army ranger.

Tobias Blackwood, PRIEST, Officer b. 2000

Ruth Blackwood, b. 2006

Doc's nephew... adopted into the family

Ruger Blackwood, BUCKY, new member, b. 2004 – Lyle's nephew. Loyal to him. Collects hunting knives. Socially awkward.

The Hollingsworth Family

The Hollingsworth family extends across all of Route 66 but the Hollingsworth family home sits in Lubbock, TX. Due to extensive real estate dealings, several members of the Hollingsworth family own property at the end of the old Route 66 highway in Santa Monica, California.

When it's time for their story, you will learn more. Consider the tall, strapping red-heads to be shrouded in mystery, obsessed with money, and hell-raisers like the other Barbarians.

Don Hollingsworth, Treasurer, b.

Annabel Hollingsworth, b.

Tanner Hollingsworth, b.

Afterword

Thank you for reading Anna & Wyatt's story.

I can't wait to share what comes next for the Rebel Barbarians.

The next book will be about Hunter 'Hawk' Sinclair and Juliette Rawlings – a story teased in this book.

I put this note at the end of this book because I plan to discuss the book with some spoilers.

Anna and Wyatt's story has a familiar start for readers who enjoy my enemies-to-lovers dark romance books... I don't know what it is about the public smutty scenes, confined spaces and the eroticism of making love to a stranger that help me set these dark but spicy scenes.

If you enjoyed how Anna and Wyatt made their baby, consider reading *Long Island Executioner* or *Pretty Little Monster...*

Inspiration for Anna's *name* did come from a Patreon subscriber, but like all my characters, I conjured Anna out of thin air. Her main connection to someone "real" is that I wanted to write a character who worked as a nurse to honor a friend of mine who has been a source of realness and support to me through this winter and who has always supported my writing.

I had Wyatt's character in my mind from the summer of 2023. I knew most of how I wanted him to behave and what type of rough af alpha male I needed him to be in the bedroom...but I didn't make Wyatt a gambler until October/November of 2023.

He turned out a little more gentle than I expected by my standards, but if you are familiar with my books, you know that the 'leader' of the series tends to be the most normal of the bunch. We are about to get into bed with some unhinged bikers in the gang as the situation spirals out of control.

I need you to dip your toes in and get comfortable in the hot and sweaty mess before we get even more unhinged.

You will meet several of the characters in this book again in the second book and in the other books in the series. I have so much more planned for the barbarians as long as you are ready to support the books.

Hawk's book will have a **plus sized female lead,** plenty of dark romance themes and the scenes they have in this book will be more detailed (with additional perspectives.) I couldn't announce this in the beginning, so pardon the author's note at the end.

The next chapters will be live on Patreon first.

Click here to learn more about my behind the scenes community: www.patreon.com/jamilajasper

I cannot thank you enough for being there on my journey.

If you made it to the end of this author's note especially, double thank you.

I hope the wait for the next book doesn't kill you.

Gratefully yours,

Jamila

ABOUT JAMILA JASPER

The hotter and darker the romance, the better.

That's the Jamila Jasper promise.

If you enjoy sizzling multicultural romance stories that dare to *go there* you'll enjoy any Jamila Jasper title you pick up.

Open-minded readers who appreciate **shamelessly sexy romance novels** featuring black women of all shapes and sizes paired with smokin' hot white men are welcome.

Sign up for her e-mail list here to receive one of these FREE hot stories, exclusive offers and an update of Jamila's publication schedule:
bit.ly/jamilajasperromance

Get text message updates on new books:
https://slkt.io/gxzM

Extremely Important Links

JAMILA
JASPER

Diverse Romance For Black Women

More Jamila Jasper Romance

Pick your poison…

Delicious interracial romance novels for all tastes. Long novels, short stories, audiobooks and more.

Hit the link to experience my full catalog.

FULL CATALOG BY JAMILA JASPER:

https://linktr.ee/JamilaJasper

Mafia Playmate (PREVIEW)

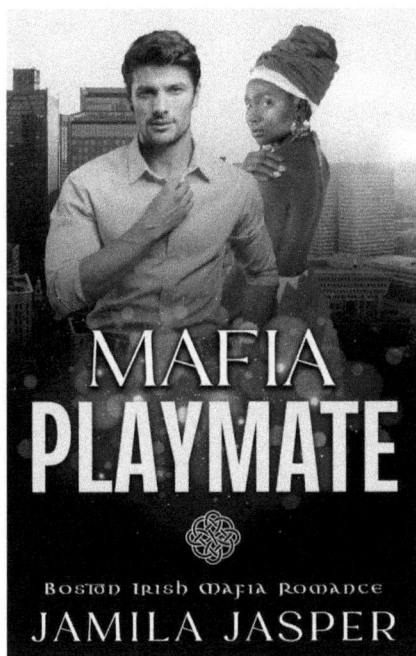

https://bit.ly/bostonirishmafia1

BOSTON IRISH MAFIA ROMANCE SERIES

Mafia Playmate

Mafia Property

Mafia Surrogate

Mafia Possession

Mafia Stalker

Click here for the complete collection:

www.jamilajasperromance.com/catalog

Content Awareness

Read this passage if you require content warnings for sensitive material. I do not give detailed content warnings that will spoil the plot, but be aware of this note.

This is a mafia romance story with dark themes including potentially triggering content of **all** varieties, violence, frank discussions and language surrounding bedroom scenes and race.

All characters in this story are 18+

Sensitive readers, be cautioned about some of the detailed romantic material in this dark but ***extremely hot romance novel.***

DESCRIPTION

A large pink box arrives on Aiden's doorstep with a woman inside. His mail-order bride arrives in her birthday suit and tied up in knots with a pretty pink silk ribbon.

Aiden never requested a dark-skinned beauty…
His family would never approve of such an impure connection.

Who is this woman? What does she want?
A note in the box reveals the truth…
The woman in the box - *Valentina* - is a gift from an anonymous sender who wants something dark and twisted in return.

CHAPTER ONE
AIDEN

You have one job in the Murray family. You grow up, you get your marks, you listen to Pa, you marry a nice Irish girl, preferably a blond or a redhead with lighter features.
You do what Padraig Murray asks.
You pray everyday and you keep your rosary wrapped in your pocket.
You stay loyal. You keep our bloodline strong.

Pa demands a meeting with me now that I'm back in the city. He claims it's important, but it can't be that important if he wants to meet me during the Red Sox game. It feels good to be home. There's something special about Boston, but maybe that's just it – paradise is wherever our family is.

After Pa, I'll go home and see Roscoe, my Rottweiler. Then get my shit together and call my younger brother Darragh to check in on his training and find out if Rian's around. Over the weekend, I'll head to Leominster to visit Callum and then Sunday after church, stop by to see Ma and Odhran. I brought a gift home with me for

Tegan, Rian's daughter, and I can't wait to see my niece's face light up when I give it to her.

If there's one thing I don't miss about being home, it's a never ending list of shit to do.

I meet my father at our usual casual meeting spot, Mulligan's, a place where we aren't afraid to celebrate Irish pride. A place where you can catch the Red Sox game and no one can catch your conversation. *It's as much home as anywhere else.*

I spot my father hunched over the bar from the street, his face illuminated by a warm orange bulb as he watches the pre-game announcer talk. I prefer football to baseball, but Pa bets on all their games, so he likes to keep his eye on the Red Sox each season.

When Pa calls, you answer, and he's desperate to know about the affair with the Italians – what the fuck happened, have I found the renegade cousins who pissed off the Italians, and whether I've killed them yet. *I haven't.*

It's all bad news and my ass is on the line if I don't find a way to sort out all the shit that happened in Long Island. At least we're guaranteed peace with the vicious Italians. *Those greaseballs aren't any better than the blacks. 'Trust 'em as far as you can throw them', Pa told me. But for now, we have peace and that's what matters. At least to me.*

I enter Mulligan's and the conversations fall to a hush. *Aiden Murray's back.* I clear my throat and the conversations continue. But there are more phones pulled out than before and two guys sitting in the back leave. I don't hate the reputation I have. Most of the bar fights I earned this cutthroat reputation in were Darragh's fault, but that doesn't change what people say about me.

Darragh, my younger brother, can still throw his weight around in the ring, but he got his practice here, in this fucking place. Our last fight here was over a girl. Darragh kicked some Puerto Rican's ass and a few of our boys jumped him outside... I don't know what happened to the guy after.

My father slides a twenty-dollar bill across the bar to the

bartender, Finnegan O'Malley, a one-eared ex-hitman, who in turn fills up two glass pints of amber Sam Adams. Pa's already several drinks ahead of me. *Great. The news can't be that bad then.*

I pull out a bar stool next to my father, who barely acknowledges me, although he must've caught me entering the bar through the reflection on the glass behind the bartender. He shoves one of the pints across the bar towards me. He knows I prefer Guinness, but I don't mind starting with this. I can see my dad's reflection in the glass. He looks older than I remember. He's pushing 70, so I shouldn't be surprised by the large streaks of gray through his slick hair which was once blond, but changed color throughout his life, settling on a dark chocolate brown, like Rian's.

I glance at the television to check the score, but the game hasn't even started yet. I can smell the alcohol coming off of him already.

"You can have a Guinness after you drink this," he says. "I heard you did good work with the Italians."

He sounds raspy, but calm. My tension dissipates. This is just a normal, father-son meeting. Nothing to worry about.

"I didn't find Eoin or Robert. Haven't heard fuck since they all screwed with Vicari," I say as I take a sip of my beer.

"Maybe the Italians killed them," he says. "They're a violent, vicious group of people."

"Yeah."

Like we're ones to talk. Pa's done with his Sam Adams already and waits patiently for me to catch up, as if I could catch up to a man who's been drinking for an hour. At forty, it's not so easy for me to keep up with long nights of drinking. I don't know how he does it.

He waits for me to have a few more sips, his eyes glued to the television. Chris Sale throws the first pitch. It doesn't go so well. My father glances down at his glass and sighs. "It's going to be a long night."

"That bad this season?" I grunt, glancing up at the Detroit batter sliding into second.

I've been too busy to keep up with baseball. My father grunts. Yeah, it has been that bad.

"Any other news?" I ask him, finishing off the Sam Adams. Dad grunts and snaps his fingers for the bartender, Finnegan. The buff, tattooed bartender hustles over as dad orders two Guinnesses without opening his mouth. Bad news if he's drinking Guinness.

"Cops got Rian last week. They're charging him with manslaughter."

Manslaughter?

"What did he do?"

"What the fuck do you think he did?" Dad responds calmly. "He killed somebody, they caught him. That boy's not careful enough and I have to pay to get his ass out of trouble. Maybe some prison time would do him good."

"That's what you said the first three times," I grunt. Sale throws a good pitch and my father's face visibly brightens.

"If it weren't for Tegan, I'd let him spend a few extra years behind bars," Dad confesses. "Your mother won't let me do that to his daughter."

"What's going to happen to her?"

"I don't know," my father says. "No one has seen the kid in a week."

"What?" I growl, sipping at my beer and hoping this is my father's idea of a joke since he sounds dangerously unconcerned.

"What do you mean no one's seen her? Is she with her ma?"

My father shrugs.

Rian's notoriously bad taste in women landed him with a child he should have never brought into the world. She's a sweet girl, but doomed by a mobster father and a whore mother.

Her ma doesn't live in Boston anymore. She wants nothing to do with Rian.

"Where does he say she is?"

"Last time he saw her was the night he got arrested," Pa says before taking a sip of his beer.

"What about the cops? Did they give her to his lawyer or something?"

I don't have a single paternal instinct in my body, but my mind courses with worry over Tegan, despite my father's calmness.

"She'll turn up," he says, pouring more alcohol down his throat.

Fuck, Rian. My brother must be an even worse parent than our father. His daughter's missing and he's behind bars and there's no one else to look for her except...

"I can find out where she is. Once I get Roscoe and take care of–

"It would serve him right if something happened to her," my father says coldly. "Her mother isn't Irish. He keeps fucking up. I'm tired of cleaning up his messes. Now *drink*. This is not why I asked you here."

I bristle at his comment, but it's just Padraig Murray. This is who he's always been and my brother should have had the good sense to keep his dick in his pants. I made it to forty without fathering bastards all over Boston. Rian should have been more careful. I drink a few more sips, but I can't let this go. *Who else will worry about the fucking kid if not me?*

"How the hell did Rian let this happen? Can I talk to him?"

"Best that none of us talk to him. The cops listen to everything. I can get messages into the prison and messages out, but I don't want you talking to him."

"Fine," I grunt, finishing off my first round of Guinness and ordering us another. I try to pay, but my father stops me and then finally answers my other question.

"Your idiot brother trusted a woman," he says. "He wants a mother for that little girl so badly, that he's willing to do anything. He's willing to kill for a woman who doesn't deserve him."

"I didn't know he had a woman," I grumble.

"*Had* is correct," Pa says. "She's dead."

I wish I could tell you a chill ran through me, or I had some other human response to my father's announcement. I don't need a university degree to understand what he's implying. Rian had a woman, she got him locked up, so my father had her killed.

"Will that affect his case?"

"No," Pa says. "It was very clean."

"Who?"

"None of your business, Aiden. You worry about your shit, I'll worry about your brother."

I want to feel sorry for Rian, but he deserves it for crossing our father. This is what happens when he pisses off Padraig Murray. More problems for all of us.

"How much time is he facing?"

"Three years since he's been in jail before. I tried to get that stupid motherfucker to get his life together, but your brother just wants to be a fuck up."

"Who's the lawyer?"

"Someone from Nigel & Bancroft."

At least he isn't cheaping out like he did for Rian's first case. I don't want to push my father's buttons, and despite his outward calm, he must be furious at Rian for drawing more attention to us, but Rian has his uses.

"It's Rian," I remind him. "Crazy fucking Rian. We need him out soon. There are some jobs only Rian has the balls to handle."

Padraig snorts. "He takes after my father. Too proud and too violent for his own good."

We created the monster Rian Murray is. He's our responsibility.

"He needs another woman."

"He needs a woman who isn't a fucking spic," my father spits. "At least the child looks white."

"What about this previous woman? What'd she look like?"

"It doesn't matter," he grunts. "She's dead. Now drink. We have more important things to talk about than your idiot brother and his shitty taste in women."

I drink because Pa commands it. I do everything he commands

and have since I was a child. I have the burns and scars to remind me of what happens when you disobey my father. At first, I hated him for what he did to me, but to keep an organization like ours together, you need to inspire fear.

YOU HAVE to be cruel to survive – that's just how the world works. I can't let Tegan go. The second I see Darragh, I'll ask about her and track her down.

I DRINK SO I don't lose my temper. He doesn't give a fuck about Tegan. No one does. Maybe he's wrong and one of my sisters took her in. But who would do that? Evie's saddled with her drunkard husband and two unruly kids of her own – Katie and Patrick. Kiara's off at university and Maeve's sixteen, too young to have any involvement.

"I need to tell you something important," my father says somberly, as if there could be something more important than my missing niece right now. I'm burning with desire to leave, but if I get up without my father's dismissal, he'll hurt me. Or someone I care about. Not like there are many of those people yet. It's foolish to get close to people in this life.

"Then tell me."

If he notices my tightening tone, my father doesn't acknowledge it.

"There's a plot against my life. I don't know who. I don't know why but... there's someone out there trying to kill me," my father says, the faded tattoos on his knuckles even more wrinkled than I last remember. He's getting older, but aside from his physical appearance, he shows no signs of slowing down. If anything, he's desperate to prove himself more. If he wasn't ordering more killings than necessary, maybe Rian wouldn't be locked up.

I don't want to dismiss his concerns as paranoid, but he's the leader of our family. There's always a plot against his life. It comes with the territory. My father doesn't have to worry because he has us. *Family.*

"Fuck that," I grunt. "No one would be stupid enough to try to kill you. April 2013, four days after the bombing. An entire decade ago. That's the last time anyone tried."

I was thirty back then, old enough to be the one who ended that war before it started. Back then, we only killed when necessary. I got five tattoos that year, one for each kill. Each a painful release, each representing a necessary act to keep my family safe.

My father smirks and keeps drinking. He shrugs. "That's what I thought. But I'm serious. This time is different. This time the bastards might just get me. I'm getting old, Aiden. Most guys in our line of work don't make it this far."

"What happened?" I grunt, urging my increasingly drunken father to get to the point. His cheeks blaze tomato red with alcohol and his blue eyes swim with tears, again brought on by drinking rather than any emotion. He grunts and knocks his biggest gold ring against the bar's surface contemplatively.

If anyone tried to kill him, surely Darragh would have mentioned it. He's responsible for keeping our father alive.

"I feel it in my bones," Pa replies. "Someone wants to destroy our family."

"Yes," I grumble. "Our cousins. But they're gone and if they were anywhere near this city, we would have heard about it."

"I don't know. Something big is coming for us. I feel it."

"We can make decisions based on feelings now?"

"Cut the shit, kid. You know my instincts are good because you're like me. You can smell shit before it hits the toilet bowl."

"I'm home. If anyone tries to kill you, they'll have to get through me, Darragh, and Callum."

My father smirks. "My boys. I'm proud of all of you. Except Rian. He's a piece of shit."

Ah, Padraig. Honest as fuck, especially when he's drunk.

He might not be proud of Rian, but he still loves my brother enough to spring for decent lawyers and to make sure Tegan goes to the best day school in Boston. Once she's old enough, she'll go to Milton or Dana Hall, or another nice private school where she can meet someone to untarnish her sullied blood, that is as long as I can find her. If Rian's behind bars, she could be anywhere. Hopefully not with her mom's people.

She belongs with us, even if Rian made mistakes. She looks like us and that's good enough to cover up his shameful behavior. I don't know what Rian was thinking with that Puerto Rican chick. Tegan's mother was low class.

Let's hope my brother's behavior doesn't come back to haunt all of us. Let's hope his daughter is safe, sound asleep somewhere and protected.

"Thanks, Pa," I mutter, uncomfortable with even this much emotional closeness between us. I love my father, but trusting him too much is dangerous. Rian found out the hard way that it isn't worth it to defy our family beliefs, and it definitely isn't fucking worth it to screw around with the wrong women.

"And Aiden? I need you to hurry the fuck up and find a wife. I'm getting old and I want to retire, but I need a family man to lead this family. You're the oldest. Why the fuck can't you keep a woman? Do I have to send you back to Galway?"

He wants a real answer.

"Not interested in chasing after girls, dad. All they want to do is take your money and ask where the fuck you're going. I've had enough."

"That old dog won't take care of you when you get old."

"Neither will some Boston snob who could take my ass to the cleaners in a divorce."

He laughs, which is the best reaction I can hope for. He quickly moves along to talking about the game and his plans for the business, and then asks me questions about Long Island. They're a mess out there, but doing better under John Vicari's leadership. We're developing a few buildings together and are prepared to make a lot of money in the real estate game. John does cleaner business than his father. Too bad the old man died of a heart attack... that's the word anyway.

"I need you to find a nice girl," my father reminds me once he's almost blackout drunk. He can barely keep his head up. *Great.* I'm not dragging his ass outta here tonight. If he wants to get so wasted he can't sit up straight, I'll leave him for Finnegan.

"We have this conversation every time we talk."

"This time, I'm serious. I want to retire. I don't want you bringing home no spics either like the Duffy boys."

"Fuck's sake, Pa. You can't talk like that around here anymore."

"I can say whatever the fuck I want. I want Irish children. Irish fucking children and I need you to have a wife so I can retire."

"Retire any old fucking day you want," I growl. "It'll be good for you to stop worrying about who I fuck or marry or the fate of the fucking family."

"The fate of the family matters," he says, taking another sip of his newest glass of beer before rubbing condensation off the sides with his napkin.

"I'm too old to have kids," I growl. "I'm too old to get tied down. You and mom were lucky you even found each other."

That's bullshit and we both know it. They stay together because they're Catholic, because back in the eighties, my dad killed someone for her father and won my mother like a prize. He also put a baby in her quickly and then kept her pregnant. There's nothing romantic about their love story or marriage in the Murray family.

"If you can't find a girl, I'll find one."

"The last girl you found me was a crazy fucking redhead who wanted to bring Roscoe Jr. into the bedroom. No thanks."

My father shrugs. "She was white. Do you know how hard it is to find a white girl around here who hasn't been fucking ruined by some fucking Puerto Rican or black guy?"

"What do you want from me, Pa?"

I know what I want. I want an end to this conversation, and I want my father to give me a fucking break about women and dating. All the Irish and Catholic women in Boston know to stay away from us, and the ones who don't learn their lesson pretty fucking quickly.

"Find a nice white girl with big tits and blond hair and get her pregnant so I know you're fucking serious about family. That's what I want."

"Give me time."

He continues, getting to what I suspect was the original point he wanted to make before the liquor got to him. "And get your ass to the site in Back Bay tomorrow bright and early."

"Why?"

This is the first I'm hearing about something wrong at the Back Bay construction site. I know something's wrong because my father doesn't do anything bright and early unless there's a problem to solve.

"You'll find out tomorrow. You just got back. Go home. Pet the dog. Your mom's tired of walking that big fuck. He nearly knocked her over near Harvard Square."

"How is mom?"

"Pissed off."

"Why?"

"Eh. Upset about another woman. It's nothing."

It's nothing. Dad just got his second mistress pregnant and even if we all know about it, we're all supposed to pretend it's no big deal that our elderly father knocked up a Irish teenager who he supposedly hired to clean the construction company office.

I hate how he treats our mother. What's the point of having a family or a woman if you hurt her? There's no getting through to him, but I have to try for my mother's sake.

"You treat her better, pa. Seriously. She needs you."

He grunts. "Get your ass home kid and get a white girl pregnant."

"Thanks, dad."

"If you can't find one, I'll find a good Irish girl who needs a green card and bring her over to you!"

My father is the last person I want picking my romantic partners. I mutter something to him about cutting back on liquor, then I pat my father on the back and leave the bar. This is the closest we've felt in years, but there's still a wall between us and there always will be. I felt closer to him when I was younger, when it was easier for me to justify the life I led. I know I'm a screw up, I know I don't belong anywhere near a woman or a family or any of the fucking things my father wants from me.

He knows it's wrong to bring a kid into this life, but he did it anyway. He knows that we're villains, but he doesn't care. Fuck, I don't care either, I suppose. I'd just rather not ruin a perfectly good woman.

I drive out of the city listening to rock classics on the radio. Just as I turn down my street – I live at the end of a cul-de-sac – I notice the large box on my front step. There are only five large houses at the end of this cul-de-sac, all of us with wide open well-maintained lawns around traditional New England colonial houses.

The box on my front step is fucking enormous – and I don't remember ordering anything for delivery. My hand moves swiftly to the pistol under my seat. I feel no fear as I reach for the gun and slip a mag out of my pocket. I feel ready.

Leaving the city for any amount of time always carries a risk, especially since I didn't exactly leave the place with a house sitter. The last time my teen brother Odhran house-sat, he trashed the place and had a threesome in my bed. I hop out of my black GMC Sierra with the gun under my coat and approach the box slowly, glancing furtively over my shoulder for anyone who might have eyes on me.

The box has holes in it. It's large. Pink. Wrapped in a bow. I reach for the bottom of the box and try to lift it. *Fuck.* It's heavy. I drop the box and I swear I hear a sound coming from inside it. *Is that possible?* I try to peek through the holes but it's too fucking dark and something's telling me opening this box will be a shitshow. It has to weigh about a hundred pounds. Maybe more. I'm no weakling, but it still takes a measure of back strength to lift a box that fucking heavy.

I open my front door and greet Roscoe Jr., my rottweiler, as he bounds towards the door to greet me. His coat looks shiny, the nub of his docked tail wags back and forth. Pa's choice, not mine. He runs up to the box and sniffs at it a bit.

There's definitely something in there and it gets his attention because Roscoe utters a low bark.

"Roscoe, go lie down."

Once he heads off to his bed, I throw my doors open wider and eye the giant box to decide how to carry the fuckin' thing. I would call Rian if his stupid ass wasn't in jail. I could call Callum, but he's still hung up on some fucking girl and won't answer my calls because I won't sugarcoat my opinion of him. Then there's Darragh... He's probably twice as drunk as Padraig. Not a good option either.

I'll have to carry the box myself. I stretch a little and then grab the edges of the box and grunt as I carry it a few feet inside my doorway. I set the box down more gently. *Is there something alive in there?* If it were an animal, I suspect Roscoe would be barking from his spot in the house, but he's laying down as I commanded, gazing at me curiously and wagging his tail.

He's probably wondering why I'm not taking him for a walk since I'm back. *At least he didn't bite the sitter this time.* I close my front doors and then search for an opening on the giant pink box. Finding none, I start with the ribbon and peel it away. The box comes up to my waist. It's *enormous.*

If it didn't weigh a hundred fucking pounds, I would assume it's a novelty gift or something extra special from one of my brothers. Which of my piece of shit brothers would get me a welcome home gift? It's not like either of them are here with a six pack of Guinness right now...

I peel the top of the box open and there's another box inside it, also pink. I open the second box and stumble backwards as I expose the contents. I don't mean to act like a fucking idiot, but I nearly fall over, because this is the last thing I expected to find on my doorstep. I just got back to Boston... How long has that box been out there?

HOLY FUCK, why isn't she screaming?

I GAIN control of myself and approach the box again, heart pounding because my second assumption is that the human female in the box might be dead and that's the reason she hasn't made a sound. The sick thought twists my stomach into an unyielding knot.

I slowly approach the box again, ignoring my heavy breathing, focusing instead on taking in as much information as possible about the situation. I move the flaps of the box open and stare at the woman's face.. Suddenly, her eyes snap open before swiveling around and looking me directly in the eye..

Holy fuck, this woman is alive.

"What the fuck is this?" I grunt to myself. Not to myself. I'm not alone. I dry swallow and run my fingers through my hair. She's black. Someone tied up a black woman in a pink ribbon, wrapped her up like a gift and put her in a box on my doorstep. This has to be a sick joke.

I'm almost too scared to reach into the box and touch her, but I have to touch her to get her out of the fucking box. Whoever this woman is, she ran into the wrong fucking people and ended up in the wrong living room.

I have tattoos and vows of loyalty to prove how I feel about people like her. "Don't worry. I'll get you out of there."

I don't know why I'm bothering with comfort. I reach into the box and grab her at the base of her spine before hoisting her out of the box and gently setting her on the ground. My stomach lurches. This is some sick, twisted shit. Whoever did this to her stripped this woman naked, bared every inch of her dark skin, the color of Arabica coffee, and wrapped her in a pink ribbon, contorting her limbs and running the ribbon over her bare breasts, between her thighs and in loops around her body so she's wrapped up like a chocolate present.

My body has an unconscious, primal reaction. I could unwrap her like the present she's been wrapped up to be, but I need answers quickly.

She has a gag in her mouth, a round white ball that keeps her lips spread open and hooks at the back. Her eyes roam around the room in terror as I reach into my pocket for my knife. I've killed people with this knife and now I'm using it to save someone.

Her skin prickles with goosebumps as I touch her. I apologize, but I need to brace myself against her to get her free. I press the serrated edge to the ribbon and make the first cut.

I cut her legs free. She groans as her legs fall in a curled heap. She cries out and tries to jerk them again, but however long she's been in that position was far too long for her to have full control of her legs and hips.

"Don't move," I remind her. I touch her skin again and my stomach lurches. Fuck, her skin is so dark. I look pale as fuck touching her and even putting my hands on her drives guilt through me. She's black. She's the wrong kind of person. I run my tongue piercing over my lower lip as I focus on all the parts of the ribbon I have to cut free.

When I have her limbs mostly free, she rolls onto her side, groaning in pain as her arms and legs curl in an awkward and splayed mess next to her. Even her wrists bend at an unnatural angle. I know she's alive, but the woman still looks dead.

I swallow slowly. What the absolute fuck is this?

"I'll take the gag out, but you can't spit or bite or do anything of that nature. Do you understand?"

She stares at me, but she can't say anything. I approach her mouth slowly and reach around her to find the clasp of her ball gag.

I unhook it and take it out of her mouth. She groans again and winces in visible pain as she attempts to close her jaw. She slowly moves her hand to her face and rubs her cheek, groaning.

I crouch next to her, staring at her in awe, knowing that I shouldn't but am completely incapable of taking my eyes off the naked woman in front of me. If her nudity makes her uncomfortable, that hasn't sunk in yet. My cock stiffens inappropriately in my pants and I clasp my hands in front of my dick, refusing to take my eyes off her.

Her breasts are small, but they protrude forward in tiny, dark orbs with nipples that are even darker than her extremely dark skin. Holy fuck, I didn't know nipples came that dark. My eyes widen inappropriately and I pray she doesn't notice my leering. Who sent this woman to me and what exactly did they send her for?

Christ, Aiden. Get a grip. You're staring at her crotch now and it's obvious.

She's waxed completely and my gaze snaps to the bare, dark brown lips. I wonder what this strange woman conceals between those lower lips and what color her flesh is between those thin, toned legs. I clear my throat.

"Who are you?"

"Read the card with the gift," she manages to say, with a raspy voice and an accent I can't place.

"I asked you a question."

"Read the card with the gift," she repeats.

I raise an eyebrow and walk towards the box. There's a large card at the bottom, about 8 x 10 inches, printed on thick paper. I pull it out of the box and read the note, muttering it out loud to myself. *What the fuck is this?*

Dear Mr. Murray,

We hope you enjoy your object. Your task is simple.

Use the object wisely. Have unprotected sex with the object and film a 4K quality video.

Compress the video file and send it to the email address below.

The object may be initially unwilling but both of you will face strong motivation to comply. The object understands that documentation of her existence belongs to us and if she fails to comply enthusiastically, we will destroy her identity.

If we do not receive the video within one week of today's date, you will both lose what's most important to you.

Tegan Murray counts on you to succeed. We have possession of the girl and you would be wise to listen to our orders if you or your family want to see her safe.

Do not call Padraig Murray. Do not call anyone else, or you will both suffer.

It takes less than a second to fire a bullet.

You must comply. When you're finished with said object, it is yours to keep.

Sincerely,

Your Benefactors

OA

"WHAT IS THIS SICK SHIT?" I growl, throwing the card back into the box, causing the woman still kneeling on the ground to flinch. My heart thuds.

These people have Tegan and this woman might know where she is and who they are. I won't be a part of this sick fucking game.

CHAPTER TWO
VALENTINA

"You have to do what they say," I say to him. "*Please.*"

It's not what I want to say, but these were my instructions if I wanted to survive. I never saw the people who put me in the box, but I heard their instructions and their threats clearly.

My throat burns raw as I attempt to plead with the man in front of me, hoping that he'll spare me. *He's involved with the people who took you. He's dangerous.*

The more I talk, the quicker he'll piece the truth about me together. I don't want this man to know *anything* about me. My voice. It's bad enough that he's seeing me naked. It's bad enough that he's about to take a part of me that I never wanted to give to strangers, that I always wanted to *mean* something.

I want to keep a piece of myself to myself. I've never had that privilege before. I won't have it tonight. He's an utter stranger to me and a terrifying one at that.

The gigantic blond man glowers at me, his blue eyes enough to melt me in place. He's 6'4", his hair looks slightly unkempt. Black ink swirls around his pale skin in a variety of Celtic knots, cursive

Bible verses and symbols that I don't understand. *Lots of tattoos. He must be a gangster. Something like that.*

I hate that I'm naked, but I'm glad that I'm free. There was nothing but pain in that box. The drugs helped at first, but they didn't last thirty-six hours. That's how long it took to get here from Idaho. Technically, the drive takes twenty-five hours, but I tried to measure time – I have a good sense of it because of the piano – and I know they took thirty six.

There's no getting out of this. Maybe this one won't be as wicked as the first.

"Who are you?" the man growls at me. "Who did this and what the fuck do you have to do with this?"

His anger sends a surge of terror through me as his face reddens with frustration. He has absolute control over this situation and he knows it. I can't afford to freeze and make it worse by proving to him what he already knows – I'm vulnerable, weak and utterly at his mercy.

I position myself to cover my breasts as much as possible as well as my *other* parts, but he's already seen every bit of me. Modesty is entirely pointless.

"My name is Valentina," I rasp out, my voice getting stronger as I tell him my name.

"Is that your real name?" he growls, stepping forward and towering over me.

I'll never know if I had another name. I've been called Valentina since I was a little girl. Sometimes Val, but never anything else. I must've had a life before, but I don't remember any of it. All I remember is Pulsifer. He was my father, my abuser, my everything. I wouldn't call this freedom, but there's still a weight lifted because this is the closest I've ever come to leaving the governor's mansion.

The blond man is even taller than I thought he was. I'm more vulnerable naked and despite wanting to stand up for myself, I shrink back from him.

"Yes," I say as firmly as I can manage.

"Who sent you? Because I'll be damned if I screw around with a n–"

He stops himself, but my skin feels a flush of outrage and humiliation as his lips hover over the n-word. I want to hit him, but I don't know what type of man my new master is yet. A racist. That part I understand. He's not the first racist I've had to deal with. He might be the richest though. *He lives in a mansion.*

"Who sent you?" He roars. His face reddens as he screams and his creepy blue eyes look bloodshot. I shouldn't cross him, but I stopped giving a fuck about what happens to me a long time ago. I've already experienced the worst.

"I don't know. All I know is they want you to do what's on that note."

I don't want that. I have to go through with it, but I definitely don't start off wanting that monster anywhere near me.

"No," he growls, his jaw tightening. "I... This is fucking ridiculous. Tell me who sent you, woman."

His anger mounts and my fear intensifies. I'm no stranger to racism, but for the word to nearly fly off the tip of his tongue like that. *How can someone who looks like that be so ugly inside?*

He reaches into his jacket and I know he's reaching for a gun before he pulls it out. The men who sent me here weren't any better than the man who received me as a gift. My throat tightens and I try not to lose control of my bladder as he pulls the pistol out of his jacket and points it straight at me.

Men are all the same and they're all violent disgusting pigs who will put a bullet in an innocent woman's head if she gets in their way. They'll use us up and spit us out and there isn't a man alive capable of real love...

"If you shoot me, you'll die," I state plainly, trying to sound like I have control of the situation. I'm not lying, but I'm also not stupid enough to mean that as a threat either. "And whoever you love enough for them to threaten will die too."

"I don't give a fuck," he snarls. "Who sent you?"

I don't believe that he doesn't care. I sense a crack in this man beneath his outrage. His anger cloaks his genuine concern. If he wanted to kill me, he would have done it already.

"Do I look like I was in control of the situation? You have their instructions. Are you going to do it or not?" I say to him sharply. Talking to him like this could be dangerous, but he doesn't react to my strengthening voice or sharp tone.

"Am I going to rape you?" He growls, lowering the gun. "Is that what you're fucking asking me?"

He has a thick accent which I can finally place. *Boston.* I'm in Boston, or close enough to Boston that men sound like Matt Damon in *Good Will Hunting.* I don't know anyone in Boston, but maybe that's for the best since I don't know any good people. Never have.

I don't respond to him. He reads the card to himself again and mutters a long string of curse words. I'm already naked and despite his apparent hesitation, the man hasn't offered me clothes. He doesn't know if he's going to do it yet, but I do.

HE'S GOING to have sex with me.

"YOU HAVE TO FOLLOW THE INSTRUCTIONS," I say to the terrifying blond man pleadingly. He still hasn't told me his name and I don't know if he will. He might worry I'll go to the police. "At least according to them." Hopefully he thinks of another solution since he's clearly some type of gangster.

I've been through enough shit to know that the police don't care about women like me. The police have *never* cared.

"This is a crock of shit," he hisses, spittle flying from his mouth as his face reddens with pure vitriol. "I have *never...*"

He glares at me like I'm responsible for this. Every inch of my body aches and I have little patience for this bastard acting like I'm the fucking problem.

"Never what?"

He glowers. "I've never been with... I don't... I don't fuck black women."

His voice drips with disgust, but I don't mind because I find this man's racism equally repulsive. He's more bothered by my race than the fact that I arrived on his doorstep naked, wrapped in ribbons, and sent to him in a box.

"You have to follow their instructions. I don't know what happens to you if you don't, but I know what happens to me."

I'll be lost to my past forever.

"Who fucking sent you?"

"I don't know."

I should have expected his next actions. He's a sicko, because the people who sent me only send gifts to sickos. My boss... My *old* boss was probably worse than this man. He was certainly much uglier, but all cruel men are the same.

He quickly racks a bullet in the chamber before re-leveling the gun to my face so I am forced to stare directly down the barrel.

"Kneel," he commands without wavering. I can see in his eyes that he's capable of shooting me. He runs his long pink tongue over his lips. He has a piercing through his tongue, a giant gold knob with a Celtic knot in the center. *What the fuck?*

My knees ache and I can't stop myself from groaning as I obey him. I have no choice but to listen to him despite the pain shooting through me. My stomach turns and if I'd eaten anything in the past 48 hours, it would've come up on this rich white man's hardwood floor.

My head lolls forward and I struggle not to cry out as more pain surges through my legs.

"Who sent you?"

"I don't know," I answer truthfully. If I had those answers, I would disappear in the middle of the night and find some way to get my real identity from the people who own me, or I suppose owned me before him.

"You must've come from somewhere," he says, his finger hovering near the trigger. It never occurred to me that he could do worse than hurt me, that he could kill me. *But he might. The men who did this to me never considered that.*

"My master sold me."

"What the fuck?" he snarls. "What the fuck does that mean?"

"I grew up... I grew up in a house with an older man. He sold me when I turned twenty-five."

"Sold you to who?"

"I never saw. I just know... I know what kind of company he keeps."

"Who was your master?"

"Governor of Idaho. Ezekiel Pulsipher," I respond as calmly as possible, even if just saying his name brings back flashes of horrific memories that still torment me every night. Who needs sleep, right?

"I don't know who the fuck that is," he spits. My chest swells with odd satisfaction that there's a corner of the universe not entirely ruled by Ezekiel.

In any other situation, his confusion would have been confusing. Old Zeke was a king in his universe and I wasn't the only girl in his harem. *He owned me since I was six years old. I don't want to tell this criminal about that, but I wouldn't feel sorry if this psychopath turned on my old master. I wouldn't feel sorry if these modern slave owners met this monster.*

I glare at him. I'm not here to give him an explanation. He's not the victim here, I am, and judging by his accent and other cues slowly coming into view, I'm on the other side of the country with no identification, no proof of who I am...Nobody knows I'm here.

It doesn't matter that I'm alone, I have to survive. I don't know what life will be like on this side of the country, but this is the best chance I've had to escape my entire life. *I can fool this white man. I know I can.*

"Why would someone do this?" He snarls.

"Maybe you're a criminal. Maybe they want revenge," I offer, perhaps pushing him too much with my attitude. His body tenses when I say the word *criminal*. Men. They think they're so careful with their emotions, but they get careless when they're underestimating you. Men get careless when they think they have the upper hand.

"I can't do what they want," he says, keeping the gun fixed at my head. This does little to warm me to him. "I can't screw... If my father found out... he would paint the sidewalk with your brains."

Charming. Now I have a definitive answer about the extent of this man's criminality.

He sets the gun on the table behind him and re-reads the card for the third time. His face turns several shades of red.

"This is sick," he spits, glowering at me with familiar, racially motivated revulsion. In most situations, I can't actually know if a man is racist. I have proof about this man.

"You have to. Whoever sent me paid a lot of money. You messed with powerful people," I tell him. "And they have someone you love and if you don't do this–

"I haven't messed with anyone," the man growls, interrupting me. "Get up."

I thought the pain shooting through me would knock me unconscious, but I had too much pride to ask him for relief. I slowly rise, my limbs barely cooperating. I look and feel ashy. I hate that I missed my routine. Spend a any amount of time in a box and you will miss the most damning prison you had before. My body still aches.

He looks me in the eye and I'm too scared not to meet this man's gaze. He's a predator and showing a predator fear gives them permission to pounce.

"My name is Aiden."

Aiden. I shouldn't care what his name is, but hearing it makes me consider him differently. The name sounds forceful and as rooted in his heritage as his Celtic tattoos.

"Great," I reply softly, unclear about what to do with the information.

He clears his throat and speaks again, "I thought you should know before we…"

"So you changed your mind?"

I shake before my body knows I'm shaking. This has happened before. Men have *taken* my body several times. Ezekiel *owned* me and believe me, he made good use of his property. Aiden. The name sounds Irish, but the man standing in front of me is All-American. He's 6'4" tall with *very* pale blond hair, but a thick crop of it. It's nice to see a man who isn't bald and who clearly works out. He's very muscular and the gun is out of the way, which sets me at ease.

"I don't know who sent you, woman. But I intend to find out. Seems like the best fuckin' way to do that is follow their instructions."

I knew it.

Aiden reaches for me and I fight my gut reaction to flinch. I don't want him to know how much I fear him. I want him to worry that I'll stab him in his sleep. I want him to feel like he's risking his life every time he rapes me.

Aiden puts his hand on my shoulder. I expected his touch to be rough, but it's very soft.

"Do they have anyone you love?"

I don't want to tell him, but his blue eyes harden and I sense that I'd better tell the truth if I want him to get this over with. His hand cups my shoulder too gently for me to describe. After the sharp angles and the pain of having my body squeezed into a box, his softness is surreal.

"I… I don't know."

"I don't want to hurt you. I won't rape you."

"If you don't have—

"I know," he growls. "But I won't hurt you. You have to consent. I…"

"I belong to you," I tell him, refusing to look away from him. I want him to gaze into my eyes and see a human being. A part of me desperately wants to shame him. It's hard to stare into those eyes and not feel something. He has intense and expressive eyes.

"No," he whispers. "You belong to yourself and once this is over, I'll have to let you go."

I fight back laughter. He won't let me go. I know men like Aiden better than he can even understand. I've lived my entire life in a world of pain and depravity.

"They'll hurt you if you don't do it. Surely my life isn't as important as yours."

"You're right," he growls. "But I've never fucked one of your kind and I don't intend to rape you either. That's not *my* thing."

He says it with the implication that he knows someone who prefers rape. And there he goes with the race talk again. *One of my kind...*

"You have to do it."

"Then agree to my terms."

"Terms."

I don't phrase it as a question and I don't want to sound too eager either.

"I'll give you money."

"So I won't be a slave, I'll be a prostitute."

His face reddens. "I'll send you away. You said they have someone you love. So you have a family?"

"No. I don't."

His hand drops from my shoulder and I glance down at his crotch. Despite Aiden's assurances that going through with this is the furthest thing from his mind, his dick bulges from his jeans. The bulge sends a deep surge of discomfort through me and my head swims.

There's no escape. All my smart-mouthed comments and my internal pleas that I might be able to survive this... I have to go through with it.

"What do you want, then?"

"A place to rest my head for a few nights. Time to get on my feet."

"Done."

He clears his throat. "I'll film it on my phone. I just... I've never..."

Aiden suddenly leans forward and kisses me. His lips surprise me with how soft they are when they first make contact. I want to scream, but it's a good kiss that draws me into Aiden's world instantly. His smell consumes me. His fingers claw at my cheeks as he holds me suddenly and keeps me still so he can kiss me.

Before Aiden, kisses felt like... cottage cheese. I want to push him away but the kiss is too fucking good for me to break away from it. I don't want to upset him, anyway. When he breaks away, his cheeks are red.

"I'm fucking dirty," he says and the revulsion in his voice tells me that he means it.

He doesn't look like he hated the kiss despite the words coming out of his mouth. He leans forward again and kisses me. This time, he spreads my lips apart and slides his tongue into my mouth. The piercing teases my tongue, sending a shiver straight through me. It's better than the first kiss and I kiss him back. He's the first man I've ever kissed back, the first man who has kissed me well enough for me to even try.

Men have done so many horrible things to me in my life and not one of them has kissed me properly. Aiden pulls away again and he pushes hair out of my face.

"We'll do this in my bedroom. Go upstairs. Third door on the left. Shower first."

Shower first. I don't like his tone, but I can't exactly blame him for it. I've been trapped in a box for several hours in a row and I probably smell exactly like it. At least he isn't pointing a gun at me anymore, and doesn't kiss me like a gross, perverted old man. He kisses me like... he would be a good lover.

That's another experience I've never had, another sad truth about my life that I never want to dwell on.

It hurts to walk up the stairs, but my body revels in the most freedom I've had in days. I almost want to race up the stairs to get to the bathroom quicker, but I walk patiently to the top and follow Aiden's instructions to find his bedroom. I can hear Aiden talking to his dog, telling him to stay on his bed for the next little while while he's busy. His house smells new, even if it's an old colonial that has probably been around since Boston's founding.

The bedroom is *extremely* neat. The floor smells clean and as my bare feet touch it, I feel like Aiden's right to wrinkle his nose at me. I'm the dirty one. *But he's sexually aggressive, and a racist one at that.* I can hear him following me up the stairs. He walks slowly, but he has a heavy gait. That may come in handy later if he tries to sneak into bed with me when I want to sleep. If I need to fight him off. That type of thing.

I had to fight off Pulsifer sometimes. That got easier as I got older. Aiden's a lot bigger than some decrepit governor of Idaho.

I find the bathroom door open and I walk inside. He has a claw-foot tub that could hold seven people. Judging by the perverts Pulsifer normally deals with, Aiden probably has had seven people in this tub at once. It sickens me to think what other secrets he could have. I flinch as he appears behind me. For a man with a heavy gait, he can apparently walk quietly when necessary.

"Get into the shower. Take your time. I'll set up the camera."

He sounds nervous, which makes me nervous. I imagine him being completely cruel. A monster would be crude and quick. Monsters *really* want you to cry. Aiden doesn't have any of those traits. He glances at my breasts, his cheeks redden and he swears under his breath.

"I can handle the shower," I say to him. He stares at me for a few seconds before leaving the doorway. I relish this alone time. I'm too grateful for my survival to think about escape. I wish I could tell you otherwise, but this is the truth. I grew up being passed around America's dirty underworld. Escape stopped being a real consideration when I turned eighteen and realized this was my destiny – permanent sexual slavery.

I clean myself as best as I can and try to ignore the numb feeling spreading over my body as I anticipate Aiden's actions. Most men are very rough. You can close your eyes and do your best to block out the pain, but nothing stops the dirty feeling of being powerless and having another person use you like an object.

Once I'm clean and have spent as much time in the shower as I think I can get away with, I step out and grab one of the insanely fluffy white towels hanging from the rack. As soon as I put it on my skin, the luxurious warmth spreads through me and the towel is so soft that I get a momentary feeling of safety.

I've carved out a life for myself despite my circumstances. I don't want anyone to feel sorry for me. I've learned how to play the piano. All the men who owned me had books that I enjoyed reading. I write poetry too, though none of it is good enough to share. Who would read my poems, anyway? Certainly not this blond hunk of muscle. His brain is probably the size of a pea.

He returns to the doorway and scowls as he watches me dry myself, reminding me that he's oversized and perpetually disgusted by me. I'm not shy about him seeing my body. He's seen it all anyway and he's going to have sex with me on camera, so there isn't a point in pretense.

"I took a vow that I would never touch a woman of another color," Aiden growls, sounding angry with me, like it's my fault that I'm black and he's racist.

I don't respond to him.

"I don't know if I can get hard," he says. "You might have to work to get me off."

I purse my lips. I have to ignore his suggestion that I'm too ugly to arouse him. White men. I try not to generalize them, but it doesn't help that all the men who have hurt me have had brilliant blue eyes, just like Aiden's. He has more of a pretty boy look, but he still has those cruel blue eyes.

"Have you done this before?"

"Yes."

I'll respond to his direct questions, but other than that, I have nothing to say. It's not like he cares.

"I'm sorry."

I give him a curious look, but I don't say anything. It's smarter not to say anything.

"If it helps, I'll make it good for you," he says in a gruff and gravely voice.

Don't bother. I want to say something cutting, but I don't want to anger him. Violence and sex are intertwined in the male brain, especially men like Aiden, a giant clearly used to getting what he wants.

This time, not responding to him provokes cheek redness. White men are always turning red when their feelings are about to take over. I brace myself for another racist comment.

"Whoever sent you must know my family. They must know about our beliefs and I want you to be clear about mine. I know my history and my heritage. I believe firmly in the superiority of my people over all others. This will not change because I stuck my cock in you," Aiden says, his voice trembling with rage as he stares at me.

I drop the towel. I'd rather him finish this than continue listening to his racist tirades.

I don't flinch, even if I want to. His words cut me deep, but Aiden, for all his complaints, still reacts like a man. His gaze drops decisively to my breasts and his teeth instinctively sink into his lower lip. His supposedly difficult to rouse cock bulges forward in his pants. *It doesn't look like he's struggling to get hard at all.*

He's even redder than before and his left hand clenches into an angry fist. I hope he's not the hitting sort. Those are always harder to deal with.

"Get on your knees," he commands, asserting power over me as my naked body renders him powerless to continue his racist little speech. I don't defy him. Despite my complete disgust with Aiden, pleasing him represents my best chance at survival, so I consent to his commands.

Any position on my knees still hurts. If Aiden cares, he doesn't show it. He walks towards me and crudely thrusts his hips into my face. His trousers smell like cigarettes and beer. His pants pockets bulge with car keys and a few other objects I can't identify. A simple, brown belt cinches over his dark blue denim.

His thighs are thick and muscular, barely held back by his pants. My heart quickens as he shifts his stance to his left side, cocking his hip. I glance down at his shoes. Brown boots. The tips are probably steel, so I don't want to do or say anything that could provoke him to kick me. I'm in enough pain as it is.

"The camera's over there," he says. "We'll have to move. I just wanted to see if you would obey me."

He leans forward and kisses the top of my head. *He's fucked up. It aches down here on my knees and I'll have to get up again.*

Aiden commands me to my feet and I follow him back out into his bedroom. He shows me where he has his cellphone set up on a bookshelf right in front of Sun Tzu's *The Art of War* and an extremely tattered copy of *The Holy Bible.*

"Kneel there," he commands, pointing to a spot in front of the lens. "It's already recording."

I obey him and quietly kneel before Aiden, facing away from the camera. He walks into the frame and commands me again, "Look up at me. I want to see your face."

When I gaze at him, he frowns with that mixture of revulsion and disapproval I already recognize as his gut reaction to me. Despite his cruel facial expression, he's still hard. I can still see the bulge in his jeans and it's terrifyingly huge the closer he gets to me.

"I don't cum from getting head," he says. "But I doubt you can arouse me without it. Take my dick out."

He's so full of shit. This man has the biggest erection I've ever seen. *He doubts I can arouse him? Something is making him unbelievably stiff and there's no one else in the room but me.*

Taking my time to remove his cock from his jeans is the only way I can postpone it. I've seen dicks before, and most of them are completely unpleasant to look at. Many of the ones I've seen are shorter than my pinky finger. The governor called some of the world's most depraved men his friends.

Aiden remains resolutely planted in place, glowering down at me as I unbuckle his belt and then slip the jean button through the loop before unzipping his pants. Because of his muscular butt, I can't rely on his jeans to fall off on their own. I hook my fingers through the back, making contact with Aiden's ass as I pull the jeans down. As I ease his jeans over his ass, I can't help but notice how deliciously round and muscular his ass feels. My hands fight the urge to cup his firm glutes and focus on the required task - getting his dick out of his jeans.

His breath catches as the jeans slide down, revealing an equally toned and muscular pair of thighs. He has tattoos everywhere, but the thigh tattoos are the most alarming. *Choose death.* He has a skull, several Celtic knots, Bible verses, and intricate designs woven together in a tapestry of a criminal's life.

A pair of crisp white boxer briefs cling to Aiden's thighs. More details of his bulging cock become apparent to me. The monster curves slightly in his briefs, the thick head oozing fluid that creates a wet spot where the tip touches the fabric.

The elastic waistband of his boxer briefs sticks to his hips and as I remove his underwear, I expose more tattoos and worse. He has scars and partially healed wounds all over his body, not to mention more muscles. He's the most muscular man I've ever seen this close and it feels wrong to notice.

All the men who fucked me were ugly and cruel with bodies and tongues that failed to arouse me. This man might be a sick mother-fucker but at least he's handsome. It's a small comfort, but I've never touched a man with such well-defined muscles, and the least I can do is appreciate it.

His cock springs free and juts forward with all the arousal Aiden claims he doesn't feel. His body doesn't lie. I haven't even touched him yet, but his cock already protrudes with pure enthusiasm. Once

I get the briefs over his ass, they remain taut and stretched around his thighs.

I can't help but stare at Aiden's dick. I've never seen one as big as this. His dick is nearly the length of my forearm and it's thick, with a dusky pink color. The tip reddens immensely, like he's sore from how hard he is. *His dick is so red.* Tufts of trimmed dirty blond hair cover the base of his cock and his shaft is so heavy, his erection leans to one side.

Clear fluid oozes from the tip.

"Don't just stare at it. The camera's rolling."

He probably doesn't mean to be insensitive. He's nervous about this too. It's not like he wants me in this position. I grasp the base of Aiden's cock to hold it up and he makes an uncomfortable grunting sound. He pulses with heat and saliva pools in the corners of my mouth against my will.

He's huge. I run my tongue over my lips so I can get them wet enough to stretch around Aiden. I lean forward and he grunts, nearly jerking back.

"I can't…"

I grasp his shaft tighter. It's too late to back out of this. Before Aiden can pull away from me and deny both of us a chance at survival and escape, I run my tongue over the head of his cock and lick up every drop of the clear fluid emerging from the tip. Aiden's next groan sounds more like an uncontrollable moan of pleasure.

Pleasing him is good. Pleasing him will bring this to a quicker end and I'll have a much greater chance at survival if I please him. The thought occurred to me that once my use has run out, he'll kill me, but I can't dwell on that. If pleasuring this man ensures my survival, it's what I'll do.

I tighten my lips around the smooth, bulging head of Aiden's big cock. He makes an ungodly pleasurable groan as I get his dick head wet with my spit and prepare myself to take the length of that enormous thing down my throat. If I gag, he could hurt me. I have to make him like it. We're being filmed, aren't we?

I tighten my lips more and get Aiden's dick even wetter. His next groan is even louder than the first and he touches the top of my head instinctively before remembering himself and jerking his hand away from me.

Men enjoy having lips around their cocks, but this man really likes it judging by the moans coming out of his mouth. I flatten my tongue along the underside of Aiden's shaft and then slide the full length of his dick into my mouth.

Tears prickle in the corners of my eyes as I stuff every inch of Aiden's dick in my mouth. He groans with pleasure again and I tighten my lips around the base of his cock as I feel the tip tickling the back of my throat, threatening my gag reflex to erupt. I squeeze my eyes shut and focus on breathing slowly through my nose.

As the tip of Aiden's cock touches the back of my throat, he moves his hips slowly with one thrust, and then he erupts. His climax happens so quickly that we're both equally surprised. The tears threatening to pierce the corners of my lids fall freely down my cheeks. I make a gagging sound as Aiden pumps thick ropes of cum into my throat.

The first warm gush fills my mouth and as Aiden tries to remove his cock from the sticky deposit of fluid between my lips, even more spills from the tip and he leaves my lips, face and mouth a mess of cum as he stumbles away and gains his composure after a few steps, making the conscious choice to put as much space between us as possible. There's surprise evident on his face, especially his eyes. *They're terrifying.*

I cough once and try to swallow the cum in my mouth, but that does nothing to remove the thick ropes coating my face and lips.

"Fuck," he says. "I've never…"

"I'm fine…" I whisper, leaning forward, trying to wipe the cum off my face and not wanting to look Aiden in the eye out of pure humiliation. I look ridiculous, I'm crying and there's cum all over me. I worry he won't go through with the instructions on the card. Then what? I'd rather stay here, thousands of miles away from the governor than to *ever* return. If Aiden doesn't finish this, I don't know who might come looking for him.

Aiden crosses the room, standing straight in front of me with his cock hanging limp. My body tenses with uncertainty. I can't predict how he'll react. He crouches in front of me, forcing me to gaze at him with concern. *Is he going to hit me?*

We're face to face and Aiden takes his finger, places it beneath my chin and turns my face so I'm staring him right in the eye. We're still on camera, but it doesn't feel like it. This moment is just for the two of us.

"That was the best head of my life," he whispers. "Once we make this fuck tape, I'll pay you back for that with my tongue. I owe you."

The touch of his finger and the intense blue gaze feel romantic, but Aiden's words emerge with a business tone. There's no romance here. I nod slowly and he rises to his feet.

"Get up," Aiden commands. "Get on the bed and face the camera."

He won't look at me as he commands me this time. I don't want him to look too closely. He's seen more than I would show a stranger, if I ever had control of my life enough to make the choice not to. I avoid gazing into the camera lens directly, but I obey Aiden and position myself in all fours on the bed.

I feel lewd on display like this. I tilt my head downward so my hair falls down over my shoulders to cover my breasts from the camera's view. It's not exactly modesty, but it's the closest I can manage given the circumstances.

I glance over at Aiden through my peripheral vision. He's hard again, with barely any time between this and his previous orgasm. The way he spoke about his ability to cum, I expected a man with some type of sexual dysfunction, not a seconds-long refractory period.

My throat tightens as I imagine my body stretching to accommodate that thing. I nearly choked on Aiden's dick in my mouth. That enormous thing could make me bleed if he isn't careful.

"Arch your back," Aiden whispers. "I want to see your ass."

It might be my imagination, but I swear his voice shakes like he believes the words emerging from his mouth represent the worst taboo. He approaches the bed slowly with that gigantic cock jutting from his hips.

"I've never filmed something like this," he murmurs as he draws closer. Aiden presses his large hand to my lower back tentatively. His hand is so fucking warm. His warmth spreads through me and I squeeze my thighs together to avoid any biological reactions to his touch.

I can't control my response to him. Aiden moves his hand down my lower back over my ass cheeks, his palm curving around my soft cheek. He makes a low growling sound in the back of his throat as he touches the inside of my thigh and discovers my wetness.

"That will make it much easier," he murmurs in response to my wetness. I think that'll be it, but Aiden slides his finger through my juices, swirling his index finger in slow circles through the juices on one thigh before moving to another. "But this is the only time. I don't fuck around with black women. Understood?"

I don't answer him. I just nod. If I'm going to have sex with this racist, I want to get it over with quickly. Judging from what happened before, maybe this won't last long. That's my best hope.

Click here to order Mafia Playmate:
https://bit.ly/bostonirishmafia1

Patreon

13 SEASONS OF SERIAL CHAPTERS

NEW preview chapters published WEEKLY on my Patreon.

Read all 6 seasons of *Unfuckable* (Ben & Libby's story)…

Unfuckable

PATREON

For a small monthly fee, you get exclusive access to over 375 chapters of my first completed bwwm dark and spicy serial romance, as well as the spin-off serial...

DESPICABLE

The second serial, despicable has 300 chapters available for all Patreon subscribers to access instantly and... we officially have a **third completed spin-off bwwm romance series.**

And yes you get access to all of this at the $5/month tier with more benefits at more pricey tiers.

The third serial is about Clover + Thomas. Thomas has a shocking connection to a character in the second serial and Clover is an all-new African American female lead.

POWERLESS

This series has three *very long* "seasons" of chapters, the length of five full-length novels all-together.

You will probably have over three months of binge-reading before catching up to current content, making this one of the most 'bang for your buck' author Patreon subscriptions out there.

Don't take my word for it.
Check the post history:
www.patreon.com/jamilajasper

PATREON HAS MORE THAN THE ONGOING SERIAL...

⚡ **INSTANT ACCESS** ⚡

- NEW merchandise tiers with **t-shirts, totes, mugs,** stickers and MORE!
- **FREE paperback** with all new tiers
- **FREE short story audiobooks** and audiobook samples when they're ready

- #FirstDraftLeaks of Prologues and first chapters **weeks** before I hit publish
- Behind the scenes notes
- Polls and story contribution
- Comments & LIVELY community discussion with likeminded interracial romance readers.

LEARN MORE ABOUT SUPPORTING A DIVERSE ROMANCE AUTHOR

www.patreon.com/jamilajasper

Thank You Kindly

Thank you to all my readers, new and old for your support with this new year.

I look forward to making 2023 an INCREDIBLE year for interracial romance novels. I want to thank you all for joining along on the journey.

www.patreon.com/jamilajasper

Thank you to my most supportive readers — my Patreon subscribers!:

Carla

Jonathan

Kelly

Jessica

Jasmine

DARSHELL

Dawn

Tiabuena3

Leigh

Yvonne

Ashlee

Crystal

Marshybabyyy

Shout

Quaniquequia

TK

Kayla

Shronda C.

Ma-Eyongerie

Kayla

Chantell

Kheiara

ophelia

Vickie

Cass

Kamil

Kaela

Love

Miryam

Charlene

Summer

Lola

Eryn

DD Davis

Symone

Deborah

Beatrice

Valescha

Khadija

makhalaab

Kaya

Glitter Garden

SavageSam

sybil arroyo

Ncsportsfan79

Jessica G.

Danielle

Yola

Joslin

Alexciz

Stacia

Ayanna

Asia

Hailey

Kaya

Nikki

Naomi O.

Jessica J

Chakiya

Noelle

kourtnee

Martha

Nikki Valentina

xjkpop

Valeria

BlkBae

SweetS

Msteeq

Rhonda

Darrah

Killa

Shavon

Misty

India

Kassandra

Imani

Nala

Chantell

Benvinda

Roger

Lexi B

Zapphire

Vbrooks

Tasha G

Kiera

Valencia

Stacy

YANITZA

Texansgurl76

Emma

Tinette

Jenny

Mariah

Nale

Tanisha

Trenita

Shelle

dulcemaria413

Shanice

Letarsha

Tania

Neeka

Julia

Linda

Lisa

Jiannie

Jillian

Tameka

Asia

Scarlette

Olwyn

R W

Fayefaefee

Brianna

Tiffany

Katie

Diamond

Kera

Tia

Love Reading

Dominique

Sheria

Jennifer

Georgette

Monique

Wendolyn

King Turtle22

Jessica

Nic M.

JustChill

DJC

Atira

TheeLastHokage

Yvonne

Chrissy

Janelle

Rian

LaRonda

LaRonda

Deanna

dlawson382

Jasmine

Haley

Belinda

Sercee

Yvonne

Jadelock

Farah

Tamiya

Quin

J.Payton

Geek Girl

Ashley

Rubi

Pilar

Sandra

Jurnee

Anni

Shannet

Joneesa

GlitzyHydra

Amanda

Barbara

Brianna

Jamica

Lyons

MARY ANN

Marketia

SarahD

LoverofHawaiiHearts

ceblue

Yolanda

MonaGirl Lewis

Dianna

Mary

amna

Nysha

fayola

Ty

Abria

Shyra

Andi-Mariee

Jamila

Naee's World

KEISHA

Jennett

Fredericka

Candece

Chante

Pholuv

Lydia A

Sabrina

JM

Jackie

Mo

Natrilly83

Ashaunte

Tolu

Margaret

Wendolyn

Lori

Dionne

ZLB

Kristina

Nicol

ELBERT

A. Harris

Jesi

Brenda

Desiree

Angela

Frances

LaShan

Only1ToniD

Debbie T.

Tiffanie

April L

shawnte

Kay

Lisema

Yvonne F

Natasha

Colleen

Julia

Amy

Jacklyn

Shyan R

Kiana B

Pearl

Javonda

Sheron

Maxine

Dash

Alicia

margaret

Love2Read

Juliette

Monica

Sandhya

MaryC

Trinity

Brittany

June

Ashleigh

Nene

Nene

Deborah

Nikki M

Dee

TyKira

Kimmey

Laytoya

Shel W

Arlene

Judith

Mary

Shanida

Rachel

Damzel

Ahnjala

Kenya

momo

BJ

Akeshia

Melissa

Tiffany

sherbear

Nini J

Curtresa

REGGIE A.

Ashley

Mia

Tink138110

Phia

Sharon

Charlotte

Assiatu C

Regina

Romanda

Catherine

Gaynor

BF

Perpetua

Tasha G

Henri Ann

sara

skkent

Rosalyn

Danielle

Deborah J

Kirsten

ANA

Taylor R.

Charlene

Louanna

Michelle

Tamika

Lauren

RoHyde

Natasha

Shekynah

Cassie

AnnaBooms

Keitheena

Nick R

Gennifer M

Rayna

Anton

Jaleda

Kimvodkna

JaTonn

Jazmine

Anoushka

Raynischa

Audrey

Valeria

Courtney

Donna

Patrisha

Jenetha

LaKisha J.

Ayana

Taylor

Christy

Monica

FreyaJo

GRACE

Kisha

Christine

Alexandra

Amber

Natasha

Stephanie

LaKisha

kristylove7

Cynthea

DENICE

Latoya

monifacd .

Doneishia

Mariah

Gerry

Yolanda T

Yolanda P

Susan D

Phyllis H

Alisa K

Daveena K

Desiree S

Kimberly B

Robin B

Gary S

Stephanie MG
Georgette A
Kathy
Marty
JanetDaniels
Megan
Shelle
Delores
Janet
Lydia
Phyllis
Freda
Charlott R

Join the Patreon Community.

Milton Keynes UK
Ingram Content Group UK Ltd.
UKHW021938080824
446615UK00015B/644